Snapped

Snapped

Tina Brooks McKinney

www.urbanbooks.net

Urban Books, LLC
78 East Industry Court
Deer Park, NY 11729

ISBN 13: 978-1-60162-367-6
ISBN 10: 1-60162-367-4

First Mass Market Printing October 2012
First Trade Paperback Printing November 2010
Printed in the United States of America

10 9 8 7 6 5 4 3 2 1

*This is a work of fiction. Any references or similarities to
actual events, real people, living or dead, or to real locales
are intended to give the novel a sense of reality. Any simi-
larity in other names, characters, places, and incidents is
entirely coincidental.*

Distributed by Kensington Publishing Corp.
Submit Wholesale Orders to:
Kensington Publishing Corp.
C/O Penguin Group (USA) Inc.
Attention: Order Processing
405 Murray Hill Parkway
East Rutherford, NJ 07073-2316
Phone: 1-800-526-0275
Fax: 1-800-227-9604

ACKNOWLEDGMENTS

This book is dedicated to the people who surround me with support and love. First and foremost, God; without Him, I would not have the inspiration to create these novels. I can't believe that He has gifted me with such a warped mind and I thank Him. Next, I would like to give thanks to my family who continue to put up with my crap while I'm writing: my husband, William, who I love with every breath in my body, and my children, Shannan and Estrell, who I'm sure are sick of me! My mother, Luetta, and my father, Ivor, who've been married forever! My sister, Theresa, she is my graphic designer and my lifeline. She gets things done for me so I don't have to worry about them. Visit her site at www.preservinglastingmemories.com.

Next my editor, Docuversion. He has helped mold the words that I put on paper into something sensible and I love this man. He's my ridedown-there.com guy. Next I want to thank the book clubs and I swear I don't want to start mentioning them 'cause I know I'm going to leave out some and I do not want to hurt anyone's feelings but I will mention the top five that have supported me from day one. Between Friends Book Club, Queens Book Club, Svvay Book Club, Books & Beignets Book Club, Baltimore Readers, Words of Inspiration Book Club. Online book clubs Raw4all, Black Expressions with Carol Mackey, Sexy Ebony Book Club, and Urban Reviews. This is a short list, folks, so please don't hate me if your group is not mentioned. I didn't get to mention anyone at all in my last book and I ain't trying to get my list cut from the book 'cause I said too much.

I would like to thank my friends who have supported me unconditionally: Angela Simpson, Valerie Chapman, Andrea Tanner, my Keough Crew (you know who you are), Talisa Clark, Ricardo Mosby—I've got mad love for you, Maceo Haywood (thanks for all your help, you've been a great promoter), Wayne Albert (I'm so glad to call you a friend now), Muriel Broomfield, Vanessa Yearby, Lasonji Strickland, Christina Fannin, Kim Robinson, and Kim Flyod.

My author friends, Black Writers With a Purpose, Gayle Jackson Sloan, Theresa Gonsalvas, Nane Quartay, Rodney Lofton, Nicole' Mitchell, Terra Little, Perón Long, Maxine Thompson, Dwyane Burch, Lee Hayes, Darrien Lee Debra

Acknowledgments

Phillps . . . There are more but I can't recall them all right now. Please charge it to the head and not the heart.

Last, but not least, I'd like to thank my new Urban family. Thanks for welcoming me into the circle. Special shouts out to Carl Weber. Thanks so much for giving me a chance! Also I'd like to thank Natalie Weber and Brenda Owens for all that you've done for me. And M.T. Pope for reaching out to me. (He got a great book, y'all.)

PROLOGUE

Tabatha looked at me as if I had just sprouted wings and was about to fly away. The expression on her face was almost comical. She paced the living room of my apartment and shook her head in disgust.

"Gina, we've been down this road before. How many times do I have to spell it out for you?"

"I don't want to hear it, Tabatha. That's my husband and I'm sticking by him."

"He's not your husband. Y'all didn't walk down the aisle in front of friends and family and recite vows. You didn't vow to love each other through thick and thin or sickness or health."

"Whatever." Tabatha was starting to get on Gina's nerves. She didn't need to have her best friend count down all the haves and have-nots in her relationship. Gina was well aware of those things.

"And he damn sure didn't promise to forsake all others, or you wouldn't be in the situation you're in now." Tabatha walked over to the other side of the room, suddenly interested in looking out the window.

It was a good thing she put some distance between them because Gina was ready to reach out and touch her.

Placing her fists on her waist, Gina stood up to face her. "Why did you have to take it there? That's water under the bridge."

Tabatha turned around, anger etched on her honey-brown face. "Because someone needs to take you there because it appears as if you've forgotten the gritty details of the life you actually live. You've been looking at your life through rose-colored glasses; it's time to take the shades off and see shit the way it really is."

"And what way is that?" Gina felt the blood rushing through her veins. She struggled to hold on to her anger.

A look Gina never recognized before crossed over Tabatha's face. "Uh—"

Gina said, "Don't get to stuttering now." She was trying real hard not to call Tabatha out her name.

They had been friends since high school, but Tabatha was wading in troubled water now. As quickly as the look appeared, it disappeared, and Gina saw a resolve that scared her.

"Fine, I'll say it. You're a fucking fool." Tabatha folded her arms across her chest and stuck out her chin. Her look was defiant, as if she dared Gina to challenge her.

"What . . . I . . ." So many words struggled to get out of Gina's mouth at the same time, she couldn't get any of them out.

"Who's stuttering now, Gina?" Tabatha taunted.

Even though Gina was pissed at her, she felt the humor in Tabatha's jest and it took the sting out. Gina sat back down, and Tabatha sat next to her.

She grabbed Gina's hand. "Girl, I wouldn't say that shit if I didn't love your stinkin' drawers."

In Gina's heart she knew that, but it still hurt. "Tabatha, regardless of whether you approve of Ronald, I can't help who I love. We don't need to practice that type of rhetoric to recognize our commitment. In my heart, we are married. Anyone who can't respect it can kiss my natural black ass."

"Thanks, but no thanks. Kissing your ass is not on my list of things to do—ever! All jokes aside, I hear what you're saying. But in the eyes of the law, he's not even your common-law husband, and what he's asking you to do is a felony."

"To quote a phrase that I've heard you say about a million times, 'fuck the law and the horse it rode in on.' I'm doing me."

"Don't misquote me. When I said fuck the law, I was talking about a parking ticket I got. I wasn't referring to something major like filing a false friggin' tax return. Not to mention claiming children you've never had. Hell, y'all done stepped over to the out-of-control side. This type of behavior is scaring the shit out of me."

"What are you talking about, Tabatha?"

"Don't make me spell it out for you, heifer. You know what I'm talking about."

"No, I don't, and I'm not a heifer."

"That is a matter of opinion."

Tabatha was joking, but like most jokes, it held some element of truth. Gina had a habit of trying to change the subject when she was called on her shit, but this time Tabatha wasn't willing to let it go.

Gina rolled her eyes and sighed. "If you got something to say, say it."

"Okay, you asked for it. When it's all said and done, you are setting yourself up for failure. This man you claim is your husband can and will walk away from you, and you will be sitting in the same spot looking stupid." Tabatha really hurt

Gina's feelings with this remark, and she had to struggle not to completely tune her out.

"Do I detect a little haterade?"

"Bitch, please. What is there to hate on?"

"You hatin' because I have a man and you haven't had one since Jimmy Carter was president."

"Say what you want, I'm not changing my mind on this." Now Tabatha let out a deep sigh.

Gina had hurt her feelings, but she refused to back down. Tabatha was tired of having this argument with a woman she loved like a sister. In Tabatha's mind, Gina was a idiot. She had wasted years on a man who had no desire to marry her. She was raising two of his children from a prior relationship. Ronald was fucking her doggie style and riding bareback while doing it.

"Okay, I give up. It's your life and I'm going to let you live it, but don't bring your ass to my door crying when the motherfucker ditches you too."

"I got it. If, and I stress the word *if*, that happens, you will not be on my list of people I call to have my back."

"Girl, stop trippin'. I didn't say I wouldn't have your back. I just said I'm going to shout I told you so before I offer one iota of sympathy."

Tabatha could tell by the way Gina threw her head back that she was through with her opinions about her relationship, but Tabatha was tired of seeing her get used. For years, Gina had been faithful to a worthless man. He had children by other women, disappeared for months at a time, and always brought those outside children into Gina's home as if it were okay.

In the beginning, she said she accepted them because she didn't have children herself, but it was a new day and Tabatha wanted her to wake up and recognize it. She was more of a mother to Ronald's bad-ass children than their birth mothers. That bugged the shit out of Tabatha. It didn't seem fair that Gina should bear the responsibilities of being a mom without the benefits of having the biological father present and accounted for.

CHAPTER ONE

GINA MEADOWS

When I woke up, the room was spinning as I rushed to the bathroom. My stomach and my intestines were battling it out; it was only a matter of time before one of them won. Frankly, I didn't give a flying fuck which one won as long as my pain stopped. I just wanted to be able to lie down and rest. I was so tired most of the time.

As I emerged from the bathroom, Tabatha loomed in my way. Obviously, I had fallen asleep at Tabatha's house because I was still wearing the same clothes I'd had on the day before. I felt grimy, dirty, and sick as hell.

"Move."

"Negro, please. You need all the support you can get." Tabatha slipped her hands under my arms to even my weight.

"Support? What kind of support do you give me?" If Tabatha was looking to piss me off, she was doing a good job.

"I am the fucking godmother, not a fucking cash cow." Tabatha swelled up with pride.

I knew this would be the first time that Tabatha had been designated for such a high honor, and she wasn't going to let my pissy attitude ruin it for her.

"Godmothers provide financial support and you ain't done none of that shit."

Tabatha all but allowed me to fall on my ass. "Hold the fuck up, heifer. Merlin and Gavin did not come from your pussy. I don't want no parts of them, but this one that you are carrying, that's another story. Are you trying to say because I didn't financially support Merlin and Gavin, I can't be a godmother to this one?"

"Hell, yeah. I need someone who is going to spoil my baby rotten."

"That's not fair, Gina. It would be different if those were your children. I never thought you would take total responsibility for children you didn't have. Besides, money ain't everything. When you need me the most, I come through, and you can't put a price tag on that shit." Tabatha made a good point.

She was always around when I needed her, and I didn't have to worry about my words coming back to me in the form of malicious gossip.

"You're right. I'm trippin'. I value your friendship and I need to start acting like it."

"'Bout time you recognized."

Tabatha was gloating, but she should be. If she weren't such an extraordinary friend, she would have drop-kicked my ass to the curb a long time ago. I was the stupid one in this friendship, and I was woman enough to admit it.

She said, "I have to ask this. How are you going to manage with another mouth to feed?"

"Tabatha, you know how long I've been trying to have a child of my own. The pain I feel because I haven't had one is changing me. I've become such a bitch."

"You ain't even lied." She smiled when she said it, but she was only stating the obvious.

"You didn't have to agree so readily."

"Hey, it is what it is. I understand how you feel, but you've already opened your home to two illegitimate children from Ronald who he isn't helping with. How are you gonna take on this additional expense?" I thought about my sparsely furnished bedroom and understood where Tabatha was coming from. It wasn't the worst furniture in the world, but none of it matched. They were all pieces I had picked up at garage sales or thrift stores.

"Maybe this baby will make Ronald change. This baby will link us together forever."

Tabatha knocked on my forehead. "Damn, what kind of dope are you smoking? People, like animals, don't change their spots. They are what they are. You either deal with them or leave them alone. He doesn't take care of the babies he already has, so what makes you think he is going to take care of this one?" She gestured to my stomach, even though I wasn't showing.

"I don't need his help. This is my baby and I'm keeping him." A look of pure horror crossed Tabatha's face. If I didn't know before how she felt, I knew now.

"Have you told Ronald about the baby?"

"No, not yet. He is coming home for Christmas, and I'm going to spring it on him then."

"Girl, you know I've got your back . . . but I have a bad feeling about this."

"Well, I don't. He's been looking for a reason to come back to Atlanta to live and this is it. I want to get married for real and raise his child."

"That sounds all good, Gina, but Ronald's track record doesn't support what you're saying. How many baby mommas does he have out there?"

"This ain't about them. I've done the work that they didn't. Being pregnant by him has to count for something," I lamented, banging my hand down on her mattress for emphasis.

"Hey, in my book it counts, but I'm not the one making the decisions. It's Ronald, and, as I've said before, his track record ain't that good."

"Everything ain't the way it seems. To you, Ronald may not look like much, but he's there for me and that's what counts," I lied. That's what I hoped for, and I knew this baby would answer my prayers.

"Ronald is only thinking about himself. He graces you with his presence only when he feels like it, he hands you a little money, and you take that shit. What I'm trying to tell you is that you deserve more than that."

Tabatha was right. If I were truly honest with myself, I actually wanted better, but I was prepared to play with the cards I'd been dealt.

"That is easy for you to say. You don't see the lives I've changed. If I weren't there for the twins, they would probably wind up in the system or on the streets, and I wouldn't able to live with myself because of it. I don't have any regrets with regard to those children."

"You don't deserve to be pregnant, you deserve a fucking medal."

We both started laughing until I noticed the look on Tabatha's face. No doubt about it, she was having one of her brainstorming moments.

"Then go into business and help yourself. Stop being a baby momma to your pimp. Take your expertise with children and make it work for you."

"Ronald is not a pimp. He's fertile. It wasn't his fault he chose to lie down with worthless women." I was struggling to come up with excuses for Ronald. I wasn't just trying to convince Tabatha, I was trying to convince myself.

"What are you saying? If it wasn't his fault, then whose was it? He did have a choice in the matter of who he was going to fuck."

"Damn, Tabatha. Why did you have to take it there?"

"Because I'm speaking the truth. Something you should be familiar with, but you aren't."

"The truth according to you. I don't care what you say. Ronald loves me and he's going to love our baby."

"Gina, the man is a walking time bomb. He doesn't even think enough of himself—or you for that matter—to wrap his dick up when he's out there in those streets. Do you know how fortunate you are that he hasn't given you some type of disease that you can't go to the doctor and get a cure for? He's playing Russian Roulette with your life."

Her words hurt me more than I wanted to admit. I had often thought about how careless Ronald was with my life, but at the end of the day, I still loved him and would do anything to keep him, including putting my own life on the line for his. But if I were honest with myself, this was taking a toll on my self-esteem. I used to think I was a vibrant woman, but lately I felt like a piece of shit stuck on the bottom of someone's shoe.

"I know you ain't stupid, but tell me this, why haven't you told him yet?"

"I told you, I'm going to tell him when he comes home for Christmas. I don't want to tell him over the phone."

"Why didn't you tell him when he was here for Thanksgiving?"

"He was only here for the day, and I wasn't sure I was pregnant. Besides, for the first time since he left, he's actually talking about moving back home."

"Ah, now we're getting to the root of the problem. You think if you tell him, he might change his mind about moving, right?"

I didn't answer her. I didn't need to because she already knew the answer to that question.

"I've got to hand it to the brother, he's good. He's got your mind so messed up you can't even tell when he's pissing all over you."

I reared back as if to slap her. She had gone too far.

"What? You gonna hit me? I'm the only one who is around for your sorry, underappreciated ass."

I got up and grabbed my purse. "You know what? I think I need to leave. Obviously, I have outstayed my welcome."

"Gina, no, I'm sorry. I just hate that you keep giving that man all your love and he continues to shit on you. I want you to wake the fuck up."

"Understand and respect this, Tabatha: I love him. For all his faults and betrayals, I love him. How he treats me is my business. Now, I love you too, but I can and will cut you from my life if I have to continue to defend my decisions to you."

"I hear what you're saying. I will try to keep my opinions to myself, but would you at least consider my idea? If you are going to take in wayward kids, why not get compensated for it? You could apply for grants and give the love that is in your heart and get compensated for it."

"Tabatha, what are you talking about? What I do for Ronald's kids, I do from my heart. I don't want to accept money for it." I sent a look that could have drawn blood.

"Gina, doing from your heart is one thing, but your purse is on empty. You need some help.

How do you plan to support another mouth when you're barely making it as it is?"

"My husband will support me and the children."

"That's the thing, sweetie, he's not your husband and those twins are not yours. He could decide tomorrow that he doesn't want to have a damn thing to do with you and there won't be anything you could do about it."

"Tabatha, I'm going to leave before I say something that I can't take back."

"Yeah, you're right. Because I am not going to allow you to sell me a line of bullshit. I love you, but I'm not going to say the things that make you happy just to make you feel better. I love you, but, damn, don't test me."

I started to gather my belongings again.

CHAPTER TWO

GINA MEADOWS

When I got home, I went into frenzy mode to make sure my meager house was spotless. I gave the house one last look before I went into the living room to wait for Ronald to come back from one of his many runs. Ronald was a street nigga. He wasn't happy staying in the house for long periods. He always had someplace to go or something to see too. He tried to make me believe that he had given up selling weed, but I wasn't that naïve. He was a born hustler, but had toned his game down since I'd first met him fifteen years ago.

In high school, I had the biggest crush on him. He didn't go to my school, but he was there so much it would have been easy to believe that he was enrolled. He supplied drugs to all the kids, so it wasn't uncommon to see him lounging around the parking lot or across the street from the school. He was smooth and all the girls loved him.

I was in my junior year when he started flirting with me. That was the year my boobs and ass finally developed. Up until that year, I was as flat as a pancake. It seemed like overnight I outgrew my training bra and added a caboose to my jeans. All the boys were trying to get my attention, but I only had eyes for Ronald. He was a boy with man-sized dreams and I wanted to be a part of them. I wasn't stupid enough to believe I was the only one vying for Ronald's attention, but I reveled in the attention he poured on me.

In the beginning, he would be waiting outside my school right next to my bus. Every day he would ask me if I wanted a ride home. At first I'd always say no, but my girlfriends persuaded me to take a ride one rainy afternoon.

My nerves threatened to get the better of me as I slid onto the leather seat of his car. I could see my girlfriends' faces plastered against the window of the bus as we pulled away from the curb. Excitedly, I waved bye to my friends. This was probably the most exciting thing that had happened to me in my whole life.

"Don't worry, Gina, I won't bite," Ronald had said.

"How did you know my name?"

He shrugged his shoulders. "I asked around."

I felt like pinching myself knowing he went through the trouble of finding out who I was. We were driving for a few minutes before I noticed that we were going in the wrong direction.

"Where we going?" The rain was coming down pretty hard. I had to get home before my mother realized I hadn't caught the bus.

"I'm waiting for you to tell me."

For a minute I felt stupid, but I quickly shrugged it off. "Well, I assumed if you knew my name, you knew where I lived as well."

"Damn, baby, I'm not a stalker. I just asked what your name was." He laughed heartily and I joined in.

"I live back the other way toward Grant Park on Boulevard. You can let me out at the corner by the zoo entrance."

"Why, you don't want me to know where you live?" He acted like I offended him.

"No, it's not that, but I don't want my mother to see me getting out of your car." Truth be told, my mother would shit a duck if she saw me in a car with a man. She was very protective of me, especially since I developed boobs. She was always asking me if boys were trying to touch them.

"Okay, I can understand that. When she gets to know me, she'll love me like all the girls do," he said with confidence, but what I heard in those words was that there would be a next time.

My tiny heart beat faster as I imagined us as a couple. All too soon it was time for me to get out of the car. This was the first of many rides in his car.

The sound of Ronald's horn interrupted my musings. I got up and grabbed my coat. For a minute, it was just like old times. I patted my stomach and ran out to meet my man.

"Where we going?" I asked as I closed the door behind me. I leaned across the seat to give Ronald a kiss, but he waved me away. I could smell the weed clinging to his clothes. He had told me he stopped smoking, but I wasn't about to bring it up, for fear of ruining our night together.

"Only your favorite place in the world," he said, laughing.

I held in my sigh of frustration. He was taking me to Copelands in Buckhead, the same restaurant he took me to every time even when we were dating. I didn't want to burst his bubble and let him know that I'd outgrown the place.

"Ah, aren't you sweet." I was so sick of their Cajun cuisine I wanted to puke. Not to mention the fact that my baby didn't seem to care for those spicy foods. But, once again, I held my tongue so I wouldn't piss Ronald off.

I was trying so hard to make this a nice visit, but my hormones were making it hard for me. I was also trying to deal with our long-distance relationship, but it was wearing me down. Ronald had moved to Ohio when the GM plant closed in Atlanta. In addition to the plant closing, he was running from the law, and this was the second time that Ronald had been back in the ATL since he left two years ago.

Ohio was supposed to have been a temporary move, but thus far he had not sent for me and the twins, and he would get upset every time I brought up the subject. Tonight, I was going to tell him about the baby because I was going to need some help as I got further along.

"Why are you being so quiet?" Ronald looked at me from the corner of his eye.

"Huh?"

He had been talking to me and I hadn't been paying attention. I was occupied with how I was going to approach him with the news of our baby.

"You were a million miles away. I guess you didn't miss me." He placed his hand on my lap.

I knew he thought he was soothing me, but his touch only made me more nervous. "I did miss you, baby. I was just thinking about the kids."

I was still concerned about leaving them home alone even though they were old enough to be left by themselves.

"Hey, don't bring them into our night out together. It's not often we get to spend time alone."

Humph, that was easy for him to say, because at the end of his "holiday" he went home to peace and quiet and I was left alone to raise his children. The situation was less than fair, and I deserved more.

"You're right. This is our night. I'm so glad to have you here. Don't get me wrong, I love Ohio, but it's much too cold in the wintertime. I hate that you had to move there to keep your job."

He said, "You ain't even lying. When I got back in Georgia, I just started peeling off my clothes. It's going to be hard making the drive back home."

Hearing him claim Ohio as his home stung. Home was supposed to be where his heart was—and that wasn't in Ohio. For a second, I started to doubt his love for me, but I quickly shook that thought from my head. If he didn't love me, he wouldn't be sending me all the money he did to sustain our household. True, I had a job and did the best that I could, but my salary was only meant to sustain me. A snippet of doubt, however, entered my mind.

***

In spite of my earlier trepidation, we had a very nice dinner at Copelands. For a while, I forgot my churning emotions.

"I can't wait to get back to the house to make love to you," Ronald whispered in my ear.

We were sitting next to each other like young lovers.

"I hope you're ready, 'cause I'm going to make you work." I was flirting shamelessly with him. My stomach was in knots with anticipation. It had been two months since we'd last made love and I was more than ready. "Ronald, when are you coming home to stay?"

Before he could answer me, the waiter came and asked if we wanted dessert. Ronald pushed his plate away, knocking over his glass of water.

"I'd like the cheesecake," I said, and smiled.

Ronald frowned. "You don't need it. Don't you think you're getting a little fat?"

My cheeks burned with shame, and I closed my eyes to keep the tears from falling. I got up from the table and ran to the restroom. I refused to let him see me cry. Ronald could be a cruel bastard when he wanted to be. Attacking my weight was just one of the things he used to keep me in my place. This was my Achilles' heel because I was not as razor thin as some of the other women he used to deal with.

I went into an empty stall and threw up my dinner. My heart ached because the blinders were falling off. Everything was good as long as I stayed in my place and didn't ask him any questions. That little glimpse of clarity didn't make me feel any better about my situation, yet I stilled loved my baby and was determined to bring it into the world. After a few minutes, I left the bathroom. Ronald was waiting by the door.

"I thought I was going to have to come in and get you."

Opting not to say anything, I walked past Ronald, straight out of the restaurant, and to the car. He let me know how disappointed he was with me by not opening my car door. We didn't speak during the twenty-minute ride home. My mind was churning with different thoughts and none of them bode well for the birth of my baby.

Ronald parked the car and for a moment we just sat inside. I wanted to ask if he was coming in, but I was afraid of his answer. Finally, he opened his door and we got out of the car. It was late and I just wanted to get some sleep. My hands shook as I tried to insert my key in the lock. Frustrated, Ronald took the keys from me and opened the door. I was feeling self-conscious and insignificant, and I didn't like the feeling one bit.

Ronald turned on the light in the living room and turned on the television. I wanted to get us back on an even keel, but I refused to beg for his affection. I left him in the living room and went into the bathroom for a shower. I felt dirty and I needed to wash away the grime of dejection. I locked the door behind me. Inside my shower stall, I cried. I cried all the tears of loneliness that I'd been holding inside. I cried tears of fear that attempted to overtake me. I stayed in the shower until the water ran cold. Shivering, I left the shower and dried off. I could not bring myself to look at my reflection in the mirror.

He was in bed when I came out of the bathroom as if nothing were wrong. I paused. For a moment, I was self-conscious about my nakedness. I didn't want him to see me, especially since he had called me fat not more than an hour ago.

"What are you waiting for? Get in the bed. The house is chilly."

He was right. The house was chilly and that was another reason for Ronald to come home to me and his children. My mother had left me the house when she passed away a few years ago, and Ronald had promised to help me fix it up. It was a two-story home. The rooms were cramped and the plumbing sucked. In the wintertime, we practically froze; in the summertime, we damn near died of heatstroke since there was no central air.

Pulling back the covers, I slipped into the bed. I stayed on my side because I was not ready to allow him to touch me. I could hear the television playing in the other room. I was so cold; I didn't feel like getting up and turning it off. "Why did you leave the television on?"

He shrugged. "I didn't know if you'd let me stay in here with you."

I turned to face him. In all the years that we'd been together, I'd never said no to him. "What do you mean?" He had me totally confused.

"I know I hurt your feelings back at the restaurant, but I didn't mean to."

I wanted to reach out and take Ronald's temperature because he had never once acknowledged hurting my feelings, which he'd done countless times. Ronald got out of bed and left the room. I held my breath because I wasn't sure if he was coming back. When he returned, I let out the air that I'd been holding. He slid back in bed and gathered me to his chest. I sighed as I sunk into his arms. Moments like these made all the pain worth it. This was the gentler side of Ronald—more like the man who I had fallen in love with.

He began kissing my neck. His hot breath sent shivers down my spine, but this time it wasn't from the cold. My back arched toward his waiting mouth. He turned my face toward his and kissed me deeply. His arms snaked behind my back as he held me close.

"I love you, Gina," he whispered as he pushed me back onto the bed.

His fingers traced tiny circles around my nipples. A low moan escaped my lips. I loved it when he took his time to bring me pleasure. I trembled in anticipation. He lowered his mouth to my waiting nipple and gently suckled it. Briefly, an image of feeding his child flitted through my mind, but I pushed that thought away.

"You taste so good to me. I missed the way you fill my mouth."

I squirmed beneath his touch. He was exciting me with his words and his fingers. He pushed my breasts together and pleasured them both as moisture leaked from my pussy. We had only been at it for a few moments and already I was cumming.

"Do you like that, Gina?" his lips murmured against my skin.

"Yeah, baby, I like it." I wanted him to go lower. I needed him to go lower. I wanted him to taste me.

As if he were reading my mind, his lips trailed lower. He blew against my stomach and my body jerked upward. I felt like a puppet on his string. He sat up in bed and positioned himself between my thighs. Instead of dipping his head down into the valley, he inserted his finger into my pussy and twirled it around.

He said, "It's tight."

His breathing was becoming labored. I opened my eyes and saw his dick pointing straight up. He was as aroused as I was. For a brief second, I wanted him to stick it in and forgo the oral pleasure, but Ronald had other ideas. He pulled his finger out and a cold chill settled inside my pussy. I wanted to yell at him to put it back. He stuck his finger into my mouth, and I sucked it like I was sucking his dick.

"Damn, girl, you still hungry?" He chuckled. Ronald was the master of seduction, and I had fallen under his spell. "Are you gonna suck my dick like that when I give it to you?"

"Try me and see." I attempted to sit up, but Ronald gently pushed me back down on the bed.

"Relax, baby, let me bring pleasure to you." He eased himself down on the bed with his mouth poised above my steamy center. Before he dipped his head down he looked at me one last time with a small smile on his face.

My juices creamed the lower half of his face as I screamed out in pleasure. Ronald entered me at the peak of my climax. As much as I wanted to feel his hot dick inside of me, he was hurting me. I cried out, but Ronald mistook my pain for pleasure. He was pounding inside of me like he was trying to punish me.

"Take it easy, Ronald, it's been a long time."

Instead of slowing down, he intensified his stroke. His mouth covered mine so I could not complain. Hot tears seeped out of my eyes as our lovemaking turned to straight fucking. Ronald held me by my hair, pinning my head to the pillow. My eyes searched his but he had them closed. I lay still, waiting for this assault to be over. Finally, he collapsed on top of me. I pushed him over and he rolled over like a hollow log. Five minutes later his snores filled the room. He came and went at damn near the same time. If I hadn't been so sore, it would have been laughable.

I climbed out of bed, careful not to wake Ronald. I wanted to make sure my baby was intact. His dick felt like it could have penetrated my womb. Ronald was larger than the average-sized man. I stumbled to the bathroom while trying to hold back my sobs. I couldn't understand why our lovemaking had become so vicious.

I used the bathroom and was relieved to find that there was no blood on the toilet paper. As I left the room, I knew one thing for certain: I could not let Ronald do that to me again.

Ronald was sitting up in bed when I came out of the bathroom. He startled me. "You're pregnant."

It wasn't a question; it was a statement. I panicked and didn't know what to say.

"Don't bother lying. I know pregnant pussy when I feel it." I turned away so he wouldn't see the panic that I knew was clearly stamped on my face. I felt my face grow warm and I felt like I was going to faint. I wanted him to know about the baby, but not like this.

"I'm not a novice, I know pussy. Your nipples are hard as rocks, your shit is wet as hell, and it feels different."

"Is that why you were so rough?" Anger replaced my fear. I never thought in a million years that he would try to hurt me, but obviously I was wrong.

"I don't want any more kids, Gina. You've got to take care of this."

I stared at him in disbelief. Surely he wasn't suggesting that I abort our child.

"Ronald, you can't be serious. Do you know how long I've wanted a child?"

"You're raising children, Gina, you're done. You're doing your duty."

"Those are your children, not mine. I'm raising the twins out of love for you." I was beyond pissed.

Ronald got out of bed and began putting on his clothes. He didn't even bother to go in the bathroom to wash his nasty ass. He just stuffed his dick in his pants and zipped them up. It was going on one o'clock in the morning.

"You're not thinking straight. We can't have a child now, especially since Merlin and Gavin are about to finish high school. That will ruin all my plans." He sat down on the bed and put on his socks.

I didn't pay him any attention since I knew that there was no way they would be leaving anytime soon.

"What plans, Ronald? You keep telling me that we are going to be together and live like a family, but at the end of the day, it's just another visit and you're gone again. That's no kind of life to me."

"And you think things will get better if you bring another child into the equation? I'll have to work even longer to feed another mouth."

"That's not true and you know it. If you would come back home, we wouldn't be spending the extra money on your apartment in Ohio. Maintaining two households is what's killing us. Can't you see that?"

"No, what I can see is a selfish person who is only thinking of herself." Ronald stood up with his chest heaving in and out.

"Selfish?" If he'd slapped me, it wouldn't have hurt more than his words did at that moment. I had sacrificed everything for this man and he accused me of being selfish. Bullshit. "You're a son of a bitch. You call me selfish? I'm not the one who is driving around in a $40,000 car and living in a penthouse apartment. I'm not the one—"

"Who fucking what, Gina? I have all those things because I work hard." He was angry but so was I.

"You have all those things because you're selfish." This was the first time that I had expressed my feelings about his opulence to him. It was true. He sent me a paltry sum to help with the kids, but it was never enough. He started flinging his shit into the duffle bag that he'd brought home with him. Fear oozed through my body. As much as I hated him at the moment, he was still my life, and I didn't want him to cut his visit short. I reached for my nightgown and put it on. I felt foolish arguing with him while naked.

"I work too, dammit, but my money goes to this house and your children," I said.

He didn't look at me as he continued to pack his bag. My pride kept me from saying anything else to him as he grabbed his cologne off the dresser.

"And don't forget to mention your freeloading friend. You run this fucking house like it's a fucking shelter and you expect me to foot the bill."

My mind was reeling. I could not believe the venom in his voice. He never complained about my friend Tabatha before. In fact, he encouraged me to let her stay when she was going through her hell. I was beyond mad now. I wanted to hurt him like he had hurt me.

"At least my friend left. Hell, you said I would only have to keep your kids for a few months and they've been here for nine fucking years!" I was screeching and I didn't even care.

Ronald dipped into his pocket and peeled off some bills from the huge knot he had in his pocket. He threw the money on the dresser.

"Take care of your problem, Gina, because if you have this kid, you're on your own and you'll never see me again." He slung his bag over his shoulder and walked out the door.

CHAPTER THREE

TABATHA FLETCHER

I met Gina in the lobby of my work place during my lunch break because she said it was an emergency.

"Ronald doesn't want to have anything to do with the baby."

I hadn't seen Gina in over two months. "Are you serious? Why is it that he can have fifty million children with other women but he doesn't want a child by you? What kind of shit is that?" I wasn't surprised by his admission, but I didn't want to say that to Gina's face.

"I know. He said he was going to leave me if I have this child."

As much as I wanted to say, 'I told you so,' I didn't have the heart to do it. Gina had been through enough and my heart went out to her. As loving as she was, she didn't deserve the treatment she was getting from her asshole man. "Stop

lyin'. What did he say?" As much as I disliked
Ronald, I could not believe he would form his lips
to say anything that cold to Gina. I expected him
to be upset, but I never thought he would suggest
she abort his baby.

"We went to dinner at my favorite restaurant,
Copelands. It was real dark and sexy. He had a
few drinks and appeared to be in a good mood.
I mentioned the children and he cut me off and
said he didn't want to talk about the children."

"You hate Copelands."

"Okay, *his* favorite restaurant. Are you going
to let me finish my story or not?" She gazed at me
through watery eyes.

"Sorry, go 'head."

"Anyway, he said he didn't want to talk about
the children."

"I guess he doesn't."

Gina paused. I could tell she was about to walk
out on me.

"Anyway, I backed off. But I really wanted to
get him to acknowledge how good of a mother
I've been to his children. You know, before I told
him I was pregnant."

"Gina, get to the point." She was dragging the
story out, but I knew this was because she was
hurting.

"I was about to order dessert and he told me I didn't need it."

"Damn, that's cold." I gazed at my friend sympathetically. She had gained a few pounds, but she was still a beautiful woman both inside and out.

"I know, I almost started crying. He didn't even apologize. In the car, I tried to act like he hadn't hurt my feelings, but I couldn't. We didn't speak the whole way home."

I tried to imagine how that ride must have been because Gina loved to talk. If she was quiet around me, I would assume she was either sick or asleep. A small smile tugged at the corners of my mouth but Gina missed it.

"I took a shower as soon as we got home. I just wanted to go to bed and sleep away my pain."

"Where were the twins?"

"My sister kept them. I told her I was going to break the news to Ronald, and she thought it would be best if they were not in the house."

"I know that's right."

Once again Gina shot me a nasty look. I wasn't trying to be funny because I knew deep down in my heart that things wouldn't go as Gina had planned when she told him about having a child.

"When I came out of the bathroom he was already in bed. I could tell that he was ready to fuck, but I wasn't feeling him."

"Humph." That was no surprise to me. Niggas always wanted to fuck. It didn't matter what else was going on, their dicks were unaffected. They could be damn near dying but would still get a hard-on. I just shook my head instead of saying the words out loud.

"Anyway, to make a long story short, he said he didn't want any more kids."

"He did not lie."

"Yeah, look, I thought I was ready to discuss this but I'm not. I gotta go." Gina grabbed her coat from the sofa and started for the lobby door.

"Wait, Gina. If Ronald doesn't want this child, then let the motherfucker go and tell him to take all of his other rugrats with him."

"Tabatha, they are my children now. It doesn't matter that I'm not their birth mother. I love them and I won't turn my back on them."

"But the nigga you slept with is willing to turn his back on you. What kind of bullshit is that? You don't deserve this, Gina. You've given this nigga everything."

"It's complicated, Tabatha, and you wouldn't understand."

"What the fuck is there to understand? He's using you. And now that you are having his baby, he wants to run and fucking hide like he did with his other babies' mommas."

"I'm not giving up on my kids."

"You can be a fool if you want to, but you mark my words, you will live to regret it."

CHAPTER FOUR

TABATHA FLETCHER

"Tabatha?" I spoke into the phone.

"Huh? Who is this?"

"It's me, Gina. I need to talk to you."

"Bitch, why are you whispering?" I turned over and looked at the clock. 1:17 A.M.

"'Cause he's in the house."

"Who's in the house? Do I need to call the police?" I rose from the bed, ready to make a run if I had to. I wasn't going to let anyone mess with my girl.

"No, Tabatha. Listen to me. Ronald came home a few nights ago and he was upset with me because I hadn't gotten rid of the baby. We fought and he left, but he just came back in."

I settled back. Even though I didn't like Ronald and the things that he did to my friend, I knew he would never hurt her. As the words replayed in my mind, something stood out. Fought? What the hell? I snatched the covers off my bed and sat up straight.

"Fought? Did that motherfucker put his hands on you? Hold up; let me clear my motherfucking head. Please tell me that nigga didn't hit you 'cause I'm on my fucking way." I picked up my panties from the floor.

"No, but I can't stand the sight of him right now I want to come and stay at your house for a minute."

"Girl, fuck him, I don't care about him. I only care about you. You are always welcome at my house."

"Thanks, Tabatha. I'm on my way and I'll be alone."

"Good, I will be waiting up for you." I hung up the phone and continued to get dressed. I had to search for something suitable to go to the door. I slept in the nude so it was a terrible scramble for me to get my clothes in order. I wasn't sure how long it would take Gina to get here, but I needed to be ready. She had been through a lot.

"What's the matter?" my bedmate asked.

"Uh, I have an emergency and you have to leave."

"Are you fucking serious?"

I could tell that he was pissed. But if the shoe were on the other foot, I would be pissed too. "Sorry, boo."

"This is some fucking bullshit right here." He got up and started looking around for his clothes.

"I'm sorry, something has come up and I have to deal with it." I felt a twinge of regret for turning down a perfectly good dick without riding him at least one more time, but there was no way I was going to be able to enjoy him once Gina got here. "Please don't go away mad. This situation is beyond my control."

"Fuck you and your situation," he said as he rammed his feet into his sneakers.

When I say the motherfucker was pissed, that was an understatement. I pushed the envelope.

"Can I get a rain check?"

"Bitch, please, your shit wasn't that good in the first place." He slammed the bedroom door on his way out.

Damn, what a waste. He didn't have to insult me; there was no call for that. I bet he had awakened all of my neighbors when he slammed the door. I went into the bathroom to wash up. I didn't want to smell like sex when Gina got here. When I finished dressing, I went into the kitchen and put on a pot of coffee. It was going to be a long night, and I needed something to clear my head.

As the coffee pot began to whistle, I decided that I'd rather have a strong drink. I turned the kettle on low just in case Gina wanted some, and fixed myself an apple martini. I had made up a batch for me and William but we never got around to drinking it. I was on my second drink when I heard her car pull into the parking lot. I went to the window and saw Gina struggling with two suitcases. I quickly went down the stairs to help. From the looks of her luggage, she was planning on staying awhile. Once again the irony of the situation struck me. There was no way in hell that she should be leaving her house and coming to me.

CHAPTER FIVE

TABATHA FLETCHER

"Are you all right?" I asked while carrying her heavy-ass bags up the stairs.

"Yeah, I just needed to get away so I could think."

I had half a mind to drill her, but I knew that wasn't what she needed from me. Even though I was thoroughly against her having Ronald's baby, I cared more about her mental health. Gina was a loving person. Her own childhood was riddled with personal drama. I knew the only thing that she craved was a happy, peaceful existence inside her own home. As a child, she felt like she was a burden to her parents, whether real or imagined, she never felt their love or support. She conveyed that to me time and time again, so I could not fault her in her decision to stand behind Ronald's children. After all, it wasn't their fault their father chose to hang his dick out the window and fuck the world.

"I'm good, just a little bit shaken up."

"Why, what happened?" I closed the door and locked it.

"Ronald came home from his last trip and he was tired. I should have allowed him time to rest before I sprang my news on him, but I was so determined to get him to change his mind about the baby. We've been together so long without any children, I was sure I could convince him to accept it so we could finally be parents. Stupid me figured that if I was able to give him children, he would stop cheating on me."

I had to hold my tongue. I knew her ability to have children had little to do with Ronald's infidelity, but I was not about to tell her. He was a lowdown, dirty motherfucker who liked variety in his life. The best thing for Gina to do right now was to walk away from him. She was still in her thirties and would get over his cheating ass in no time.

I said, "As much as I want to say it, I'm not about to say I told you so. So the number one question is, what are you going to do?"

Gina slumped down on my sofa and started crying. My heart went out to her. I went over and wrapped my arms around her. She lifted her head and placed it on my shoulder. No one should be subjected to the pain she had dealt with, and I vowed to be there for her and to support her decisions, whether I agreed with her or not.

"I don't know. I want to be a parent so bad, but I don't want to be a single parent."

My anger rose again, and I realized that keeping my vow was going to be more difficult than I thought it was. "Gina, you've been a single parent for years. The only difference is that the children you mothered weren't yours."

Gina tensed up in my arms, but I didn't let go. She might not have liked what I said, but it was the truth. We rocked together for three or four minutes before she pushed away from me.

"It's okay, boo, you're safe now." I continued to comfort her. I eased the duffel bag purse she had on her shoulder to the floor. It was so heavy, it was like she tried to pack her whole life into it.

"Damn, girl, what you got in these bags?"

Sniffling, she replied, "I just grabbed everything I could. I just needed to get out."

"Gina, I know you don't want to hear this right now, but I have to say it. That is your grandmother's house. There is no way that you should have had to leave it."

"Tabatha, I know it's mine, but you didn't see his face. He was so angry, I thought he was going to hit me, and for what? Because I wanted to keep my baby."

"So why are you the bad person? Doing the same thing that his other babies' mommas have done?"

Gina pushed me so hard I fell off the sofa. "I'm not like those other bitches. I love that man and I care for his children."

Even though I wanted to get mad as I pulled myself off the floor, I had to admit she was right. Unlike those other whores, she was there on the battleground fighting for two of the kids Ronald had delivered into the world. "Gina, I'm sorry. You are right, you've been there and I can't deny it. My bad for even suggesting such a thing 'cause I know better." Bile rose in the back of my throat. While I believed Gina did everything she could do to raise a happy family, Ronald was like dirty laundry, if you didn't wash it, it began to stink. "I can't help it if I get mad every time I think about how he treats you. I want to whup his ass."

"Nobody wants to whup his ass as bad as I do, but I can't."

"Hold up, I'm going to stop this negative thinking right now. The bottom line is you're my friend and that is your man for better or worse." Even as the words fell out of my mouth, I wasn't feeling them, and I was sure Gina saw right through me. I paused to see which way she was going to take them. To my surprise, she actually believed me.

"Are you for real?" Gina said.

That answered my question. I could see the happiness on her face. She was only hearing what she wanted to hear. I wasn't mad at her. She was dealing with what she could while she was in a compromised state. With any luck, she would regain her sanity once the baby was born.

"Looks like I better start getting ready to be a godmother."

Gina looked at me and shook her head.

My forehead wrinkled. "What do you mean no? Who else is going to be the godmother?"

"I'm not having the baby, Tabatha. I know you don't understand this, but I'm gonna do whatever it takes to keep my man."

I smiled, but it didn't match my thoughts. I really wanted to tell her that she was the dumbest bitch in the world. But for better or worse, I was in it for the long haul with my friend.

CHAPTER SIX

GAVIN MILLS

Four Years Later . . .

I was taking a trip down memory lane, and I wasn't pleased by the memories that came rushing back to me after I saw my brother. Practically every ass whupping that Merlin ever got from ages five to sixteen was a direct result of something that I had done. I was not proud of that fact, but it was what it was.

As children, Gina always told us to never back down from a fight and to always have each other's back. More times than not, I wasn't around when the fighting began. This, of course, was by my design. It wasn't because I had some death wish for my twin; it was because I was tired of competing with him for my mother's affection. So having someone else take him out seemed like a viable option to me.

Merlin was the good kid, but he was easily misled. He did well in school, minded his manners, did his homework without being prompted, and kept his side of the room spotless. I, on the other hand, was the complete opposite. The only way I knew how to level the playing field was to create situations to bring him down a notch or three. It wasn't personal, it was survival. Merlin used to love me and would do anything that I told him to do. Although I was ashamed of the things I'd done to Merlin, I was helpless when it came down to the love of our mother. As far as I was concerned, there was only one spot available in my mother's heart and I aimed to claim it. Thus, it wasn't hard to understand why he hated me now.

"Merlin, get your ass in here!" He sat up in bed. I assumed he was confused as to why our mother would be calling him while it was still dark outside.

"Huh?" he yelled back.

I snuggled down deep in my covers and pretended not to hear the ruckus she was making. For good measure, I faked a loud snore.

"You heard me. Get your ass down here."

"Shit," he mumbled under his breath.

My heartbeat quickened. Merlin was in for an ass whupping, and I could tell by the sound of

my mother's voice it was going to be a long night.
For a fraction of a second, I pitied my brother
because he was about to walk into the bowels of
hell and had no clue why he was headed there. A
slow smile came across my face.

I watched as he pulled on his pajama bottoms
and threw on his robe. If he knew what I knew, he
would have hurried downstairs because Mother
hated to be kept waiting. Technically, Gina wasn't
our real mother, but she was the only mother we
knew, so she'd earned the title. Mentally, I went
through the list of chores that I'd been given and
subsequently assigned to Merlin. I knew he finished his chores, but mine were lacking.

Gina worked a part-time job on Mondays and
Wednesdays, leaving me and Merlin home to
fend for ourselves, which was no problem because we were old enough to stay home alone.

"Don't make me come up there and get you."

He walked out of the room still half asleep.
I felt a tinge of regret for setting him up, but it
didn't last long. Her voice was coming from the
guest bathroom. Because of that, I knew it was
about to be on. I was supposed to clean the bathroom, but instead I pissed over everything. Even
though I had pretended to be sleep, I couldn't
help but follow Merlin and witness the fireworks.

"Hey, Mom, what's wrong?"

She whirled around to face Merlin, her eyes squinted in anger. "Don't be sneaking up on me, boy." She had her hands on her hips, blocking the rest of the bathroom from our view.

"I wasn't sneaking," Merlin sputtered.

"Shut up."

He stood before her, shifting from foot to foot. Suddenly, I had to go to the bathroom in the worst way, but I didn't want to do anything that would draw attention to me.

"What day is it?" she demanded.

Clearly Merlin had no idea where this conversation was leading him. I had switched days with him on the calendar our mother kept on the refrigerator.

He said, "Wednesday."

"And what happens on Wednesday?"

This was not a trick question, and I was sure he knew the answer to it. On Wednesday night, my brother and I cleaned. We each had a long list of chores that would keep us busy until it was time to go to bed. It was Gina's way to keep us occupied so we didn't notice we were home alone.

"Cleaning day." Merlin was smooth. He didn't flinch when he answered our mother because he was certain he had finished his chores.

Usually, Merlin was responsible for cleaning the first floor. I was given the job of doing the upstairs, which included straightening up my mother's bedroom. I hated that detail because she was always throwing her bras and panties around the room. No child should have to pick up his mother's dirty underclothing.

"Exactly. So telling me you forgot won't cut it. You know the rules, right?" Mother began to undo her belt from around the waist of her denim jeans.

"What's wrong, Mother? I did my chores."

She whirled around and surveyed the room. I knew for a fact that the bathroom was in total disarray. I had planned it that way, right after I switched Merlin's name with mine on the calendar.

"You call this clean?" She stepped to the side with a sweeping motion of her hand. "I gave up my own child for bullshit like this. Fuck that."

"Mother, I cleaned the first floor."

I could see the fear etched on his face. The last thing you wanted to do in life was piss off my mother. Merlin was pleading with her, but she wasn't hearing him. I was ecstatic. Things were playing out just like I wanted them to. She was ready to inflict some pain. Once again, I felt sorry for my brother, but not enough to step up and admit that I had a hand in this mess. I didn't really hate Merlin per se. I just didn't want to compete with him for the affections of our mother.

"So what are you saying? Are you trying to act like I'm senile or something?"

If my brother wanted to say something at all about the state of my mother's mind, he wasn't given the opportunity, because she hit him across the lips with her belt. Immediately his upper lip split and began to swell. In spite of myself, I gasped. I wanted her to punish him, but not in this manner. I was thinking more on the lines of no television or not being able to go to the movies.

"What are you doing in here? Did I call you?" My mother demanded as she shot me a beady-eyed look. "I should have kept my own damn baby."

My eyes bucked in horror. I had walked right into the trap I had created, and was about to face some of her wrath for the messy bathroom and for the baby my deadbeat dad forced her to abort.

"Look at what your brother did." She splayed her arms to show me the damage, but I already knew what the room looked like.

Comet was spread all over the sink, walls, and floor. She yanked me into the bathroom so I could get a better look. Wet wads of toilet paper littered the walls. A note was written on the mirror in toothpaste: Merln hates chors.

Gina slapped Merlin in the back of his head, bringing tears to his eyes.

"Mother, I didn't do this," Merlin stammered.

"Do you think I'm stupid? I know your dumb-ass brother did this. Hell, he can't even spell your name let alone 'chores.' But you didn't stand up for yourself and that is why I am punishing you. This is a mean world you're stepping into and you've got to learn, hook, crook, borrow, or steal to make your way in it. Your dumb-ass brother knows this, and he sets you up every time and you allow it. You need to check his ass! I can't do it for you." She popped him in his head again.

I wanted to take offense for her calling me a dumb ass, but when I realized what I wrote on the mirror, I couldn't argue with her. In my haste, I had spelled his name wrong.

"If there is one thing that you will learn from living with me, it will be to stand up for yourself." She dragged him closer to the toilet.

If he thought things were bad before, he was wrong. Floating among the Comet and the piss I'd left in the toilet was my mother's toothbrush.

"Oh, God!" Merlin shook his head as if he couldn't believe it.

My mother turned another shade of black. She was almost blue, and her eyes looked like they were about to pop out of her head. Once again, I felt sorry for my actions, but I was too far into it to back out. I inched my way out of the bathroom. My brother was on his own.

"Is that my toothbrush?" my mother demanded.

I was so sure that she already knew it was hers before she even asked him, but he didn't know how to respond.

"Oh, God!" he said again.

I was afraid—really afraid.

"Don't you dare take the Lord's name in vain." She whacked him upside the head with her fist.

"Momma, I swear I didn't do this," Merlin shouted, but it was too little too late. He bent down under the sink to get something to fish her toothbrush from the toilet with but instead of finding a rag, her wet silk headwrap fell out along with the empty can of Comet. Merlin's honey-bronze face turned bright red. He knew he was in deep shit when he realized what he held in his hands.

"If there is one thing that I will not tolerate in my house, it's a fool. I know you had nothing to do with this, but you did nothing to stop it. That is why I am punishing you. I work too damn hard to have to come home and see this bullshit."

"How can I stop something that I didn't even know was happening?"

He had a good point, but Mother wasn't buying it.

"You should have double-checked." She slapped him upside the head again. Even though she held her belt in her hand, she used her fist to let him know she meant business.

He continued to tell her that he didn't do it, but she couldn't care less. She was on a roll and there was nothing he could do about it but take his licks. I was satisfied with another successful mission.

"I know you didn't do it, but you're too stupid to tell me who did."

Damn, why should he have to tell her? We're the only ones who live in the house. She should've known. I slipped out of the room because I wasn't in the mood to get slapped upside the head.

"You're going to learn how to be a man."

So what is she saying? Does she mean real men rat on each other? Those words reverberated in my head as I sought my bed.

I heard Merlin say, "But, Momma—"

"Momma, my ass. Now clean this shit up, and you will be paying for my toothbrush and my headwrap from your lunch money."

***

"What are you grinning about?"

A feeling of dread came over me. My mother had snuck into the room.

"Huh?" I rolled over and tried to grab my covers, pretending I'd fallen back to sleep.

"Huh, my ass. I know it was you who fucked up the . . ."

I waited for her to finish her sentence, but she left it hanging in the room like a stale fart. I hoped she wasn't waiting for a confession, because it would be a cold day in hell before I'd confess to throwing her toothbrush in the toilet. "Ah, Ma, you messed up a perfectly good wet dream." My intent was to shock her, but not to piss her off. Boy, was I wrong.

"You nasty little pervert. How dare you say some shit like that to me!" She started beating me over the head with her hands.

In hindsight I was glad it was her hands and not a bat, 'cause she would have whupped my ass to death. "I'm sorry. I was sleeping, Momma. I didn't mean any disrespect. I said the first thing that came to mind."

"What do you take me for?" She stopped beating me about the head as if she seriously expected me to answer her question, but I was not falling into that trap.

I didn't understand why she was punishing Merlin if she knew I had been the one to do it. Clearly she could see I'd targeted her when I destroyed the bathroom, because all of the items I used belonged to her. I couldn't understand why she didn't see that I was calling out for attention.

"Get up. I want you downstairs to mop the kitchen floor and vacuum the living room."

"Mom, I have to go to school in the morning. Don't you know how important it is to get a good night's sleep before school?" I was laying it on thick, but I could tell she wasn't buying it.

"You'd have to go to school before that lie would work with me. Don't think I don't know you're spending all your time on the corners instead of in the classroom."

Damn, she knows! I thought I was slick and shit and she saw right through my game. Maybe now would be a good time to tell her I'd dropped out. I gave up all pretense of being asleep. "Well, Ma, since you know I haven't been going to school, don't you think this would be a good time for you to sign my work permit and let me get a real job? With the money I make I can help you out around the house." I raised up on my arms and looked into a face contorted in rage.

"You little pissant. Who do you think will hire your retarded ass? You need an education so you can better yourself."

Her comment stung, and even though I k
it was her anger talking, it still hurt. I wante
ask her how that worked for her because sl
been slaving at three jobs just to maintain
raggedy-ass house, and she had her diploma

"Wipe that damn smirk off your face and
mop the floor, and while you're down there,
it, too!"

I rolled out of bed under her watchful gl
Even though I wound up with additional cho
I still made out better than my brother, 'ca
he had to clean the bathroom with a toothbr

"And you're going back to school in the m
ing, mister." She walked off in a huff toward
bedroom. "Should have had my own damn b
and let Ronald raise his own damn kids."
face felt tight, and I was afraid one sharp mo
could cause it to crack in half.

I gave her the finger behind her back.

"I saw that, you rotten bastard."

CHAPTER SEVEN

GAVIN MILLS

Moms wasn't playing about my going back to school. She took off from her day job and personally escorted me. The whole way there, she talked about how she should have never given up her baby for me and my sorry-ass dad.

"You didn't have to come with me." I was dragging my feet because I didn't want anyone to know we were together.

"Like hell I didn't. You're going to get a high school education even if I have to sit up in the class with you every damn day."

I paused midstep. Surely she had to be kidding. I would look like the biggest loser in the world if that were to happen.

"Come on, boy. You don't want us to be late."

I felt like crying when she yanked open the front door to the school I'd sworn to never step foot in again.

"Which way to the office?" My mother reached back and yanked me beside her. Her voice was so loud it practically bounced off the walls.

I was so embarrassed I was afraid to look up. "Down this hallway and on the right." I started walking faster.

The sound of her heels clicked harshly against the ceramic tiled floors. Fortunately, the first bell had already rung, so the hallways were clear of other students. The morning announcements were being read as I held open the office door for my mother. She marched past me and made her way to the secretary's desk.

"May I help you?" the secretary said.

"Yes, my name is Gina Meadows and I would like to see about getting my son back in school."

She looked past my mother's shoulder at me and her eyes narrowed in recognition. "Isn't he already a student at the school?"

"When was the last time you saw him?"

I prayed the floor would open up and swallow my body.

"Well, uh . . . now that I think about it, it's been a minute."

"That's my point." My mother looked back at me with a smug expression on her face.

If it was her intent to embarrass the hell out of me, she succeeded.

"Have a seat and someone will be with you."

My mother grabbed me by the arm and pulled me over to a bench in the corner of the office. Part of me wanted to snatch my arm away and find my own chair, but I was no fool. If I'd have done that, she would not have hesitated to go upside my head.

"Don't you buck up at me, boy, or I will wear your ass out right here in this office."

"I didn't do nothing." I shoved my hands in my pockets to keep from giving her the finger again.

They kept us waiting for at least half an hour before the principal finally came to meet with us.

Principal Gaynor said, "Ms. Meadows?"

My mother stood up and pulled me to my feet with her. "Yes, that's me."

"Come with me." Principal Gaynor turned and started walking to her office, which I was very familiar with. She held the door open for us, then we took a seat in front of her desk. She closed the door behind us.

I slumped over in my seat.

"Sit up straight," my mother prodded.

I sat up.

"How may I help you this morning?" Principal Gaynor asked.

"It has come to my attention that my son has not been attending class. I want to see what I need to do to get him back in school."

"Ms. Meadows, the school year is almost over. Gavin has missed a lot of time."

I hated that they were discussing me as if I weren't in the room with them.

"I know, but he has got to get an education."

"I agree, but we can't make him come to school." Principal Gaynor left the comment hanging in the room, but her message was clear.

"Oh, I'll make him come to school," my mother threatened.

The air in the room became uncomfortable, and I started to squirm in my chair.

Principal Gaynor cleared her throat. "Ms. Meadows—"

"It's Mrs."

I turned to her, surprised she'd said that as if my dad would actually marry her. Shit, he didn't fuck with me and my brother. He only came around her when he wanted a piece of ass and needed a place to stay the night without paying while he was in town. Dad might have been into some dark shit, but he was my type of dude.

"I'm sorry, Mrs. Meadows, I didn't mean any disrespect."

"None taken."

"As I was saying, the school year is almost over and your son did not do well in the few months that he did attend school this year."

"I understand, but can he come back?"

"That's up to him. He's sixteen years old and still in the tenth grade."

I could feel my mother staring at me, but I refused to look up.

"Excuse me, Mrs. Gaynor, but this is not up for debate. This boy is going to go to school and he's going to apply himself. Right, Gavin?" She said this as if I had a choice.

"Yes," I said between clenched teeth.

"Yes, what?" my mother demanded.

"Yes, ma'am," I mumbled.

"Fine, but it's not going to be easy. He may need a tutor."

"Don't worry about that. His brother is a good student. I'll get him to help Gavin."

"Oh, yes, Merlin is an excellent student and an absolute gem to have around. Our school is lucky to have him on our basketball team."

I felt like puking. I was sick and tired of living in Merlin's shadow. I just got no respect. "I don't need no damn tutor."

My mother knocked me in the mouth so fast, I didn't even have time to duck.

Principal Gaynor jumped up from her desk. "Mrs. Meadows, we don't condone that type of behavior in this school."

My mother's face contorted in rage. "I'm sorry, Principal Gaynor. You're right, but sometimes this boy just pushes all my buttons. He reminds me so much of his father."

She continued to stand as I rubbed my face. Tears pricked at the back of my eyes but I refused to cry.

"Well, I . . ." The principal seemed to be at a loss for words.

This was the second time my mother mentioned a father who didn't give a fuck about any of us. I wanted to ask if her dead baby, empty bed, and ringless finger weren't proof enough, but I didn't have a death wish. My mother would have opened up a can of whup ass on me right in the principal's office.

Instead, I said, "I don't need a tutor. The work is too easy so I stopped going to class." I slouched down in my seat as all eyes turned on me.

"Is that so? Perhaps we should test your son's abilities." Principal Gaynor sat back down at her desk and opened the folder that she had been carrying in her hands when she greeted us.

"So what are you saying, you think you're some type of genius?" My mother's voice dripped with sarcasm. Her eyes told me that she didn't believe a word coming out of my mouth.

"I ain't saying all that. I just said that I can do that stuff they teaching me in them classes in my sleep."

Ma said, "How would you know what they are teaching if you haven't been there?" She had me there, but I wasn't about to admit it.

"I've seen Merlin's homework." A smile inched up from the corners of my mouth, but I wasn't out of the woods yet.

"Fine, test him since he thinks he's so smart." My mother stood up to leave, and I got to my feet as well. "Where do you think you're going?"

I was confused. "I thought the meeting was over." I looked down at my feet.

"It is, but this is a school day and you've got a test to take. I'll see you at the house." She shook the principal's hand and walked out of the office with her head held high.

I sat back down.

"Gavin, it's going to take me a minute to get a proctor to handle the test. Sit out in the waiting area and I'll have someone come and get you when we're ready for you."

CHAPTER EIGHT

MERLIN MILLS

I was leaving my second period class when I heard the news.

"Hey, man, I guess they finally caught up with your brother. I just saw him down in the principal's office," Braxton Harris, my best friend, said.

"Huh?" I froze in my tracks.

"Your brother. He's sitting down in the office." Braxton pointed. "Go see for yourself."

"Shit." Instead of going to my next period, I detoured to the office. "What are you doing here?" I took a seat next to my brother.

"Mom brought me."

He was pissed, but so was I. My life flowed better when my brother wasn't in it.

"For what?" I was not happy about this latest development because Gavin was always in trouble, and people tended to lump us into the same category.

"She said I got to finish school."

I could tell that he wasn't happy about being here. "So what you going to do?" I secretly hoped he would say fuck it and walk away.

"Finish. She said she would kick me out the house if I didn't stay in school."

I didn't understand. Gavin hadn't been in school in months and it never seemed to bother my mother before. "So when did she become a concerned parent?"

He grinned. "When I threw her toothbrush in the toilet."

Damn, with one stunt Gavin had managed to fuck me twice.

"That was some foul shit you done. Why you always got to be fucking with me?"

"Man, I don't feel like hearing your whining right now."

I wanted to argue with him, but now was not the time. "So what you waiting in here for?"

"They supposed to give me some type of test to find out what grade I belong in."

I almost told him exactly what I thought, but decided to keep my big mouth shut. The last thing I needed right about now was to get into a fight with my brother and risk being cut from the basketball team. I saw basketball as my ticket out of my mother's house and to a better education, and if basketball didn't land me a scholarship, I was headed straight to the military. It wasn't that I didn't love Gina for all that she'd done for us, but ever since she let my dad talk her into aborting her baby, she had become such a bitter person. I didn't want to be around her any longer. "All right then, I'd better get to class before I get into trouble."

Gavin just nodded. He didn't look too happy, but then again, neither was I. I went back to class with a heavy heart. Fortunately for me, I made it before the bell. One of the hardest things about being on the basketball team was that the teachers used that shit against you to keep your ass out of trouble. If I missed doing my homework, I sat out a game; if I was late to class, I sat out a game. Because I planned on using basketball as my ticket out, I couldn't afford to miss shit.

CHAPTER NINE

COJO MILLS

Nine Years Later . . .

Lazily, I stretched my arms over my head and allowed a hearty yawn to follow as I wrapped a towel around my body. Droplets of water dripped from the ends of my hair onto my shoulders, but for the time being, I didn't care about it. Sexual satisfaction made the small stuff seem trivial, and I was indeed satisfied. My husband, Merlin, made it home safely from his short deployment in Iraq, and he'd just worked his magic on me!

"Umph, umph, umph. There ought to be a law against feeling this good." I grabbed a washcloth from the cabinet over the toilet and used it to wipe a clean spot on the mirror. My dark brown eyes twinkled back at me. A satisfied smile tugged at the corners of my mouth. While I had managed to cover most of my head with my shower cap, I noticed that the cap was haphazardly skewed in the back, which allowed the ends of my hair to get wet.

"Oh, fucking well." I giggled as I turned away from the mirror. I wasn't about to let something as miniscule as wet ends ruin my luxurious mood. I grabbed a bottle of lotion and sat down on the side of the tub to begin my moisturizing ritual. I liked to apply lotion while my body was still damp and my pores were open. I rested my slender leg against the sink as I applied the lotion; I could not get the image of my husband's face between my thighs out of my mind.

"He ate your pussy like he was starved," I said to my reflection in the mirror. "I guess that old saying is true: absence does make the heart grow fonder." Rubbing the lotion between my hands to warm it up, I used long strokes to deeply penetrate my sore muscles.

"You should have taken a bath instead of a shower," I spoke again to my reflection while shaking my head.

Merlin twisted my body like a pretzel. I was so engrossed in getting mine, I didn't complain about the complicated positions. In fact, I welcomed the abuse; it had been a long time coming. He fucked the shit out of me.

Merlin had just gotten home from his first active deployment since he joined the Army. He'd enlisted when he got laid off from his job with the state of Georgia. Enlisting in the Army was the last thing either of us wanted, but jobs were difficult to come by. Unemployment was so high, college graduates were competing with high school students for jobs at fast food restaurants.

Although I managed to keep my job with the state, there was no way that I would've been able to keep us afloat with my meager salary. The military offered career opportunities for Merlin that he wouldn't have had without the benefit of a college degree. According to his recruiter, after his mandatory stint of four years, he could attend college for free.

I allowed a small squeal of excitement to escape my lips as I jumped up from the tub. I was about to trapeze over to "what if" land without talking to Merlin to see if anything that we'd be told was actually the truth. With my feet back on the floor, I went into our bedroom to get dressed.

As I entered our room, my breath got caught in my lungs. Merlin was standing in front of the mirror, flexing his newly defined muscles. He was drop-dead gorgeous, and I felt like the luckiest woman in the world just for being his wife. His bald head glistened in the mirror, and his honey-bronzed skin appeared to glow.

My pussy dripped in anticipation of another go round. His eyes met mine in the mirror and my body seemed to float over to him. The muscles in his chest flexed, drawing my eyes to them. My hand reached out to touch him as I closed my eyes. A shiver passed through my body as my hand touched his warm skin.

"Umm, you ready for round two?" I suggestively said. A sudden arctic blast froze my hand to his chest; the chill caused my lids to snap open.

Merlin's seductive eyes turned stony as he stepped away from me. "Round two?" His voice seemed to rumble deep within his chest. His nostrils flared, which caused me to take a step back as well.

My fingers sought the edges of my towel that I'd almost flung to the floor only moments before. "What's the matter?"

Merlin's whole demeanor was different and it threw me off as well. "You said round two. What do you mean?"

I assumed he was joking and wanted me to reiterate how much I enjoyed our last lovemaking session. I coyly smiled at him and took a step closer. "Oh, you don't remember ripping off my clothes and fucking my brains out on the living room floor?"

"Cojo."

There was a warning in his tone that I failed to pay attention to as I continued to taunt him.

"You don't remember sucking my lips and teasing my clit with your tongue?" I closed my eyes and started twirling my hips to a song that played only in my head. I allowed my towel to fall to the floor as I danced for him.

"Cojo."

Once again I ignored the warning in his voice. I was caught up in the moment, and I was anxious to feel his hands on my body again. "You said my pussy was the sweetest nectar that you'd ever tasted . . . umm." My fingers trailed down my body and I finger-fucked myself. "Wanna taste?" My eyes were still closed.

The sound of his fist connecting with my jaw reverberated throughout the room. My arms flailed about helplessly as I sailed through the air. I was so surprised by the blow that I didn't feel the pain, not until my body collided with our bedroom wall. Stunned, I struggled to get to my feet. My jaw throbbed. I felt a mixture of emotions all at the same time: shock, fear, anger.

"Have you lost your rabbit-ass mind? What the fuck is wrong with you?" I demanded, holding my jaw. Perhaps I should have chosen some gentler words to gauge where all this anger came

from, but I was beyond pissed. One thing tha
would not tolerate in a relationship was a m
putting his hands on me.

"No, what the fuck is wrong with you?"
grabbed a shirt from the dresser and yanked
over his head.

"Is that the shit they taught you in Iraq? 'Cau
if it is, then you need to take that shit right ba
where you got it from."

Merlin started at me as if this was the fi
time that he'd ever laid eyes on me. The look se
a chill up my spine. And, for a moment, I did
even recognize my own husband.

"One hour ago we were making love and n
you want to hit me?" I rubbed my jaw for er
phasis and winced in pain. My entire body hu
but my physical pain was nothing compared
the mental anguish I was going through. Nev
in my wildest dreams would I have believed th
Merlin would put his hands on me.

"I've only been home ten minutes."

What the hell did he just say? "Huh?" O
viously, I was the one suffering from del
sions. There was no way he could've said wha
thought he said.

"I said, I've only been home for ten minut
Who the hell were you fucking an hour ago?" I
chest swelled before my eyes as fear replaced t
anger in my heart.

Something was very wrong with this picture, and I was having a difficult time trying to figure out what it was. "I, uh . . . I don't understand."

"Neither do I." He took a step toward me and I backed up farther into the corner.

I needed a moment to think. One of us had obviously lost his mind, and I was quite sure it wasn't me. "This isn't funny, Merlin."

"Do I look like I'm laughing to you?" His nostrils were flaring again and his hands were balled up in tight fists.

I looked around for a weapon. There was no way I was going to allow him to hit me again. Frantically, my eyes searched my corner of the room. The closest thing to a weapon I could find was a pair of high-heeled shoes. I inched my way closer to the closet as he took a step closer.

"I'm waiting." He beat his fists against his thighs as his eyes narrowed. Gone were the lust and longing I had seen in his eyes when he was beating the breaks off my pussy.

"Merlin, stop. Something is wrong."

"Ha, ain't that the understatement of the year. I come home after getting my ass kicked for six months to find my wife acting like a fucking tramp!"

"Merlin, please." Tears began to flow down my face. I felt like I'd stepped onto the set of some horrible movie, and I wanted to wake the fuck up.

"Please, my ass. I ought to kill your trifling ass. Who was it?"

I dove for the closet, but he swooped me up before I could hit the floor. I'd never been so afraid in my entire life. My body trembled uncontrollably as his fingers tightened around my arms. He lifted me over his head as I screamed.

"Hey, bro, what's up?"

My head jerked toward the door at a man who looked like the spitting image of my husband. Merlin paused as his fingers dug into my skin.

"Gavin?" Merlin asked, stunned to be looking at his brother.

I felt the floor rush up to greet me as Merlin dropped me like a useless dumbbell he had tired of.

"Yeah, man, what's up with you?" The stranger took a step into the room with a shit-eating grin on his face.

"How did you get in here?"

I sat up, wincing in pain.

"You're still leaving the key under the mat just like you did when we were kids."

"Merlin, who is this man?" I was reaching for my towel to cover my nakedness. I knew it was a stupid question even before it had left my lips, but rational thinking wasn't something I was capable of at the moment. Both men stared at me like I'd just stepped off the short yellow bus.

Merlin's shoulders slumped. "Man, please tell me you didn't just fuck my wife." The fire had gone out of Merlin's body as my eyes bucked at the implication of his words.

"Wife? When the fuck did you get married?" The stranger laughed, as if he had told a joke.

"Aw, man . . . shit." Merlin's face was pinched, and for a moment, I forgot about how I was feeling and my heart went out to him.

"Hell, man, I didn't know. She came through the door looking all good and shit, it just happened. She ran up on me, wrapped those chocolate legs around my waist—it was a wrap." He shook his head as if he was sorry, but he was smiling.

A feeling of dread came down on me. Merlin had a twin brother? *How come he didn't tell me? Where the fuck has he been all this time?* Too many questions and too few answers were racing through my mind. I stood up, but the room was spinning. I stumbled over to the bed to sit down, but Merlin pushed me to the floor. Venom spewed from his eyes as he glared at me.

"She was my wife, dammit," Merlin yelled as he pounded the mattress for emphasis.

"Was? Did he just say was?" I thought This nightmare I was living was dramatic. "Wait just a fucking minute," I said as I angrily got to my feet. I marched over to the evil twin and slapped him across the face. I was hoping to wipe away the smile, but it didn't work.

His grin turned into a menacing leer. "Come on, baby, you weren't acting like that a little while ago." He mocked me and it took all my strength not to head-butt that motherfucker.

"You bastard," I spat.

"True that, Dad never got around to marrying our moms." He chuckled and that just made me madder.

I wanted Merlin to come over there and punch him like he'd punched me, but he just sat on the bed and stared at his feet. I whirled back around and faced his brother. "How come you didn't tell me who you were?" Outraged, I placed my hands on my hips for want of a better place to put them. Although I wanted to hit him again, my fingers were still stinging from the first slap.

"How come you didn't know my dick from his?"

I reared back as if he struck me. His words pierced me like a knife.

"I . . . uh." I heard the wail come from my husband's mouth seconds before his body collided with mine.

He rushed me like a linebacker. "You bitch," he yelled as his fingers found their way around my throat.

I struggled to get him off of me as his grip got tighter. He was going to kill me, and I was powerless to do anything about it. My eyes sought to convey how sorry I was, but Merlin wasn't looking at me. It was as if he were lost in the past.

"I'm sorry," I gasped as Merlin abruptly let loose.

Hot tears streamed down his face and dripped into my open mouth as I struggled to breathe.

I said, "I'm so sorry."

He pushed me one final time before he rolled off of me.

CHAPTER TEN

MERLIN MILLS

Brushing past my brother, I headed for the bar in our living room. I needed a drink in the worst way. Gavin reached out and grabbed my arm, but I batted his hand away. I wasn't ready to deal with his ass just yet; I needed to wrap my mind around what had just happened. In my entire life, I had never put my hands on a female. I was deeply ashamed of myself.

I grabbed a glass from the hanging rack and filled it to the brim with Absolut. I didn't even bother going into the kitchen to get some ice, I just turned up the glass and drank the whole thing. The liquor burned all the way down my throat and landed in a fiery ball in my stomach, but it did not dull the pain that I felt in my heart. I quickly refilled my glass, but this time I began to sip it. I walked over to the sofa and took a seat.

In our bedroom, I could still hear Cojo sobbing, but I could not force myself to get up and go comfort her. I felt like she had betrayed me even if it was by mistake. "Lord, if it would have been anybody else, but my damn brother." I didn't bother to wipe the tears that flowed from my eyes.

"You talking to yourself, bro?" Gavin had walked into the living room. He wore a satisfied smile on his face.

It was all I could do not to leap over the sofa and bust him dead in his mouth. "Not now, Gavin," I said between clenched teeth.

"If not now, then when? We haven't seen each other in ages. Don't you want to catch up?"

"Look, haven't you done enough already?"

"What did I do?" He looked at me with his big, round eyes, which looked so much like mine that it just made my stomach hurt.

"Man, fuck you." I didn't want to talk to him. I didn't want to talk to anyone. I just wanted to be left alone to wallow in my misery. I could not believe he had come back into my life and ruined the only thing that belonged to me. I wished they would have left him in prison forever. Seven years just wasn't long enough.

"Damn, dude, are you crying?"

I threw back my glass and finished off the rest of my drink.

Gavin said, "Hey, do you think I can get some of that?"

My brother had some big-ass balls. Any other man would have gotten the hell out of dodge as soon as he found out that he had fucked another man's wife and he knew it. He was lucky I wasn't wearing my service weapon. I do believe that at that moment I would have shot first and asked the questions later that I needed answers to. "Gavin, I'm about ten seconds from killing your ass so you need to get the fuck up out of my house."

"Shit, I said I was sorry. What the hell do you expect me to do, kiss your ass?"

I could feel the rage building behind my eyes. I just wanted to be left alone so that I could think. "Stop playin', Gavin, I said enough. I am way past my breaking point so please leave it alone."

"Or what? I ain't scared of your punk ass. You won't be putting your hands on me like you did your wife."

I could not believe he was still goading me. I felt like I was a child all over again. "Not now, Gavin," I warned. I was burning on a slow fuse and I knew that if he actually touched me, I would have punched him square in the mouth.

Gavin had always been the bane of my existence, and even though I loved him, most times

I couldn't stand him. As a child he was always getting into trouble and I wound up getting punished for it.

"You think this is a fucking joke." I snatched my glass and went back to the bar to refill it. I tilted the glass up to my lips, anticipating the burn.

Cojo was still crying in our bedroom and I tuned her out. Although my head knew it was not her fault that my brother had deceived her, my heart wasn't trying to hear it. Putting my feet up on the coffee table, I picked up the remote, hoping to drown out the sounds coming from my bedroom.

Gavin came over to me and kicked my feet off the coffee table.

"Fuck off, Gavin, I ain't in the mood."

"Stop acting like a punk, man. This ain't the first time that we've shared some pussy. Remember Kim?"

I pointed toward my bedroom. "That pussy belongs to my wife." It took everything in me not to bash him upside the head with my glass.

"Damn, my bad. But I still don't see why you're getting so upset. How was I supposed to know that you were married?"

My head jerked up. I just stared at him. I could not believe that he was taking this so lightly. "What are you doing here, Gavin?"

"Damn, I've been in the joint all those years, not one letter or visit from you. Can't a brother come see about his kin?"

Any other time, I would have been happy to see him, but he'd ruined our reunion when he slept with my wife. "How did you find me?"

"Moms, she gave me your address when I showed up at her house." Gavin let out a wicked laugh, but I failed to see any humor in the situation.

"Remind me to thank her if I ever speak to her again." I went and got the bottle and brought it back to the sofa with me.

Gavin mentioning Gina brought up another bone of contention. Thinking about my mother only made me depressed.

"What? So you mad now?" Gavin pushed his foot against the table, causing me to spill some of the booze on the table.

"Why shouldn't I be?" I sulked.

"Man, I said I was sorry," Gavin replied.

"No, you didn't. You said 'my bad.'"

"Same difference." Gavin picked up the bottle and turned it up to his lips.

"I see prison hasn't changed much for you." I snatched the bottle back from him and wiped it off.

"Bro, you need to lighten up. If you keep treating me like this, I am going to get a complex."

"Fuck you and your complex. That's the problem with your ass now. Everybody babied your ass and you believed people owed you something for nothing."

"Nigga, please, ain't nobody babied me. It was your ass that was always running around trying to suck on Momma's tit."

"I'm not going to argue with your ass. Tell me what you want and leave."

"Oh, it's like that?"

I threw my hands up in the air in frustration. Gavin was a superior manipulator. Whenever I went against him, I came out with the shorter end of the stick.

"Gavin, I am in no mood for your games."

"I need a place to stay." Gavin reached for the bottle again, but I quickly moved it out of his reach.

"Get your own bottle," I said, pointing to the bar in the dining room.

"I like yours better," Gavin said as he faked a left and moved right and grabbed the bottle out of my hand. Although he was laughing when he said it, he had never spoken truer words. He always liked what I had, but the bigger part of the problem was that he always got it. I buried my

head in my hands. Part of me wanted to just ha
it out with my brother, but the saner me kn
that I couldn't win.

"You can't stay here," I spoke into my han
It hurt me to my heart to tell him no, but the
was no way that I was going to allow him to st
with me after what he had done to my wife.

"Why not?"

I fought the urge to scream at him becau
I knew it wouldn't do any good. Gavin was t
type of guy who got off on getting somebody e
rattled—especially me.

"Hello, you just fucked my wife!"

"Oh, yeah, I'd forgotten about that." He start
laughing.

Before I could stop myself, I lunged at hi
but Gavin pushed me aside before I could wr
my hands around his neck.

"Stop playing." He brushed himself off as
had somehow soiled him.

Cojo's sobs got louder when she opened c
bedroom door. She was holding a rag to the rig
side of her face with one hand and her suitc
with the other. For a moment, I forgot about I
ing mad at my brother.

"Where the fuck do you think you're going?"

She looked at me as if I had just bumped
head. "None of your business." She walked in
the kitchen with me close on her heels.

"Cojo, I asked you a question."

"And I gave you an answer." She continued looking around the table as if I weren't standing there.

It was bad enough that she'd admitted to screwing my brother, but my ego couldn't take her clowning me in front of him, too. I reached out to grab her arm, and she snatched it away from me.

"Don't you dare touch me." She pulled down the rag and allowed me to see what I'd done to her in my rage.

My heart clenched as I looked at her swollen jaw. My anger dissolved immediately. I forgot about the macho image I was trying to maintain. "Ah, damn, baby, I'm sorry." I took a step forward. I wanted to take her in my arms and comfort her.

"You damn right you're sorry. You lucky I don't have your ass locked up."

I took a step back. I didn't take kindly to being threatened with the law. But truth be told, in this instance I deserved it. I swallowed my pride. "I understand how you feel, there is no excuse for what I've done."

She stopped searching the table and looked at me. I guess I surprised her with my admission, but the words were coming from my heart.

"Tell it to my lawyer."

If she was trying to hurt me, she was doing a damn good job. Despite what had happened here today, I didn't want a divorce and I didn't want her to leave me. "Baby, please, can we just sit down and talk about this?"

"Oh, now you want to talk after you tried to bash my brains in?"

"Babe, I said I was sorry and I meant it."

She just stared at me. But I felt hopeful because she hadn't left the house. I knew that if she left me, she would never come back. She would go home to her mother and, since she didn't like me anyway, it would be a wrap.

"I think I need some time by myself to think." Her voice was barely over a whisper so I had to lean in close to hear her.

"Can't you do your thinking here?"

"The sight of you sickens me."

I was about to respond until Gavin walked into the kitchen.

"Yo, bro, I know you ain't begging that bitch to stay."

Cojo and I both swung around and stared at Gavin. I'd forgotten he was even here.

"You . . . rat . . . bastard," Cojo yelled. She grabbed a knife and was heading straight for my brother.

I said, "No, Cojo."

Gavin was backing out the kitchen with his hands up in the air. He was smiling as if this were all a big joke. I grabbed her arm but, once again, she snatched it away from me.

"I told you to keep your hands off of me." She wielded the knife at me.

"I wasn't going to hurt you. I just didn't want you to do something you would regret for the rest of your life."

"What? You think I care about that fucker? After what he did to me?"

"Put the knife down, Cojo," I pleaded.

"Punk ass," Gavin replied.

I could not believe he was still egging her on instead of keeping his mouth shut and letting me diffuse the situation. "Shut up, Gavin. You're not helping matters."

Acting like Billy Bad Ass, he turned his back and walked away, almost daring Cojo to put him out of his misery.

She whirled around and faced me. "I'll stay, but that motherfucker has to go." She lowered the knife, but she didn't put it in the sink, so I wasn't out of the woods yet.

"Baby, he just got out of prison and he doesn't have any place to go."

"And am I supposed to care?"

I knew exactly how she felt, but putting [...] out would be easier said than done.

"Look, stay here. I'll be right back."

She turned away from me, but I was ha[...] that she didn't just say fuck it and leave. I [...] back into the living room.

"Man, you ain't going to be able to stay he[...]

"You letting that bitch tell you how to t[...] your own family?" He hawked up a bunch of [...] as if he was going to expel it on the carpet. "[...] we ain't talked or seen each other in seven ye[...] We're brothers."

"Kill that noise, it ain't even about her. I d[...] want you here."

Gavin raised his eyebrows, as if he ha[...] heard me correctly. There was no way that I [...] going to side with him over my wife.

"I guess I got to go back to Mom's and tell[...] you wouldn't help me out." Gavin got up off [...] sofa and walked toward the door.

I looked around the room for his bags [...] I didn't see any. "I don't give a rat's ass v[...] you tell our mother, but you can't stay her[...] slammed my hand on the coffee table just t[...] him know I meant business. He had manipula[...] me enough. I was done. I pulled out my wall[...] had just gotten paid so I was going to give hi[...]

few bucks to tide him over. Counting out $200, I folded up the bills in my hand. "Gavin, wait."

"You changed your mind?" He turned around all smiles. "Thank God I don't have to wait for another cab. I'm broke as it is."

"Naw, just take this. Maybe you can get a hotel room until we can figure out something else."

"Shit, I don't want your money. I came over here because I wanted to spend some time with my only brother. Keep that shit." He pushed away my hand as if I offended him.

"Man, take the money. You can get a room and not have to worry about going by Mom's. We can get together in a day or so and I'll look out for you."

"Whatever." He snatched the money from my hand and went out the door. He didn't say bye or kiss his ass.

Part of me wanted to run after him and allow him to stay, but the other part of me really didn't want him around. With him out of the way, perhaps I could pick up the pieces of my life and try to put them back together.

CHAPTER ELEVEN

GINA MEADOWS

"Tabatha, I need to talk with you. Pick up the phone." Three times I had called Tabatha and each time she ignored my call. I really needed to get her opinion before I accepted Gavin back into my life.

She picked up right as I was ready to hang up. "Bitch, why you blowing up my phone?"

A part of me wanted to get mad, but the other part of me was grateful she was on the line.

"Girl, stop playing. You know I love you. I just need some advice."

"I should have known that your ass wasn't just contacting me because you missed me."

It had been a few months since I'd talked to Tabatha and, truth be told, I did miss her in my life, but I was not about to tell her that. She was nosey enough without that little bit of information.

"It's Gavin. He's out of prison and I don't know what to do."

"What do you mean you don't know what to do? Shut the fucking door in his face. That boy is bad news. After all the shit he did, I'd be scared to have him around me."

"Tabatha, he is my son."

"Son of a fool. You don't owe that man anything."

"Tabatha, you've never had children. Even if his father was an asshole, I still owe his child."

"Tabatha, Gavin's twenty-five years old. The debt has been paid."

There was some truth in Tabatha's words. I didn't have to continue caring for the child of a man who'd dogged me all these years, but I still loved Ronald and we continued to see each other. "You have a point. He just showed up at my door as if I owed him something."

"I don't see why. As hateful as you've been to him and Merlin, I don't see why he darkened your doorstep in the first place."

"I was not hateful."

"Bitch, please. Ever since you aborted your baby you've been a hateful heifer to them boys. And you're still a hateful bitch behind that shit to this day."

"Tabatha, I didn't call you for all of that."

"The truth hurts. Why you think you and M⟨e⟩lin haven't spoken in all these years? If you ⟨⟩ that shit to me, I wouldn't be bothered with y⟨⟩ ass either."

"I've got to go, Tabatha." I hung up on h⟨er⟩ without waiting for her reply. Her words ⟨⟩ home and hurt me deeply.

I sighed and thought back to the day Mer⟨⟩ and I fell out. We had been drifting apart ev⟨⟩ since he started dating Cojo in his senior ye⟨ar⟩ of high school. He spent more time at her hou⟨⟩ and less time with me. Things really hit the f⟨⟩ when he announced that he was getting marri⟨ed.⟩

"What do you mean you're getting marrie⟨?⟩ I yelled. I felt like he was much too young to ⟨⟩ married.

"Yes, I'm getting married." He poked out ⟨his⟩ narrow chest and stared at me.

"Is Cujo pregnant?"

"Her name is Cojo, not Cujo. And no, she⟨'s⟩ not pregnant."

I wasn't really trying to piss him off, but ⟨⟩ had thrown me for a loop. "Then why the ⟨⟩ rush to get married?" I demanded.

"We're not rushing. We just know what ⟨we⟩ want and there is no point to waiting."

"Yes, there is. You hardly know this heffa."

"If we are going to continue this conversation, I would appreciate it if you would stop calling my future wife out of her name."

I was stunned. This was the first time in Merlin's entire life that he ever stood up to me. I reached back and slapped the shit out of him. He rubbed the side of his face but he didn't back down. I immediately regretted hitting him. "I'm sorry. I didn't mean to do that." He did not respond right away, and I assumed that he was trying to get his emotions under control before this conversation went to a whole different level.

"We're getting married on May twenty-third, one week after we graduate. I'd like you to be there, but if you don't feel like it, I will try to understand." He turned and walked out the door.

That was the beginning of the end for my relationship with Merlin.

I staggered down the aisle. I had no intentions of going to the wedding, but liquor has a way of making you do stupid shit. I had spent the entire week drinking until I passed out. I was so upset with Merlin I didn't know what to do.

"If I could just get him to listen to me, I'm sure I could make him change his mind," I muttered out loud.

The church was full with the students Merlin went to school with, and, I guessed, Cojo's family. I don't even remember how I got to the church; I was so drunk. I looked around to see if Ronald was there, but I didn't immediately see him. I took a seat a few rows from the back. I would have walked up closer, but I wasn't sure my legs were going to support me.

"This is some bullshit." I was getting angrier by the second.

Merlin stood facing the altar with the priest and waited for his bride. He turned around and looked to the door at the back of the church, and I saw the eagerness on his face. Suddenly, he didn't look like Merlin to me; he was Ronald. I shook my head in confusion.

"Ronald." I struggled to get out of the pew. I could not believe that my dream was finally going to come true. I rushed down the aisle to get to him. "I'm coming, Ronald," I whispered. I didn't see Cojo walk up the aisle until she joined hands with Ronald.

"No!" I yelled.

All eyes were on the front of the church, so no one was really paying me any attention. She looked lovely, but there was something wrong. Cojo was wearing my dress! I looked down to see what I was wearing, and I was appalled to see I was wearing blue jeans and a tattered robe with slippers on my feet.

"This isn't right." I looked up to see if Ronald noticed that she was wearing my dress. He wasn't even looking at me; he was staring at Cojo.

"How did you get my dress, you bitch?" I reached for Cojo, but she jumped behind Merlin.

"Ms. Meadows? What are you doing?" Her face was twisted up into an awful grimace, and she kept turning her head as if she smelled something foul.

Merlin frowned. "Mom? What are you doing?"

"She's trying to steal you away from me, Ronald." I reached out to Cojo again, but Merlin guarded her well. "Let go of that heffa and let's get married." I saw the ring that he was about to place on her finger and I grabbed it from him. "Give me my damn ring."

"You're drunk." He turned his nose up at me and looked at Cojo.

Everyone in the church was talking with shocked looks on their faces.

"Who is that?" the crowd whispered.

"I think that's Merlin's mother."

"Get out of here."

"What the hell is she wearing?"

"I think she's drunk. I heard she wasn't stable, something to do with Merlin's father."

"Who is this Ronald she is talking about?"

"That's Merlin's father." I slipped the ring on my finger and it fit perfectly.

"It fits, Ronald. She tried to ruin things for you and me, but I'm not going to let her."

Cojo started to cry. "You're trying to ruin my wedding."

I reached for her again, but only managed to grab the flowers out of her hand. "Let's do this, Ronald. I've been waiting all my life to be your wife."

"Mother!" Merlin yelled.

I didn't understand why he was yelling at me on the day that I was finally marrying his father. I reached for Cojo again and managed to grab the bodice of her dress. I yanked it hard, trying to get the dress so I could finally get married. I felt the fabric tear, and I yelled out in frustration. "Give me my dress, bitch." I had lost all rational thought.

I wanted the heifer to go away. I could see the anger on Merlin's face. I never thought I would live to see the day he'd hit me, but he did. He slapped me across the face, breaking me out of the trance I was in.

"Merlin?" My head started spinning. I looked around at all the faces in the church as the reality of what I'd done rushed back to me. "Oh, God,

I started to fall on the floor, but Merlin caught me before I could hit the ground. "I just wanted to say I do . . ." Cojo rushed up and grabbed my other hand. I turned to her to apologize for my behavior. The bile in my stomach rose to my mouth and before I could stop myself, I puked all over Cojo's beautiful dress.

CHAPTER TWELVE

GAVIN MILLS

After struggling with the unfamiliar door, I nally managed to get it open, and tossed my ke on the kitchen counter. I was so deep in though I didn't even see my mother draped over the li ing room sofa.

"How did it go?" She looked at me and I want to smack her. She was a tricky bitch and I w lucky to find her. This was the third apartme she had moved to since I was locked up.

"All right." I was not ready to discuss my vi with Merlin just yet. I still had some figuring do. Something had changed about him, an had to figure out what it was before I proceede

"Just all right? Was he there?" she demande

"Uh, yeah, he was there." I took off my jack and was about to head back to my room, but was obvious my mother wasn't done with o conversation. "He paid for my cab fare."

"Don't you walk away from me, boy, while I'm talking to you."

My skin bristled as I digested the comment. It really pissed me off that my mother insisted on calling me a boy, despite the fact that I was halfway through my twenties. I bit my tongue to keep from telling her exactly how I felt, because Gina could be a vengeful bitch. She would kick me out of her house and not even bat an eye, so I treaded carefully. "Sorry, Mother, I didn't realize you had something else you wanted to discuss." I lifted her feet off the sofa and sat down with her tiny feet on my lap. Gently, I massaged her toes. I knew this was one way to bring out her other half, the half that I loved. Growing up with a Gemini woman was a stone-cold trip. You never knew who you were talking to until you felt the backside of her hand upside your head.

"Umph." She sniffed.

I could tell that she accepted my peacemaking attempt. Truth be told, the last thing I wanted to do in this world was to rub her crusty feet. If I had more money in my pocket than the measly $200 my brother gave me, I would've treated her to a pedicure.

I looked at the room and I felt like I had stepped back in time. The sofa that we were sitting on was the same one that had graced our

living room when Merlin and I were younger. I
was still encased in plastic, which had yellowed
over the years. Part of me just wanted to take off
the plastic and let the sofa breathe.

"Was his trick there?"

"You mean his wife?" I knew exactly who she
was talking about, but refused to go there with
her.

Gina had yet to tell me what exactly she had
against sexy-ass Cojo. Until she did, I was going
to walk softly.

"I said exactly what I meant and you know it."
Gina folded her arms across her ample chest.
For a minute, my gaze lingered. The size of her
breasts never ceased to amaze me. For such a
tiny woman, she had the biggest natural breasts
that I'd ever seen. I suppose that's why I'd always been attracted to busty women. They could
be dumb as a doorknob, but if they had a set of
knockers, ooh whee, I was in lust.

"Yeah, she was there." I kept right on massaging my mother's toes, hoping that she would give
up her third degree. For a brief second, I felt a
tinge of jealousy because my mother was more
interested in what my brother was doing at his
house than in me. After all, it had been seven
years since we had seen each other and the first
words out of her mouth when she opened the

door were about whether I'd stayed in contact with him. Shrugging, I pushed away those ugly thoughts and tried to enjoy being with her again.

"Why are you being so damned secretive?" She pulled her feet off my lap and sat up on the sofa.

Part of me wanted to rush to the bathroom and wash my hands, but I knew that would send her into a tizzy, and I did not need the bullshit. All I wanted to do was go in my room and take a nap. Merlin's wife wore me the fuck out, and I needed to re-energize. "I ain't being secretive, it's just nothing that I want to talk about right now. I'm tired. The trip here was three hours; I need a bath and a bed, in that order." I was hoping my little plea for sympathy would get me off the hook for a few hours, but my mother wasn't having it.

"You've got all night to sleep. I want to know what your brother is up to."

"He ain't up to nothing. How come you didn't tell me that he enlisted in the Army?"

"He did what?" She jumped off the sofa and started pacing the room. She grabbed a cigarette from the pack on the coffee table and struck a match to the end.

The acrid smoke filled the room; I stifled the urge to cough. I hated cigarette smoke, and I felt like she lit it just to torment me. As an asthmatic, I tried to stay away from it because it forced me to use my inhaler. It'd been three long years since I had to use it, and I didn't want to start back using it now. "Must you smoke that thing while I'm in the room?"

"Negro, please, this is my damn house. If you don't like it, you can get the fuck out."

I just shook my head; some things never change. She had been telling me to get the fuck out, it seemed, for my entire life. I stood up.

"Where the fuck do you think you are going? I wanna hear about your brother and the service."

"I'll tell you, Mother, but I cannot stay in the room if you insist on smoking." I held my breath just in case she told me to get the hell out of her house.

"Fine, I'll put it out. Now tell me." She snubbed her cigarette into the ashtray and flopped back against the cushions of the sofa, as if I had stolen her lollipop.

"He just got home from Iraq. From what I gathered, he's been gone for about six months."

"My baby has been gone for six months, and he didn't even bother to tell me?"

Gina was a fucking trip. She chose the damnedest times to claim us as her children. Most of the time, she ignored the shit out of us and complained about not having her own child.

"I don't know nothing about it. None of y'all wrote to me and told me shit. If I hadn't shown up when I did, I guess I wouldn't have known either."

She frowned at my spicy language. "Did you ask him why he made such a foolish move?"

"No, frankly, I didn't. I'm going to take a shower. Perhaps you will be done with your cigarette by the time I'm finished and we can continue our talk." I walked away knowing full well she might pick up any object and swing it at my head. Luckily for me, she didn't exercise that option.

"Yeah, take your ass to bed. Maybe when you wake up, you won't be in such a stank mood."

If she thought my mood was stank, it was obvious that she hadn't checked herself out in the last thirteen years. "Are there towels in the bathroom?"

"Yeah, in the closet, and don't go messing up my fancy ones on the wall. And make sure you put the toilet seat down when you use it. If I dunk my ass one time, your black ass is out of here."

"Yes, Mother," I whispered through clenched teeth. If she'd told me once, she had told me

three thousand times about letting down
seat, and I was sick of hearing it. Althoug
loved my mother, she could work my last ne
I gently closed the bathroom door, even thou
I wanted to slam it. For the umpteenth tim
wondered if I'd made a mistake by coming ba

After a seven-year bid with the Federal Bur
of Corrections in Edgefield, South Carolin
didn't have a lot of options. Although I got
GED while in prison, and graduated from Oas
novel writing class, I had no real work expe
ence, and my cash flow was nonexistent. My p
was to come home, regroup, and try to get on
feet in familiar surroundings; however, I'd f
gotten how dysfunctional home really was, an
was beginning to wonder if the security of a r
over my head was worth the mental torture t
living with Mother brought.

Taking off my clothes, I filled the tub, hop
to revive my spirits. It had been a long time si
I'd been able to take a bath, and I planned on
joying every minute of it. I stepped in. I imme
ately began to relax, and the things that I'd be
stressing over moments before no longer seen
important. I hadn't realized until that mom
how much prison had changed me. Just be
able to close the bathroom door was a lux
that had been taken from me. I grabbed a yell

bar of Dial and smelled it. "Ah, I feel like I've died and gone to heaven." Anything that didn't smell like prison-issued lye was heaven sent to me because I didn't have money to buy anything while I was in. That prison shit made your skin itch something terrible, and the smell followed you around for hours. I inhaled deeply, fully appreciating something as simple as a bar of soap.

I soaped my washcloth thoroughly and reveled in the feeling of the bubbles gliding over my skin. I was feeling so good, I wanted to break out with a song, but since I couldn't carry a tune in a bucket, I decided to leave that alone.

As my hand glided over my dick, I froze. My thoughts went back to Cojo, and I began to stiffen. A slow smile slid across my face as I remembered her fat pussy lips and the way they wrapped around my dick and sucked me in. She was quite a handful and just what the doctor ordered after my imprisonment. "I'm gonna have to hit that again."

Gina banged on the door like she was a CO. "Gavin, don't you be in my tub jacking off and shit."

"Damn, she can ruin a wet dream." I rinsed the remaining soap off my body, then stepped out of the tub. I looked down at my clothes in disgust. I didn't feel like putting them back on. I stuck my head out the door. "Mother, do you still have my old clothes?"

"Hell no. I know you didn't think I would be carting that stuff around with me when I moved," she hollered back.

My heart sank because I would have no choice but to put on my dirty clothes again or walk around in the buff. "I just asked." As much as I wanted to argue with my mother, I knew it would be pointless, and I didn't want to be out on the front porch for the night.

"Call your trifling brother and see if he can bring you over some clothes. I sure would like to see him."

Wow, that was actually a good idea, and I was surprised that I didn't think of it myself. Wrapping a towel around my waist, I padded out to the living room to make the call. "What's his number?"

"Hell, you were just over to his apartment, why didn't you get the number while you were there?"

Sometimes I just wanted to strangle her. "I forgot. Things were happening kind of fast. Do you have the number?"

She got up off the sofa and went into her bedroom. I could hear her grumbling, but I pretended not to notice. She came back a few minutes later carrying a small phonebook. After flipping through several pages, she finally called out the number.

The phone rang three times before Merlin came on the line. "Long time no hear from, Mother."

I hung up the phone. The last thing that I wanted was for Merlin to know that I was staying with our mother instead of in the hotel he'd given me money for.

"Why did you do that?" Gina demanded.

Thinking fast, I blurted out, "His wife answered."

"Well, I don't blame you then. I hate her."

I kept my hand on the receiver just in case Merlin decided to call back. If he did, I would have to make up something to say that would explain my presence.

"So what are you going to do now?"

"Can I wash my clothes here? I'll stop by and see Merlin in the morning about getting some other clothes."

"I guess, but don't be making this no habit. Ain't nothing in this apartment free, and I don't have money to be wasting it on extra water and shit." She lit up a cigarette.

"Okay, Mother, I get it. Just give me a few weeks to get on my feet and I'll be out of your hair."

"Humph. I'll believe it when I see it. I've heard it all before . . . Just can't do right."

There was a hint of sadness mixed with sarcasm in her voice and it hurt. She blamed me for my shortcomings, but I blamed her. If she'd been more loving and nurturing, maybe things would not have turned out as they did. As it was, she pitted me against my brother from as far back as I could remember. I wanted to say all those things and more, but I was forced to suck it up until I could do better.

I placed my clothes in the washer and went into the spare bedroom to take a nap. Gina was still on the sofa watching television as I gently closed the door behind me. With any luck, her other half would be around when I woke up.

CHAPTER THIRTEEN

GAVIN MILLS

I lay across the bed. Sleep claimed me, and almost immediately I fell into the same dream that had haunted me since the fateful day I tried to steal something else from my brother and ended up in prison behind the shit, trying to get my dick wet.

I'd made a date with this cute little honey named Cheryl who thought the sun rose and set in Merlin's ass. She flirted with him shamelessly, but he wouldn't give her the time of day. He was too busy trying to be a basketball star. One day I asked her out, and she accepted thinking I was Merlin. So I borrowed—actually, I took—Merlin's car and picked her up. She didn't live that far from our Covington home, so I wasn't worried about not having a license. I'd practiced driving before and felt like I was competent enough to do it. Perhaps things would not have turned out as badly as they did if I'd asked permission to borrow his car.

Cheryl was looking hot when I picked her up. She came out to the car after I tooted the horn, and stood by the door with her arms crossed across her breasts. I could not remove my eyes from their swell.

She cleared her throat. "Aren't you going to open the door?"

This bitch was tripping. I fought back the urge to ask her if her fingers were broken. I wasn't used to playing the role of gentleman. For some pussy, though, I was willing to play along. I got out of the car, sauntered around the back, and stood facing her. I wanted a kiss but knew it was too soon to be taking it. I reached past her and opened the door. "You look nice," I said as I closed the door behind her.

She seemed to unthaw with those few words.

"Thanks, Merlin, you look cute too."

I was wearing black jeans, a black Frankie Beverly and Maze T-shirt, and a black hat. I walked back around the car with a little pep in my step. I was feeling cocky and sure of myself as I got back into the driver's seat. Although, I never heard a single song that Frankie Beverly sang, he just seemed like the type of artist Cheryl would appreciate, so I borrowed the shirt from my brother. I didn't actually borrow the shirt, 'cause that would require my asking his permission, so I guess you could say I stole it too.

"Where are we going?" Cheryl was looking in the mirror and putting on lipstick. She wore a tight pair of blue jeans and a yellow tank top.

My eyes kept going back and forth from the road to her breasts.

"Merlin?"

I heard her talking, but I forgot I was pretending to be my brother until she nudged me.

"Huh?"

"I asked you where we're going." Her voice was beginning to get on my nerves.

Up until this moment I hadn't spent much time around her, so I never noticed the whiny quality in her tone. I was taking the shortcut though the Indian reservation when the car sputtered and jerked.

"What the fuck?" I muttered as the car quit moving altogether.

"Did you just run out of gas?"

In my haste to get the car out of the driveway before my mother stopped me, it didn't even occur to me to check if there was any gas in the car. "Shit." I hit my hand on the dashboard in frustration. All week long Merlin had been catching rides to school and work with his buddy

Braxton Harris, but he never said why and now I knew. He hadn't gotten paid and was broke. He couldn't afford gas.

"Please tell me you didn't run out of gas." There was attitude in Cheryl's voice.

This was not good. We were on a deserted part of the reservation at the bottom of the hill, which was a disaster waiting to happen.

"You are going to have to steer the car while I push it off the road." I opened the door and went around to the back of the car.

"I don't know how to drive."

I wanted to tell her neither did I, but time was running out. "Just turn the wheel to the right and keep your feet off the brake. Put it in neutral."

She slid over in the seat. Any hope of getting some pussy tonight went right out the window. I'd be lucky if I got a kiss on the cheek.

She put the car in gear and I started to push. Getting the car to move was harder than I thought it would be. I had to dig real deep before it began to move.

"Now straighten up the wheel," I yelled, grunting with exertion.

"How do I do that?" she yelled back.

Ooh-whee, I was sick of her, I thought. Instead I said, "Turn it a little to the left."

She stomped on the brake, stopping the car.

"Get your fucking foot off the brake."

"Who the hell are you cussing at?"

That had to be a rhetorical question since we were the only people out here.

I counted to five before I answered, "Cheryl, please. We have to get the car off the road before someone comes and hits us." I pushed again and the car glided to the right. "Okay, that's good. Put the brake on and put it in park." I leaned against the bumper as I tried to catch my breath.

Cheryl got out of the car and stomped around to the back. Her four-inch heels made a clicking sound on the pavement. "What now?" She had her hands on her hips and was working her neck like some ghetto chick. It was not a good look.

Wiping the sweat from my forehead, I said, "I guess we walk."

"Walk? Are you out your mind?"

"Do you have another suggestion?"

She was quickly getting on my nerves.

"Merlin, there is no way that I can walk with these shoes on." She was whining again.

"Fine, stay here. When I get some gas, I'll be back."

"You expect me to wait here all by myself?"

Her question didn't even warrant an answer. I just wanted to get as far away from Merlin's car as my feet would carry me. I had a couple of dollars in my pocket, so I was going to get some gas, drop this bitch off at her house, and park the car back like nothing ever happened.

I said, "If we stay here, we're liable to get hit, so the choice is yours." I opened the trunk. I prayed that Merlin had a gas can in there, but luck was not on my side. "Shit." I slammed the trunk and started going toward Salem Road.

"Why are we going this way? My house is back there." She was pointing her finger back in the direction we came from.

My blood was starting to bubble. "I have to get gas, don't I?"

"But if we walk that way, we will have to walk back."

"Duh!" I was done being nice to her, and if she thought I was going to walk her home first then go get gas, she was silly in the head.

"You don't have to be an ass, Merlin. It's not my fault you ran out of gas."

So now the bitch wanted to play the blame game. I started walking again at a fast pace. The way I figured, the quicker I got the gas, the quicker I could get rid of this pesky clickety-clacking heifer next to me.

"Must you walk so fast?"

"I ain't tryin' to be out here all night. I told you you're welcome to wait in the car." I could tell that she was thinking about it, but while she was thinking, I was walking. The road going through the Indian reservation was dark and without a sidewalk, so we had no choice but to walk on the road.

"Did you see a flashlight in the trunk?"

Dumb bitch. "If I saw a flashlight, don't you think I would have brought it along?"

"You don't have to be so nasty, I was just asking a question."

Once again, her comment did not deserve an answer. The walk was beginning to take its toll on me. We had just started up the hill when we heard an approaching car. Without thinking, I grabbed Cheryl's hand and quickly crossed to the other side of the road. The car rushed past us.

"What are you doing, idiot? That car could have given us a ride."

"And they could have run us over. Didn't your mother ever teach you to walk against the flow of traffic?"

"You leave my mother's name out your mouth."

The second she said it I realized my mistake. Cheryl's mother had passed away a few months before.

"I'm sorry, Cheryl, I didn't mean it the way it sounded." I felt like kicking myself. Even though she was getting on my nerves, I didn't mean to hurt her like that.

She stopped walking. "We could have hitched a ride."

"You would have gotten into a car with a stranger?"

She said, "I wouldn't be alone, you would be with me."

"What good will that do if they have a gun," I started walking again.

"You wouldn't throw yourself in front of a bullet for me?"

I couldn't tell if she was being serious or not so I didn't respond. I kept walking, and she started following me again. I was glad because I really would have hated to leave her.

"My feet hurt," she whined.

I ignored her and kept on walking.

"How far is it to Salem Road?" she asked.

"After we get off this reservation, probably about two to three miles."

"Miles? You have bumped your head. I'm not walking no three miles." Once again she stopped walking.

"Suit yourself." I kept walking.

"You're going to leave me out here by myself?"

"If you don't come on, yes, I will. We've got to get to the gas station before it closes and pray that they have a gas can for sale. If it makes you feel any better, we can try to get a cab from the station."

She appeared to think about it for a minute before I heard the distinct sound of her heels clacking against the road.

"Some date this turned out to be." She ran to catch up with me.

I ignored her chatter.

"I can't wait to get back to school and tell everyone on my cheerleading squad what an ass you are."

For a second I almost stopped, until it dawned on me that she wouldn't be smearing my name, she would be attacking Merlin. A chuckle slipped from my mouth. Hell she didn't even go to my school

"Oh, you think that's funny?"

I wanted to tell her so badly that it was, but I wasn't ready to disclose my true identity. Cheryl would have never gone out with me in the first place. According to her Facebook page she was on the A–list at school, a good student, and the vice president of the senior class. A bad word from her would be the kiss of death. I, on the other hand, was a second-class citizen. I failed twice, was always in trouble, and if I didn't find a way to cheat on our next test, I would more than likely fail again. So yeah, it was funny to me. I had nothing to lose.

"I wish your feet would move as fast as your mouth."

She punched me in the shoulder. Part of me wanted to slug her but I held my composure. It wasn't her fault that we had to walk, but it wasn't mine either. If Merlin had put gas in his car, we wouldn't be in the situation we were in.

She nudged me. "So what are you trying to say? Are you saying I talk a lot?"

"A hit dog hollers."

"What's that supposed to mean?" She started walking so fast that she breezed right past me. I didn't complain because it gave me the opportunity to watch her ass jiggle in her jeans.

"I know you're watching my ass. Take a good look, 'cause this is the closest you will get to it."

This time I didn't bother to stifle my laughter. She was so full of herself I just couldn't control it. "Girl, your ass is okay, but I've seen better. Leave the jiggling to Jell-O and firm that shit up."

She fell back in step with me and raised her hand to strike me as Braxton's car came barreling down the hill. I don't know what came over me, but something told me to push the big-mouth bitch, so I did. Her screams permeated the air. The awful sound of crunching bones met my ears. The car rolled right over her stomach-cutting off all sound.

"No!" I yelled.

Braxton was fighting to regain control of his car. I rushed to Cheryl. Blood was pouring out of her mouth, and her eyes were wide open. I knew she was in pain.

"Cheryl, I'm so sorry."

She looked as if she wanted to say some-thing, but her mouth was not cooperating. Tears streamed down my face. "I didn't mean it. I swear I didn't mean it."

Braxton's car finally managed to stop in the middle of the road. The passenger door opened.

"I don't have a phone. Could you please call for help?" I pleaded.

"Gavin?"

I looked up, confused. The voice sounded so much like my brother's but that just couldn't be.

"Call for an ambulance, please," I begged.

"Oh, God, what have you done?" Merlin ran toward me.

"It was an accident. I swear it was an acci-dent." I felt like I was losing control. Faces that shouldn't be there were popping in and making me nervous. I saw my mother's face. She had a perpetual frown. My father's face had a look of disgust, but the facial expression that hurt me the most was my brother's. His had a look of horror.

"Is that Cheryl? Oh my God!"

I tried to shake Merlin's voice from my head, but his face remained. He was crying and yelling at me at the same time.

"What have you done?" Merlin leaned down and started beating me about the head.

Since I thought this was all a dream, I tried to protect Cheryl as best I could, but her eyes were no longer open. I prayed that she had passed out and was not dead.

"Gavin?"

Slowly, I came back to the present after reliving my first murder.

My mother stood over me. "Didn't you hear me calling you? I need to wash some clothes so you need to get yours out the way." She walked out of the room without another word.

I was glad that she snatched me away from the memory that changed my life, but at the same time, I was kind of pissed that she didn't put my clothes in the dryer herself.

I guess that would have been too much like right. She had abandoned me when I needed her, so why should I expect anything different now? I retied the towel around my waist and went to finish drying my clothes.

CHAPTER FOURTEEN

MERLIN MILLS

My heart was heavy as I closed the door behind me. This was not how I'd envisioned my homecoming. I had tackled the hardest part, which was leaving, so coming home from Iraq should have been the reward.

"Cojo?" I thought she would still be sitting in the living room, but she wasn't.

"I'm here."

I followed her voice to the kitchen. She was laying on the floor in the corner. She was my queen, and I'd reduced her to this. I rushed forward and gathered her up in my arms. She did not fight me as I lifted her from the floor and carried her into our bedroom. As I walked, I left a trail of kisses over her face. My heart was beating double time. I could not believe that I had used my hands against the only person in the entire world who loved me unconditionally.

"Baby, I am so sorry."

She started to struggle against me, but that only made me hold her tighter.

"Let me go." She was fighting me now as if she wanted to hurt me, but I couldn't let her go.

"Please, baby, let me explain." I didn't know what I was going to say to her that would make things better, but I had to try.

"You promised—"

"I know, sweetie, and it will never happen again. I lost my head for a minute and couldn't see what I had before me."

She didn't have to finish her sentence because I already knew what she was referring to, and she was right. I did break my promise. When she pushed me this time, she appeared to have the strength of ten men. I fell off the bed.

"Fuck that. I will not be your punching bag. You disrespected me and our marriage. I'm leaving you."

"Baby, you don't mean that. Just give me a chance to explain." I got up from the floor, and she scrambled over to the far side of our king-sized bed.

"I said exactly what I meant. You violated our marriage vows. I just need to think about how I'm going to get away from you." A long wail followed her sentence.

Deep in my heart, I knew that she still lo
me. I just had to find a way to bring it to
forefront. "Can I talk to you while you're try
to figure this out?"

"Do I have a choice?"

I wanted to get mad about the bitternes
her voice, but I understood the role I play
"Yes, you have a choice, but I am begging yo
please listen to what I have to say. I don't w
our whole marriage to go down the drain beh
this stupid shit."

She turned around and faced me. My en
demeanor changed. I saw the damage that
done to her face and wanted to whup my o
ass.

"Oh, God, baby, I am sorry. I swear to yo
never meant to hurt you. If you want to pick
a pan and beat my ass, then do it. I deserve
love you more than life itself. I am so sorry. S
ing you like this . . . I don't know if I can e
forgive myself." I couldn't explain it, but I
a shift in temperature in the room. I lifted
arms from around her waist.

"You went crazy. I didn't know you," she s
watching me closely.

"I know, and none of that has anything to
with you. Please believe that." I was crying on
inside for all the pain that I'd caused her.

"I need to understand." Her voice was barely a whisper, but it resounded in my head like a cannon.

"That's fair. Gavin is my twin brother. From the first day that I can remember, I had to watch over him. You would think that he would be someone I could look to for guidance, but that wasn't the way it was."

"You know what? I thought I was going to be able to do this, but I can't. Just looking at you makes me sick to my stomach. I have to leave." Cojo got up to go back into the living room, but I stopped her.

"Sweetheart, I know this is difficult right now, but we can work through this." I was determined to get through this no matter how painful it was for both of us.

"That's easy for you to say because you don't have a swollen jaw." She yanked her arm from my grasp.

Although I wanted to reach out to her again, I didn't want to cause her further pain. The bottom line was that there was no excuse in this world that would make this better. She began pacing the room like a caged animal.

"Baby, would you just sit down?"

"I can't do this . . . I just can't do this."

"Shit." If I could have beaten myself up, perhaps I would've felt better. I could understand

Cojo's pain because I broke the promise tha[t] made to her when we first started dating in hi[gh] school to never put my hands on her in ange[r.] honestly didn't know what came over me. C[ojo] left our bedroom carrying a small suitcase, a[nd] my heart stopped beating. This was definit[ely] not the way I had planned on spending our union night.

"Cojo, where are you going?" I rushed to h[er] side, but I didn't make the mistake of touchi[ng] her.

"I don't know, but I need some time to thin[k.]"

"Baby, please don't do this."

"I have to. I can't look at you without wanti[ng] to bash you in the head." Her voice was tre[m]bling and it tore at my heart.

My mind was going a mile a minute, tryi[ng] to think of something to say that would chan[ge] things. "Hit me then if it would make you f[eel] better, baby. Here, use this." I picked up the lam[p] that was sitting on the end table and pushed [it] into her hands. I bowed my head and prayed th[at] I would be able to withstand the pain. The ba[se] of the lamp was all metal. I closed my eyes a[nd] braced myself for the assault. Several secon[ds] passed and I felt nothing. I opened one eye a[nd] peeked up at her. I didn't know if she was waiti[ng] to catch me on the upswing or not. "What are y[ou] waiting for? Knock my lights out." I remembered hearing the same line in a movie, and it almost caused me to smile.

She put the lamp down on the table and shook her head. "I don't believe in violence. I thought you felt the same way, but obviously I was wrong." She kept throwing little verbal jabs that felt like rock-solid punches.

A single tear leaked from my right eye. "Baby, please. Don't do this." I knew that I said that before, but I didn't know what else to say.

Her eyes were uncertain when she looked at me, but I was comforted by the fact that she didn't immediately turn away from me.

She said, "I just need some time to think."

My mind raced. What was there to think about? I fucked up, plain and simple. I was sorry and we would get past it. I could not understand why she needed to make things more complicated than they already were. "You have to know that I will never put my hands on you again." I spoke with conviction from my heart, but her look was skeptical.

"Yesterday I believed that." She started walking backward toward the door.

"No, baby, I can't let you leave." I started in her direction.

"You're going to hit me again?"

Her words froze my feet and stabbed my heart. Another tear followed the path of the first, and it started a flood that I couldn't control.

"Oh, God, I'm so sorry. I never wanted this to happen."

She started crying too. I wanted to take her in my arms and tell her that everything would be okay, but now I was beginning to have my own doubts.

"I don't want you to leave. If you can't stand to look at me right now, I'll go. Perhaps in a few days we can sit down and talk about this rationally." I said what I thought would make things better, but in my heart, I didn't want to go. Secretly, I hoped she would say it was unnecessary for either of us to leave and we would work on patching things up together. It didn't play out.

She put down her bag and waited rather impatiently as I repacked my things to leave. For the first time in my life, I prayed and packed. I prayed Cojo would change her mind and that we could get things back on the right track before I had to leave again. I only had a two-week furlough, and I didn't want to spend the entire time fighting. As I was flinging things into my duffel bag, I thought about where I was going to go.

There was no way I was ever going to my mother's house. Therefore, I either had to check into a hotel or try to catch up with my homeboy Braxton to see if I could play on his sympathy. In fact, that was probably my only solution because I didn't want to blow the money I'd managed to save while I was away on a stupid hotel. Times were too hard in 2009 to be foolish with money.

"Cojo, I'm being redeployed to Iraq in two weeks. I wanted to house hunt while I was home so we could stop renting this apartment. We've been living here since we got married." I was begging hard. I knew that this wasn't the best time to throw this at her, but I felt like I was running out of time.

"Oh my God. You just whupped my ass for something that wasn't my fault and now you are asking me to house shop with you. Am I hearing you correctly?"

"Baby—"

"Stop calling me baby. That shit ended when you raised your hand and struck me. You threw away a seven-year relationship with your fist."

"You're right. I'm sorry—"

"I should have kept going when your mother showed her ass at my wedding."

I was in the begging mode now and would have agreed to anything that would have kept me from walking out the door and kept her from reliving our wedding day. Leaving was an expense

I had not calculated and would mess up
three-year plan. "I'll go, but can I call you late
I didn't know what I would have done if she t
me no, but I asked anyway.

"Yeah, but I need time."

It was a small concession on her part, bu
was thankful she was even open to dialogue w
me.

I said, "I know you can't feel it right now, b
believe we can make this right."

Cojo followed me as I backed up to the do
In my heart, I believed she would stop me bef
I crossed the threshold, but it wasn't so.

"Give me your key." She held her hand out.

"Huh?" I wasn't ready for that one.

She wasn't just content with my leavi
she wanted to make sure I didn't pounce b
into her world without permission. Part of
wanted to object, but the other part of me kn
I had fucked up. I slipped the keys off my rin
had to be willing to do anything to keep my m
riage.

"Can I take you out to dinner tomorrow?"

She said, "I don't want to go outside looki
like this."

Her comment was like a lead weight in t
room. I had to decide whether to let it go or
to fix it.

"Can I bring the fixings and come over and prepare a meal for you?" I saw a hint of a smile on her lips. I could tell she knew I was trying to make this right.

"We'll see."

It wasn't the answer I was hoping for, but it would have to do. "Do you have a preference?"

"My preference would have been for this not to have happened at all."

"Darling, if I could take things back, then trust me, I would. But it is what it is, and I am going to do my damnedest to make things right between us again." I wanted some assurances from her that my efforts would not be in vain, but I guess I was asking for too much.

She just stared at me until I was uncomfortable. As much as I didn't want to go, I knew that I had to. Opening the door, I paused. There was so much I wanted to say, but every time I looked at Cojo, the words stopped short of my lips.

"I love you." I waited for a few seconds just to see if she would respond.

She didn't.

I walked away from the best thing that had ever happened in my life.

CHAPTER FIFTEEN

COJO MILLS

I crumbled onto the sofa as the door closed behind Merlin. My body shook uncontrollably as I fought the urge to run to the door and beg him to come back. Vivid images from the last two hours of my life flitted through my mind. It was a nightmare that I didn't want to relive, but I couldn't turn it off.

How could I not know who it was I was sleeping with? The thought made me think I didn't know my husband as well as I thought I did. How come I didn't even know he had a brother? Questionable thoughts kept coming but the answers evaded me. I wanted answers to stop the feelings of guilt that kept trying to invade my body. I buried my head in the sofa as hot tears came to my eyes. They burned my face, but I could not stop them even if I wanted to. I cried for what we had and what we'd apparently lost. Although I still loved my husband, I didn't think I would ever be able to look at him the same again.

Rising from the sofa, I went into the kitchen to get some ice for my jaw. It was swollen, and crying wasn't helping the situation. As I passed the telephone, it rang. My heart skipped a beat as I debated whether to answer it. Part of me hoped it was Merlin calling, but the other part of me wasn't ready to speak with him, even if it was on the phone.

"Hello?" My voice was barely above a whisper. I cleared my throat and tried it again. "Hello." My hands gripped the kitchen counter tightly as my knees wobbled.

"Hey, girl, y'all fucking yet?" Tiffany laughed as if she were caught up in her own joke.

"Huh?" I was holding my breath. When I finally exhaled, I saw tiny stars before my eyes.

"Don't play dumb, girl. Your man was due home today, and I just wanted to interrupt y'all's flow for a second and give the man a chance to rest."

Our phone connection was lousy. I could hear music blasting in the background and what sounded like glasses rattling. "Where are you?"

"At Taboo Two, it's ladies' night and you know I'm a sucker for them free drinks."

"Oh."

"Damn, what's wrong with you? Merlin did make it home, didn't he?"

"Yeah, he was here." I debated how much I was willing to tell my inquisitive friend. I loved her and all, but I wasn't ready to tell anyone about the assault that had happened here tonight and my role in it.

"Whoa, hold up. What do you mean *was*?"

Shit, I didn't mean to say that. Now she would be all over me like white on rice. "Girl, stop tripping. We're cool. Just chillin'." I hoped she couldn't hear the beating of my heart. If Tiffany knew what really went down, she would have been over here faster than I could hang up the phone, even if she was on the other side of town.

"What's up, boo? You don't sound right."

"Uh . . . I was asleep, a brother wore me out."

"Shit, I know that's right. If my man had left me for six months and came back home, I'd be asleep too." She started giggling.

I couldn't tell if she was happy for me or if her ass was already drunk from the free liquor. "You've got to get a man first." *Damn.* I knew I had gone too far as soon as the words left my mouth.

Tiffany was a player. She had a different man every day of the week. And so far, it was working for her. She didn't want for anything. If one man didn't do her right, she always had a backup waiting to fulfill her needs.

She said, "Hell, don't hate the player, hate the game."

She must have been drunk 'cause the Tiffany I knew would have cussed me out for insinuating she was pimping the game.

"Okay, since you interrupted my beauty rest, was there another reason for your call?" I needed to get her off the phone before I started crying again.

"I told you why I called. I just wanted to hear you answer the phone panting and shit. Give the dick a chance to breathe."

"You're sick."

"I love you too."

I chuckled because if things had worked out differently, she would have interrupted the greatest sex I'd ever had.

"So where is Merlin the magician? I wanna holler at him too."

Panic set in. *What was I going to tell her? Why must she ask for him at a time like this?* I wanted to tell her to go take a flying leap and mind her fucking business, but deep inside, I knew that she loved him too. "Girl, I worked the nigga over. He's out cold."

"That's what I'm talking 'bout. All right th
I'll holler later. You two have fun."

"Thanks, girl. You be careful out there."

"I'm cool. I've got two or three niggas ready
take me home. I'm good."

"If that was supposed to make me feel bett
it didn't. Don't go hopping into cars with fo
you don't know. I don't want to turn on the te
vision in the morning and hear about you."

"You worry too much. Go back to that sleepi
dick in your bed and leave the grown-up stuff
me." She laughed as she hung up the phone.

Part of me wanted to scream at her and let h
know I wasn't okay, but it was too late. I was alo
with my thoughts once again. "Shit. Why didn'
tell her what happened?" Even as I said the wor
out loud, I knew why I had kept my silence. I
had told Tiffany what had happened here tonig
she would have arranged to have Merlin killed
seriously fucked up, and she would have nev
forgiven me if I decided to speak to him agai
Truth be told, I didn't want my marriage to en
Even though I didn't understand why Merlin to
his frustration out on me instead of his broth
I knew he loved me. I just had to find out why
reacted the way he did.

Taking the ice from the frezer, I made my w
back into our bedroom. I tried to fight the d

mons that waited for me inside. The biggest demon was my dresser mirror. It mocked me. Before I could stop myself, I hurled the ice pack at the mirror and it shattered into a million pieces. The shards of glass littering the floor were like the pieces of my life, all broken up.

I collapsed onto our bed as all the anger drained out of me. I'd never felt so lost in my life, and I didn't know how I was going to be able to go on if I didn't manage to salvage something of my relationship.

I can't give up now, Lord. I wasn't trying to convince God; I was trying to convince myself. I'd always believed I would never allow a man to put his hands on me, but this had to be an exception to the rule. It wasn't that he just hit me for the hell of it, he was provoked.

"That shit doesn't even sound right to me," I whispered. The fact remained that even though he was upset, taking his anger out on me was not the answer since I clearly was as much of a victim as he was. I buried my face into my pillow, trying to hide from the pain.

CHAPTER SIXTEEN

COJO MILLS

The sound of the phone roused me from a deep sleep. I inched across the bed to silence the ringing instrument. "Hello?" My voice was hoarse and raspy. I felt dehydrated from all the crying. My eyes burned as they sought out the clock: 9:27 P.M.

The voice on the other end of the phone remained silent.

"Hello." I was irritated because whoever it was wasn't speaking.

"Cojo."

It was Merlin. My heart clenched as the fight replayed in my mind.

"Yes." I was still hurt, but regardless of what happened, I still loved my husband.

"Are you okay?" He was breathing heavily over the phone.

I wondered where he was and what he was doing, but I refused to ask. "Yeah." Did he really expect an honest answer to his question? I waited to hear what else was on his mind.

"Sweetheart, I'm so sorry."

Bitterness struggled to erupt from my mouth, but I fought hard to hold it in. I didn't want to fight with him, but didn't know what to say.

"Are you still there?" he said.

"Yeah." Unwanted tears fell from my eyes. I tried to hold them in but that only made me cry harder.

"Are you crying?" His voice broke, and I could tell he was about to cry too.

"I'm okay." I gulped back the sobs that kept trying to escape my throat.

"I didn't call to get you upset. I just wanted to hear your voice, to know you were all right."

"Okay, well, I'm alright."

"I love you, Cojo."

"I love you too, Merlin."

He broke down crying then; my heart went out to him. If he felt one-tenth as bad as I did, I knew that he was hurting.

"I want to come home." His voice was so low, I barely heard him.

My heart wanted to tell him to hurry up, but my brain needed some time. "Not tonight," I

whispered. It didn't feel right telling my husba
no, but it would have been worse if I allowed h
home and found I still could not stand to look
him.

"Have you eaten yet?"

"I'm not hungry." I searched my brain f
something else to say to him, but my mind w
blank. It wasn't that I was trying to make h
suffer, I just needed some time. For a few s
onds there was silence on the line.

"Well, all right then, I won't hold you up a
longer."

A pregnant pause filled the air.

"Okay," I said.

"Can I come see you tomorrow?"

I could hear the desperation in his voice, a
even though this wasn't the first time we'd sle
in separate beds since we'd been married, it w
the first time that either of us had gone to sle
unhappy or sad. "Yeah, I doubt if I'll feel like g
ing into work tomorrow."

"Fine, see you tomorrow."

Merlin knew that if I called into work, I h
to be feeling pretty bad. He hung up the pho
quickly. I wanted to call him back to assure h
things would be okay, but I had no idea whe
he was. More importantly, I didn't know who
was with.

A tiny devil landed on my shoulder and whispered in my ear: *He's probably out fucking someone else. Serves you right for kicking him out of his own home.*

"Stop it," I yelled into our empty apartment. I felt like I was losing my mind. I got up from the bed and began pacing the room. I didn't want to start speculating on where he was, but the seed had been planted. I snatched the phone from the wall and tried to call him back. I was going to tell him to come home, even if it meant I would have to sleep on the sofa.

I dialed the fast access code to display the last caller, but unfortunately the number was blocked. "Damn." I dialed his cell phone and it went to his voice mail. I didn't leave a message so he wouldn't think I was weak. I shoved the phone back onto the cradle and continued to pace the floor. The phone rang and scared the shit out of me. I snatched it before it could ring a second time. "Hello." I was ready to have my husband home.

"Let me speak to Merlin."

Anger replaced the fear that had just vacated my heart as I struggled to maintain my composure. My mother-in-law was the last person on the planet I wanted to speak with at this particular time. What made her call after so long anyway? Ignoring the fact that she didn't even say hello, I answered her, "He's not here at the moment." My hand stood poised to disconnect the phone.

"Where is he?" she demanded.

I wanted to tell her it was none of her fucking business, but I held my tongue. "Out," I replied. Over the years I had tried a few times without Merlin's knowledge to make friends with this woman, but she made it very clear she wasn't interested in being my friend. I wasn't the one who ruined her wedding.

"Now you listen here, missy, I want to speak to my son, and I want to speak to him now."

"I'll be sure to tell him when he gets home." I hung up the phone before she could say anything else. That simple act of defiance made me feel better. I went back into the living room, curled up on the sofa, and went to sleep.

CHAPTER SEVENTEEN

GAVIN MILLS

When I looked up, my mother was standing in the doorway to my room.

"I can't believe that bitch hung up on me," she said.

"What bitch?" I was standing in my underwear, and she didn't even have the decency to knock on the door or turn away when she realized that I didn't have any clothes on.

"That bitch your stupid-ass brother married."

I struggled to hide my irritation as I pulled on my socks. My mother's tirades were nothing new to me because she hated everybody or thought they were stupid. I grabbed my pants from the bottom of the bed and slid my legs into them as I turned and faced my mother. If she was the least bit embarrassed about seeing me in a state of half dress, she didn't show it.

"Why she got to be a bitch?" I zipped up my pants and reached for my shirt. I changed my mind about taking a nap. I wanted to go out to get something to eat and a beer.

"Are you taking her side now?" She had this crazy look in her eyes, and I instantly regretted saying anything at all.

I should have agreed with her and kept it moving. "No, Mother, I'm not taking sides."

"Good, because I was about to send your ass packing tonight."

I ignored her as I put on my shoes.

"Where are you going? I thought you were going to take a nap."

"I was, but I got hungry, so I was going to go out and grab me something to eat."

"I thought you said you didn't have any money." She eyed me skeptically.

For a minute, I thought she was going to demand that I empty my pockets like she did when I was a kid. "I got enough to grab a burger and some fries."

"Umph. If I were you, I'd save that money just in case you find yourself out on the street." She turned and left my room.

The veiled threat hung in the room like a stale fart. I was going to have to do something about my financial situation quick, fast, and in a hurry. "Can I make a sandwich then?"

"Yeah, but don't make a mess." My mother was a real piece of work. She didn't want me to go out, but she didn't want me there with her, either.

"I won't. Do you want me to make you a sandwich too?" I didn't really want to fix her a sandwich, but I knew that if I didn't offer, I would have to hear her mouth for the next twenty-four hours.

"No, I ate already."

I wanted to ask her why she didn't bother to share her food with me, but I let it go. I learned a long time ago to pick my battles with my mother. Since I was not in a position to do any better for myself, I would just have to suck this one up.

Opening the refrigerator, I searched the practically barren box. The only things close to edible were a few pieces of cheese and some questionable bologna. "Dag, Ma, how long has this stuff been in here?" I brought the bologna to my nose, but immediately pulled it back.

"What?"

"Never mind." My appetite had suddenly gone away. I walked back into the living room.

"You ate already?"

"Naw, I changed my mind." I sat down in the loveseat across from my mother.

She didn't even look at me. She was watching *The Real Housewives of Atlanta*, a reality show everyone seemed to enjoy. Even the dudes in prison watched it every week. I was surprised she was watching the show because she had not a housewife bone in her body.

"You actually watch this shit?" I did not attempt to hide my personal feelings about the show, which was about a bunch of broads living off their husbands' success. It would have been different if at least one of the ladies had something going for herself other than marrying well.

"Watch your language."

With the exception of the television, the room was silent. If I'd had a television in my room, I would have gone in there to watch it, but the room only contained a bed. "How long have you lived here?"

My mother tore her eyes away from the tube. "Huh?"

"This apartment. When did you move in?"

She took her sweet time answering me, and I was beginning to believe that she had placed me on ignore status. "Why?"

"No reason, I was just making conversation."

She settled back onto the sofa and continued to ignore me. "I ain't stupid. You are looking for an excuse from me for moving and not letting you know, but I don't have one. If you hadn't taken someone's life, you would have known what I was up to."

I was silent for a moment. "It was an accident."

"I know that, but it doesn't change the price of tea in China."

"What does China have to do with any fucking thing?"

"Don't you get snippy with me. I don't have to tell you anything. I'm your mother."

"Mom, I am not blaming you for anything you've done. Obviously, you did what you thought you had to do. I was just trying to find out where my shit is."

"Your shit, as you call it, was thrown out in the trash. I never expected to see you again, and I damn sure wasn't going to cart around that crap with me."

A pain settled deep in my heart. I hated my brother for turning a once loving woman into a callous bitch. "You used to love us?" My voice was barely above a whisper.

"You stupid bastard. How the hell could you form your lips to say that to me? If I didn't love your stinking ass, I would not have gone through the pain of raising you instead of my own."

I was sick of hearing about the child she wanted. It didn't have anything to do with me. "Don't ever call me stupid again. I may be a bastard but that was beyond my control." I threw my head back in defiance. While I was locked up I'd grown used to expressing myself, but now was not the time to share this.

"Excuse me? Who the hell do you think you are talkin' to?"

Reality struck me in the face. I was staying with this woman who made all the difference in the world to my comfort. Hell, it wasn't the best existence, but it was the only one I had at the moment. "Mother, I'm sorry. I lost my head." I practically choked on the words as they left my mouth.

"Humph. You damn sure did. I didn't have to take your ass in. I've done my job with raising you two boys, and what thanks did I get? Nothing. Both of you shit on me every chance you get."

"Mom, I said I was sorry. You've always been there for me." She knew I was lying but didn't bother to correct me. Truth be told, she was the first one to sell me out when the police tried to figure out which twin had pushed Cheryl.

Mother told them that it was me who had taken off in Merlin's car.

"You got that right. I've always been here for you and Merlin, but you made my life hell while you were here, and I don't intend to go through that shit again. So if you are even thinking about starting some trouble, you can just get your shit and go."

What shit? I didn't have anything and she knew it. My blood started to boil as I struggled not to respond to her latest jab. "I see that I have awakened some bad memories. I'm going to bed because I don't want you going back down memory lane. It wasn't good the first time, and I don't feel like going there again."

"Stop it. I don't base my opinions of you on the past. I'm thinking of the here and now, and you are nothing to be proud of. You were worthless when you were born. Your damn daddy did that to you. I tried to beat that shit out of you, but I know who you are—you are rottten."

"Mother, you are talking crazy." The words slipped out of my mouth before I could catch them. I spent my entire life in my brother's shadow, and it hurt to be reminded of it now. Even though I wanted to fight her on this issue, I could not afford to because, at the end of the day, I still needed a place to stay.

Her words hurt me to my heart, but I would not allow her to see the pain she had caused me. I wanted her to know that she was the only woman who I cared about, but she couldn't see me for my brother. He was the object of my hate!

"Momma, are you saying that you never loved me?" This time I wasn't asking if she loved my brother and I.

"Of course I loved you. What choice did I have? That doesn't change the fact that you're evil. You don't have the same thought process as your brother. Everything is twisted for you."

"And how much do you play into the that? I am a product of my environment."

She had gone too far. I only had love for her, and she turned it all around.

"I will not take the blame for that. Your father's sperm destroyed you."

"Is that how you really feel about me?" My heart sunk into my chest. I never believed that my own mother had such a low opinion of me. If I was thinking clearly, I would have understood that this anger was with my father and not me, but I wasn't there yet.

"I raised you, wasn't that enough? I can think what I want. You were a disappointment to me back then. Now you have to make your own way. I'm done."

"Why? Why was I a disappointment? I was a fucking kid."

"'Cause you were just like your damn daddy."

"Your issue is with my father and not me!"

"You are right about that. I do have issues with your father, but your father has not shown up on my doorstep asking to move back in. You did!"

"But what about your influence? Didn't you have a part in shaping me into the man I am today?"

"So are you tryin' to say I made you the failure that you are?" She planted her hands on her hips, and I wanted to slap the hell out of her.

I was not a failure, and I was bound and determined to prove it to her. "I'm not a failure." My chest was heaving. I was so hurt by the words coming out of her mouth, I wanted to slam my fist into her face. "I'll admit I wasn't the best child a parent could have, but I was never a failure."

"The proof is in the puddin'. You will have to prove it to me 'cause I'm not about to take your word on it. As far as I can tell, you don't have shit, you still don't want shit, and you ain't never going to be shit." She turned away as if the conversation were over.

"How you gonna say some shit like this to me and just walk away? Your ass ain't perfect

either." I knew I was out of line, but she wa
going to continue talking to me out of the
of her mouth without my saying somethir
didn't ask her to raise me. Hell, I didn't even
to be born, and she was punishing me for bor
those things that I didn't have any control ov

"Nigga, have you lost your motherfucl
mind? I ain't some hood chick you done me
the street, I'm your momma."

I wanted to scream at her and tell her
needed to act the fuck like a momma, but I di
Instead I seethed inside. Regardless of what
thought, I treated people—friends and far
alike—just as I had been treated all my life. If
ways were fucked up or unconventional, it
because I didn't know any better. "I'm sorry
feel this way, but have you ever thought ab
how I feel?" The words burned as they exited
mouth.

She had only been thinking about hersel
years, and I was sick and tired of that shit.

"You damn right you're sorry. I have half a n
to kick your stupid-ass right out of my house,
I'm a woman and women don't treat men
that." As usual, she focused on what she wante
hear and not what I said.

"Okay, Ma, I'm just delusional. Please for;
me." I was ready to leave before I said someth

that would force me to take up residence in a homeless shelter or some other shit like that.

"I just need you to get out my face. Go on back in your room. I'll deal with your ass tomorrow." She held a bottle of gin around the neck and was swinging it as she spoke.

When I saw the bottle, I knew that there would be no reasoning with her, so I quickly left the room and said a silent prayer that she would go into her own room and go to sleep. Walking away without telling my mother exactly what I thought about her was probably one of the hardest things I'd done in quite a while, and it left a sour taste in my mouth. The urge to hit her was so overwhelming I could actually feel it.

"Stankin' bitch," I retorted as I quietly shut the door to my room. I wasn't sure about what I was going to do about my future, but I damn sure knew I would have to make a decision soon. I wouldn't be able to continue living under my mother's roof if this was any indication of how things were going to go.

CHAPTER EIGHTEEN

COJO MILLS

My fingers were trembling when I hung up the phone. Why did I ever agree to see him tomorrow? I had to remain strong. Merlin had to know that what happened between us was totally unacceptable. He had to know I was not going to tolerate being his punching bag no matter what—I didn't care what the circumstances were.

He should know I was not the one. I told him I had watched my mother go through it, and I wasn't interested in following in her footsteps. Compassion nagged at my resolve. I loved Merlin liked I'd loved no other, but I was not going to relive the horror my mother went through. I'd just as soon end up alone for the rest of my life if I was going to travel down that road.

As much as I wanted to believe my husband that this was an isolated incident, I needed some answers from some people who knew him longer than I did. We had dated for a few months when I started going to his school in the twelfth grade, and we married right after graduation.

I picked up the phone, but embarrassment made me hang it up. There was no one in our lives who I was willing to confess my troubles to. Tiffany and Braxton went to school with Merlin long before I did, but I was going to have to deal with this situation all by myself. Hanging up the phone was a humbling experience. Once again I felt alone, and I never thought I would feel that way again when I married Merlin.

I am an only child. My mother died when I was eight. My father remarried when I was twelve, and I lost the love of the only person in life who mattered to me. My dad emotionally abandoned me when he started caring for his new wife. She had three daughters, and I got lost in the sauce. He didn't turn me out into the streets, but for most of my life, I felt like I was on a deserted island. We moved from Baltimore to Georgia in my senior year, and I found someone to share my island with.

Merlin had thrown me a raft of love, but now I didn't know if this was a raft of love or of entrapment. Had I set myself up for failure by depending on him? Questions kept ringing in my head as I tried to make heads or tails out of what had happened in our home.

Merlin was a first for me: the first man who I had relations with; the first man who I'd loved; and the only man who I wanted in my life forever. But he showed me a side of him tonight that scared the fuck out of me.

Was I wrong about giving this man my love? This thought replayed in my head like a damn mallet beating against a hollow surface, and each beat hurt like a pointed dagger stuck in my heart. I couldn't figure out who I was maddest at: Merlin, for not believing that I was deceived by his brother, or Gavin, for taking advantage of my forced celibacy.

"Bitch, please, I will not let you turn this around on me," I said aloud. Blaming myself would be easy for me. I was always hardest on myself, but this time I hadn't done anything wrong. I looked around the room as if someone were there to witness my mental breakdown, but thankfully I was alone. My shoulders heaved when I realized I was alone, but my heart hurt when I realized that I was on a deserted island by myself again.

"Dear God, what have I done to deserve this?" I wailed at the ceiling. I buried my head into my pillow. I tried to burrow deep, but my head kept bopping up because I knew in my heart I didn't do anything to deserve this pain that I was going through.

The phone interrupted my thoughts. I scurried away from it as if answering it would have burned me. Who would be calling me this late? I allowed it to ring two more times before I answered. "Hello."

Merlin said, "Babe, just in case you're wondering, I'm at a hotel not far from the house."

I let his statement hang in the air. If I'd admitted to caring where he was staying, he might get the wrong impression.

"I miss you, baby, I'm so—"

"Save it, Merlin. In fact, let me get off the phone, because talking to you is only making me mad. Call before you come in the morning." I hung up before he could say anything else, and before I could start crying. It felt like my heart was breaking in pieces.

I threw myself on the bed and had another good cry. I remembered once reading that crying was good for the soul, but I doubt they meant this type of crying. I went through a whole gamut of emotions until I got sick and tired of my damn self.

I pulled myself out of bed and went to take a shower. In the past, showers always refreshed me. While I was bathing, I didn't think about what I was going to do next, I just went through the motions. I knew that I would not be going to work tomorrow, but I had to do something with my time or I'd go crazy.

I started cleaning up the mess that Merlin made in the bedroom. I wasn't claiming any of that shit 'cause I wasn't a part of the deception. As I cleaned, I tried not to think about the violence I saw in my husband that I had never known existed. Without a shadow of a doubt, there was some very bad blood between the brothers. I tried to keep moving so I wouldn't dwell on the past twenty-four hours.

I changed the sheets on the bed and vacuumed the carpet, getting up the smaller pieces of glass that I was not able to get with my hands. When I shut off the vacuum, I heard the answering machine going in the kitchen.

"Merlin, this is your mother. Pick up the phone."

I rolled my eyes. The very last person I wanted to hear from at this moment was his meddling mother. Talking to her was bound to make me feel even worse than I felt right at the moment, so I continued to listen to her talk to the machine.

"I know you're back in town 'cause your brother told me. Now be a good boy and pick up the phone." She was speaking to the machine as if Merlin were actually standing there ignoring her ass, which he was known to do.

"Merlin, we need to let bygones be bygones. Well, you're probably busy, but you need to stop by and see me." She hung up the phone, and I breathed a sigh of relief.

As long as she stayed her ass on the other side of town instead of coming over to our house, I would be all right.

In the six and a half years that Merlin and I had been married, she came to visit one time. She was drunk, and all she did was complain. Most mothers would have been proud to see that their children were doing better than they had, but not Gina. She acted like Merlin owed her the same creature comforts that we'd been able to obtain. I walked into the kitchen to erase the message because I was not about to allow Gina to cause us any more drama.

The next morning I woke figuring I'd fix myself a stiff drink. I needed something strong to help me forget the ass whupping my husband gave me and the thorough fuck his brother laid down.

The doorbell interrupted me. I wasn't expecting anyone, so I approached the door with caution. My husband and I were not that popular, and we didn't have a bunch of friends who stopped by unannounced. I tiptoed to the door and peeked through the peephole. I was shocked to see Merlin standing there. I snatched open the door, fire burning in my eyes. "Merlin, I said in the morning, but I didn't mean the crack of dawn."

"You trying to make the same mistake twice?" Gavin was grinning at me like we shared some type of special bond. These brothers looked so much alike I couldn't tell them apart.

I stumbled back from the door, and he took this as an invitation to come inside. He turned and shut the door behind him.

"What are you doing here?" I was very nervous about being alone with Gavin again after our last little encounter. Something happened between my legs that I needed to ignore.

"Merlin told me that I could come by and pick out a few outfits to wear until I get my shit together."

"Merlin is not here."

"I gathered that." He walked over and took a seat on the sofa as if he had every right to be in my house and in my presence.

Any other time I might have found his cockiness appealing, but something about Gavin rubbed me the wrong way. It was like fingernails scratching against a chalkboard. "I don't remember asking you to come in."

He sat up from his lounging position with a sinister smirk on his face. "But you didn't ask me to leave, either."

I wanted to knock that silly smile right off his face. I could tell that Gavin was used to having his way with women, but he had come against the wrong sister this time. We may have wound up in a compromising position once before, but that shit would never happen again, despite the excitement soaking my panties.

I walked over to the phone to call Merlin. I was not about to play this little game with Merlin's brother. Keeping my eye on Gavin, I dialed Merlin's number.

He answered on the first ring. "Baby, I'm so glad you called. I've been up all night, and I just can't get it together. I've been so worried about us."

I still wasn't ready to have that conversation with my husband, but I needed his help to get his brother out of my house. "Merlin, your brother is here." I cut right to the chase so there would be no confusion as to the nature of the call.

"He's what?" Merlin shouted into the phone.

"He's here in the living room. He claims that you told him to come over today to pick up some clothes?"

"Shit, I forgot about it. He called me last night after we talked last. I'll be right there."

I felt better knowing that he was on the way. I hung up the phone, and this time it was me who had a smirk on my face.

"What? You had to call out the troops? If I didn't know better, sis, I would think you didn't like me or something."

I had to fight back the urge to fling my crystal vase at his head. I could tell he liked to get a rise out of people, and I refused to allow him to see me upset again. "Think what you like. My husband will be here soon."

"Damn, do you want me to wait outside?" He was trying to be funny.

"As far as I'm concerned, you can sit out on the curb with the rest of the garbage." The remark slipped out of my mouth before I had a chance to stop it. There was just something about this man that brought out the worst in me.

"Ouch, that hurt. I know you're still mad about yesterday, but can't we just put it behind us?"

I was outdone. I could not believe he would sit right in my face and say some stupid-ass shit to me after what he did.

The devil whispered in my ear: *But you liked it.*

"I'm not going to even dignify your question with a response." I left him sitting in the living room. I went into the kitchen to make myself something to eat. I wasn't really hungry, but I was trying to dispel the nervous energy I felt. Regardless of how much I disliked my husband's brother, I had to give it to him: he knew how to get down in the bedroom. So keeping my distance from him was a very good idea.

I pulled some bacon from the refrigerator and placed several slices on the microwave rack. It wasn't until I had turned on the microwave, I realized I'd cooked more than I'd intended to fix. It was too late to turn it off, so I went ahead with every intention of making breakfast for my husband.

"You fixin' some for me too?" Gavin called from the living room.

"When donkeys fly."

"Now, sis, is that any way to treat your family?" Gavin had snuck up behind me. He was standing so close, I could feel his breath on my neck. Electricity flowed through me and landed between my legs. I grabbed a knife from the dish rack. I was prepared to cut him if I had to.

"Whoa, it's not that serious." With his hands in the air, Gavin backed out of the kitchen.

"Either you wait for your brother in the living room or wait outside. The choice is yours." I punctuated my words with the point of the knife.

"Damn, if I didn't know better, I would swear you needed some dick in your life." He made it out of the room before I had a chance to throw the steak knife I was holding tightly in my left hand. I immediately remembered how he'd pinned my legs over his shoulder and gave me every inch of his business. The smell of burnt bacon and the ding of the timer brought me back to my senses. Gavin just didn't know how close he had come to being a casualty.

Grabbing a hand towel, I removed my breakfast from the microwave and threw it in the trash. I turned on the vent to get rid of the smell and opened the window to allow some fresh air into the house. I had just finished washing up the rack when the doorbell rang. Drying my hands on a towel, I went to answer the door, but to my chagrin, Gavin had beaten me to it.

"What's up, bro? You lose your key?"

I could see the vein jumping on the side of Merlin's neck, and I knew I had to do something to diffuse the situation. Walking past Gavin, I gave Merlin a big kiss on his lips. I could feel his body relax against mine.

Merlin closed the door behind him. "How long are you here for?"

"Dag, what is up with y'all? I said I was sorry about yesterday. It was a honest mistake."

Merlin tried to step past me to get to his brother, but I grabbed his hand and pulled him back. The last thing we needed was a repeat of the day before. Besides, it wouldn't do anything to make the whole nasty situation disappear.

Merlin said, "All right, man, I'm not about to press the issue. Let me just get you a few things so you can be on your way."

Gavin frowned; his nostrils flared. "Well, I missed your ass too."

My head swung between the brothers. If I hadn't seen it with my own eyes, I would not have believed that two men could look so much alike. Even their mannerisms were the same. It was as if the egg was split in half. I tore my eyes away from Gavin, who was trying to stare a hole in me.

Not wanting to get into another conversation with Gavin, I followed Merlin into the bedroom as he went through his clothes that I hadn't managed to snatch from their hangers and fling to the floor.

Merlin looked up when I walked into the room. "I guess I deserve this, too," he said as his eyes surveyed the mess.

For a moment I felt ashamed of my childish actions. Throwing his clothes on the floor or even setting them on fire, which was my first instinct, would not make the situation any better. "Merlin, I've been thinking. Yes, this is a fucked-up situation, but you are not entirely at fault. I have to share in some of the blame." I could see the hope dancing in Merlin's eyes.

"I fault myself for not knowing the difference, but you have to promise me you will never ever put your hands on me again."

"Baby, I swear to you on everything I hold near and dear to my heart that I will never do anything to hurt you ever again." He took a step toward me, but I instinctively backed away.

"Not so fast. I'm not finished."

He stepped back.

"We are going to have to get some counseling before this thing festers and gets even more ugly than it already is."

"I'm cool with that, but I'm only here for two weeks, minus a day now. But I will do whatever you say."

I walked toward my husband with my arms outstretched. Even though I was afraid of the decision I'd made, I knew that I was not ready to give up on my man and what we'd built together.

Merlin wrapped his arms around me and we cried together. We were so in tune with each other that we forgot about Gavin in the other room. I was startled when I heard the refrigerator door shut, and I pushed away from Merlin's embrace.

"Your brother doesn't have any manners."

"Don't remind me. When he leaves, I'll tell you all about my brother."

"I'm going to hold you to that because I find it strange that we've been together all this time and you or no one else ain't never mentioned you had an identical twin. Is there anything else I should know about?"

"Naw, that's it. Let me get this fool some clothes so he can get up out of here."

I left Merlin in the closet while I went into the bathroom to wash my face. It was bad enough I had to see myself looking like a boxer; I didn't need anyone else looking at me.

CHAPTER NINETEEN

GAVIN MILLS

Being in the house with Merlin and his wife was starting to get on my nerves, and it was not what I had planned when I slipped over to their house unannounced. In fact, I was banking on Merlin sleeping somewhere else and ol' girl being ripe for the picking. As much as I had tried to get the image of her naked body out of my mind, she'd kept swirling around my dreams all night long.

For a moment, I wondered how long they had been together and just how tight their relationship was. If their relationship was on the rocks, I wasn't adverse to stepping in and helping Merlin if he was having problems getting the job done in the bedroom.

"Damn, did y'all forget I was here?" I yelled into the bedroom from the kitchen. I went in there to see if Cojo had any leftover bacon. The smell was lingering in the air. I didn't care that it was burnt. My ass was hungry, and I'd rather eat up their food than spend the money that my brother had given me.

"Hold your damn horses," my brother yelled back.

I was going to have to check his ass sooner or later. He must have forgotten how badly I used to tear that ass up when we were growing up. So what if he went to the Army and came home a little swollen? I could still take his ass because I could out think him. Merlin was a sensitive guy, and he thought more with his heart rather than his mind. I, however, was a fighter through and through; I had no problem getting mine by any means necessary.

Cojo had already thrown the bacon into the trash, so I couldn't munch on it. I pulled open the meat drawer and saw that she still had a half a pack of bacon in there, so I proceeded to fix me some. After all, we were family.

"What the hell do you think you're doing?" Cojo asked. She had crept up behind me without my hearing her. She scared me so badly, I almost dropped the bacon I was holding.

"Damn, girl, why you wanna creep up on a brother like that?"

"You have no business in my damn kitchen

"Hell, I didn't think you would mind. I t•
you earlier I was hungry. Why don't you bri
your fine ass in here and cook me up someth
so I don't get your kitchen all messed up.
winked at her.

"Merlin, you'd better come and get your brotl
before I have to hurt him." She snatched the I
con from my hand and threw it into the trash.

I wanted to hit her ass so badly, I was shaki
"Girl, you'd better stop playing with me. Shi
ain't your husband."

"You damn right you're not."

"You're kind of feisty. I like it, but don't ,
ahead of yourself or you might not like the cc
sequences."

"So what, is that a threat? Am I supposed to
scared of you or something?"

"Naw, I don't have to threaten you. I work
promises."

Before I could say anything further, Mer
came into the room carrying a small duffel b•
which he thrust toward me. "This should hold y
for a few days." He tossed me a set of car ke
"That's my old Malibu in the lot. Take it. We'll ;
the registration taken care of later. Now, I've dc

all that I'm going to do for you. I ain't fucking with you, Gavin."

"Thanks, bro, good looking out."

We stood around the kitchen staring at one another until I decided it was time to make my exit. I was definitely going to have to come back so I could whisper in Cojo's ear. Right now she was playing all hard to get and shit, but I was willing to bet I could get her to change her mind about spending some time with me.

I said, "Well, I hate to break up this party. I'm gonna bounce."

"All right," Cojo replied.

I waited for a few beats to see if Merlin wanted to get together later, but the invitation didn't come. I turned and left the kitchen, working my way to the door with both of them hot on my heels. It was a very uncomfortable moment for all of us.

Cojo stepped up from behind Merlin and opened the door. She was playing the victim role very well as I stepped through the doorway. Once I had cleared the path, the door slammed behind me. All I could hear from the apartment was the sound of the locks being engaged.

"Damn, that was cold," I muttered to myself. I stood there for a few seconds, pondering what I was going to do next. I didn't want to go back to my mother's, but I had very few options outside of that. It had been a long time since I'd been home, and even when I did live in Atlanta, I didn't have many friends.

I tossed the bag over my shoulder and made my way to my new car. As I pulled out of the apartment complex, I looked back just in time to see the window flicker shut. I felt a tinge of guilt about the whole situation, but I quickly forgot it as I made my way to McDonald's to get something to eat. My plan was to fill up on a few of their Dollar Menu items and go back to my mother's to crash.

CHAPTER TWENTY

MERLIN MILLS

Once Cojo and I were alone, I began to feel nervous. It was like a large elephant had stepped into the room and neither one of us wanted to acknowledge its presence. I paced around the living room trying to work up the nerve to speak to my wife. She had moved away from the window and was standing behind the sofa. She appeared as nervous as I was.

I took a seat on the sofa and asked her to join me. I waited until she looked comfortable before I began. "I really don't know where to begin." It was a lame statement and I knew it, but I was afraid.

Cojo just stared at me for a few seconds. "You can start with why you felt it was necessary to keep your brother a secret."

"Honey, it wasn't that I was trying to keep a secret. It's been so long since I thought about my

brother that I just forgot him. He dropped out
school so long ago, no one remembers him."

"How does one go about forgetting such
important part of his life?"

"You would try to forget too if you had som
one in your life who caused you so much pain

She cocked her head to the side as if she w
trying to figure out if I was telling the truth.

"Gavin was a major pain in my ass when
were growing up."

"Most siblings are."

"No, you don't understand. It was more th
just being a pain in the ass. He did things, t
rible things, and used to blame them on me."

"What kind of things?"

I was trying to gauge Cojo's tone to see h
she was feeling, but her tone was noncommitt
"Damn, now that I'm talking about it again
sounds stupid even to me. But back then, it w
drama city."

"Well, you are going to have to make me u
derstand because it feels like you lied to me, a
I don't like the feeling."

"I'm telling you, baby, it was an error of om
sion. I just needed to close the part of my life th
involved Gavin." I got up and started pacing t
room again. I knew that I had to make her u
derstand if we were going to have any chance

stay together. "When I was in high school, before I met you, Gavin talked this girl who had a crush on me into going out with him." Just thinking about it left a sour taste in my mouth. I shook my head, trying to clear my thoughts.

"And?" Cojo still had a hint of attitude in her voice, but I tried not to let it bother me as I continued the story.

"Well, I guess I didn't phrase that right. He tricked her into going out 'cause she thought she was going out with me."

"Oh, so you got mad? That's not enough to deny your brother even existed."

I ignored my wife's comments as I got lost in that painful night. "He had been pursuing her for weeks, I later found out. He would get on my computer after I went to work and would speak to her for hours using my login. Hell, I didn't even know she liked me until after the fact."

"Did y'all go to school together?"

"No, she went to another school. She was a cheerleader for an opposing team who always flirted with me, so I guess that's why he was able to trick her."

"That's messed up, but why wouldn't he just talk to her on his own since you didn't even know her?"

"To be honest, I have no idea why he sucked me into the whole mess, but it was ugly, especially when the police got there."

"Wait, this isn't making any sense. What did the police have to do with it?"

"I don't even know if it was part of his plans, but he took my car and went to pick her up. He wound up running out of gas and they had to walk. Apparently she got pissed, and somehow or another she wound up getting hit by a car. The police thought I had something to do with it because my computer records showed we were corresponding and, according to her mother, she left with a boy named Merlin." I paused. "And Gavin told the police I caused her to get hit, like he always blamed me for stuff he did."

"Oh my God. How terrible, was she okay?"

I got up and started walking around the room. I didn't want to admit to her that I saw Gavin push the young lady into the street. "She died, and the only reason Gavin went to prison and not me is because Braxton and Gina stepped up and told the truth. Gina told the police that Gavin had taken off with my car."

She nodded. "Yeah, that's kind of jacked up, but it still isn't a reason to disown him." She didn't appear to be moved by my explanation, and I felt compelled to further explain my thinking at the time.

"Cojo, that was just the tip of the iceberg. Our relationship was always troubled. He always wanted what I had. If he couldn't steal it, he would fuck it up so it was taken from me. He competed with me for everything. Most of the time I didn't even know the competition was going on until I lost whatever it was I wanted. "

"That's not unusual, is it?"

"How the hell would I know? But things changed when he killed that girl. When he blamed me, I had to accept that my own blood hated me."

"Hate? That's a pretty strong word, and you know words have power."

"Cojo, he caused me to get arrested for something I didn't do. They came down to my job in the middle of the day and handcuffed me. They took me off the clock and kept me there overnight for something I had nothing to do with. I wound up losing the very first job I ever had as a result of his fuck up. And let's not forget that the girl's brothers kicked the shit out of me because I couldn't convince them that I didn't have anything to do with her death."

"That's unfortunate, but it's not enough to forget or ignore your family."

"Are these the words of someone who
found out she had a family after all these yea
I regretted the words the moment they left
lips. I knew that Cojo was sensitive about
family situation, and I vowed to never use
words against her. I felt like punching myse
the face. "Wait, please don't respond to tha
slipped off the sofa and got on my knees. "B
I was way out of line with that one. I am sensi
to my family dynamics, but it does not give r
pass to hurt you about yours. I am so sorry."

I could tell she was hurt because she woul
even look me in the eye, but that was what
brother did to me. He changed me when he
around. I would do things just to spite him
were normally not in my character. I thoug
was done with that when he was finally out o
life. I waited for her to respond to my apol
but she continued to avoid my gaze. A single
dropped from her eye, and I quickly reache
and wiped it away.

"Sweetheart, I'm sorry. I didn't mean to
you."

"Twice in twenty-four hours."

Damn, that couldn't have hurt worse if s
stuck it to me with the tip of a sword.

"Ouch." I had to fix this, but I had no idea
I was going to do it. I got up off my knees and

next to her on the couch. I held my arms open, not at all sure she would fall into them, but it had always worked before.

She used to find comfort in my arms, and despite all that had happened, I still loved and worshiped her. She stared at me for a few seconds before she allowed herself to slip into my arms. Her shoulders shook as she wrapped her arms around my waist. I allowed my head to rest on hers. The fact that she was willing to let me hold her told me she still loved me, in spite of our problems.

She said, "I get it that siblings fight. I get it. I get it that they sometimes feel jealous. I truly do, but because I haven't lived through that, I can't help but feel envious."

"Baby, I'm sorry. What I said was insensitive. I know you are just getting to meet your brothers and sisters, but to be honest, I don't think anyone in your family is like my brother was to me. He was and is a rare breed. To this day, I don't know if he ever found love in his heart for me. I had to divorce him from my life in order for me to go on."

"Why?"

"Because I loved him too much to allow him to continue to hurt me, and it was clear to me that he didn't give a damn about me."

Cojo pulled against my embrace. As much as I wanted to yank her back to my chest, I allowed it.

"Why do you say that?" She cocked her head to the side, and for a split second I began to believe that he had gotten to her enough to turn her heart against me.

"It wasn't one action, it was the summation of all his attacks that made me close my heart to him. He didn't leave me much choice." I wanted her to sink back into my arms; instead, she lay back on the sofa, deep in thought. On one hand, I should have been thanking my lucky stars that she hadn't sent me packing, but on the other hand, I missed my wife. I'd yet to show her all the pent-up love and frustration I had in my body after our forced separation.

A red-winged devil flew onto my shoulder and started talking in my ear. *She don't need you like you need her because her needs were met by your brother.*

I gritted my teeth against the visual that played out in my mind.

CHAPTER TWENTY-ONE

COJO MILLS

Merlin paced and talked. "Sweetie, as I said before, I can't imagine what life was like for you, but I do care."

"Caring isn't enough. Family means everything to me. You turned on me yesterday without finding out what the circumstances were. That is what bothers me most, because you are my family, and the most important person in my world. I would never do that to you."

"I know, sweetheart, and I am deeply sorry. I acted on emotion without any thought. Haven't you ever felt like that before?"

He made a good point, and for a moment I just wanted to forget this whole incident had ever happened.

He said, "So what do we do now?"

That was a good question and one that I didn't have an answer to. My heart wanted to hold my husband in my arms and have him make sweet love to me, but I didn't know how to say it to him. This whole situation was very confusing to me because I never had a problem communicating with Merlin before. In fact, most times I didn't have to tell him what I wanted; he knew. The silence that followed was irritating and neither of us was strong enough to stop the irritation.

He took my hand. "I love you, and I want us to work on saving our marriage."

No sweeter words could have been spoken to me. I was hoping my husband believed enough in our marriage to make it work. I wasn't wearing silk blinders, thinking that he would not have his moments when he remembered that I'd slept with his brother, but I hoped that our love would prevail.

"I believe in us." There was nothing left to say as I melted into his arms. All the pain and anguish over the last twenty-four hours were forgotten. I got to enjoy the feel of my husband's arms around me, and I was excited about what would happen next. My clit came alive, yet not how it had when Gavin showed up at my door the previous morning.

"Are you sure?" Merlin pulled me away from his chest and looked me straight in my face.

I felt so much love for him at that moment it was difficult to speak. After all that we'd been through within the last twenty-four hours, he still thought enough about me to ask me if I was sure.

"I've never been so sure of something in my life." The lines that had etched his face moments before dissolved, and he stood before me looking like a twelve-year-old child.

My heart swelled again with love. This was my soul mate and I loved him. He picked me up and carried me into our bedroom, and gently laid me down on the bed. He stretched my arms out, a clear indication that he didn't want me to do anything.

"I've been waiting for this moment for six months." His voice was a low growl, and it turned me on just listening to him.

I tried to keep my eyes open and focused on him, but my mind wandered as he started to strip for me. Since I'd been with both brothers, I couldn't help but notice that they were both gifted in the drawers. Even though I'd been with my husband before, it had been a minute. But Gavin was freshly painted in my mind. Merlin wore his desert fatigues and a tan wife beater that showed off his pecks, but I wasn't craving his pecks. I needed him to bring on the dick in spectacular style. I needed him to erase the thought of his brother from my mind and body!

"You're taking too long." I said. I needed him to fill my body so my mind could stop the doubts that were flowing through it. I wanted to make sure that he was still able to fulfill me after I'd had a taste of the forbidden.

"Girl, I can't go at this too quick because it's been a minute for me." His arms were raised over his head as he was taking off his shirt, but he stopped and his shoulders shook.

I could tell in that moment he was remembering what I was trying so desperately to forget. That's when I knew that I had to take matters into my own hands to get our relationship back on track.

As he stood there frozen in time, I slipped out of my clothing. At first I was going at this with my mind, but now my heart got into it. I didn't want to lose my marriage and the man who I'd grown to love. "Open your eyes." My voice was sultry and commanding.

"Damn." He couldn't say anything else, but he didn't need to. His dick fought against the confines of his shorts and told a story that his lips didn't have to.

"I love you," I whispered as I turned over and got on my knees. Even though I would have gotten more enjoyment from a frontal assault, I knew he needed to be in control of the dick slinging. I pointed my ass in his direction and prepared myself for the punishment. Mere seconds passed before I felt the head of his dick pressing against my hole. He wasn't going for the pussy; he was pushing into my ass without lube or chaser. Instinctively I clenched up. I wanted to stop him, but I stopped myself. He had to discipline me somehow and this was going to be my punishment. It would be rough for a few strokes, but eventually I would feel the groove.

That's what I told myself, but truth be told, he hurt the hell out of me. I could not produce enough lube to make the encounter even remotely enjoyable. He actually chased me around the bed before he gave up. Not wanting to lose the sexual bond that we'd formed, I slipped into the bathroom and wet a washcloth. I washed my ass and spent a considerable amount of time washing his dick with the warmed washcloth. When I finished, I replaced the warm cloth with my mouth.

"Ah . . . shit, baby, what are you trying to do?" He stood on his tiptoes.

I took a moment to allow his dick to slide out of my mouth to answer. "I just want you to know how much I missed you."

Once again he tightened up, but as my lips sought his dick again, he had no choice but to give into the feeling.

He said while I deep-throated him, "Baby, I thought of you every night. I love you so much." He palmed the back of my head.

Even though I had him in a compromising position, I knew in my heart he was telling the truth. I could just feel it.

"Can I cum inside of you?" His voice was low, but I was close enough to hear it, and it was like music to my ears.

"All day and every day." I relinquished my hold on his dick and flipped over so he could sink his shaft deep inside of me.

He climbed on board and let me have five great pumps and let go. Normally I would have felt deprived, but tonight it was all I needed to get off my damn self. We came together, but my mind was working overtime. *Is he better than Gavin?* I was treading on dangerous ground and I knew it, but I couldn't control my thoughts any more than I could control the weather.

"Damn, baby, that was good." Merlin sighed. He ran his hand down my back and rested it on my ass.

It was good for me too, but it wasn't great like what I'd had yesterday with his brother. I couldn't get his brother's dick out of my mind. "Yes, it was." I felt as if I should say more, but I couldn't figure out what to say without giving voice to my thoughts.

He snuggled closer, and I wondered what was going through his mind. Was he doubting me as well? I tried to fall into a comfortable nap, but I could not help but compare Gavin to Merlin. As much as I hated to admit it, the chemistry between us was unlike anything I'd ever experienced before, and part of me wanted more. Gavin was only the second man I'd slept with in my life, and he was truly fucking with my mind. If I had to choose between the two sexually, I would have chosen Gavin even though I knew he was trouble. But to be honest it excited me more.

CHAPTER TWENTY-TWO

GAVIN MILLS

I knew that coming back home would to be difficult, but I had no idea that it was going to be this hard. Momma was acting like a pure bitch and didn't waste a second telling me how she felt about my coming to stay with her.

"This is just temporary," Gina said.

"I know that, Mother." I was trying to slip past her and go to my room, but she obviously had other ideas.

"Did you look for a job today?" She stood there with her hands on her hips like she was about to climb in my ass if I didn't give her the answer that she wanted.

"I went to the library and put in a few applications online."

Her eyes widened in apparent shock. I know that she didn't expect a response from me, and I tried to hide the smile that threatened to creep up on my face. I was lying my ass off, but she didn't need to know all that. I just needed to keep her off my back for a little while.

"Humph. Online, huh? Ain't nothing like a face-to-face interview."

"I'm going to do that, Mother, but I had to make an appointment first. I can't just show up all unannounced."

"Why not? That's the way that I found my job."

"And that was like a hundred years ago."

Her mouth twisted into an evil frown. I could have worded it a little differently, but I was just trying to let her know that times had changed since she last looked for work.

"You trying to get smart, boy?"

I bristled because my days of being a boy were over. I was twenty-five years old and didn't appreciate her trying to act like I was still a teenager. I wanted to tell her exactly how I felt about her evil ass, but I still needed a free place to stay until I found my next hustle. Working nine to five was just not for me. First of all, since I had never finished high school, my options were not that great. And if she thought that I was going to work in some fast food joint, she had obviously lost her happy mind.

I needed to find something that would allow me to get the hell out of her house quick, fast, and in a hurry. My mind went back to Cojo. If I could turn her out, there was a good chance that she would allow me to crash with her. She looked like she was handling her business and handling it well. I was sure that I could sweet talk myself into her life if I could just get rid of my brother.

Gina snapped her fingers to bring me out of the daze. "Are you going to answer me?"

"Huh?" I had completely forgotten what she had asked me.

"I asked if you were trying to get smart. I ain't going to have you living up in my house and disrespecting me."

"No, I wasn't trying to be smart. I was just saying that things have changed. Nowadays everybody is on the Internet. I'm surprised that you aren't on it."

"What do I need a computer for?"

"You could shop."

"Shop for what? I have everything that I need."

I looked around her sparsely furnished apartment and stifled a grunt. "You could even find a man on the Internet."

"I don't need no man. And if I did, I damn sure wouldn't be looking for him on the Internet."

I didn't agree with that statement because I thought some dick was definitely what she needed. Perhaps if she got broke off in the right way, she wouldn't be such a bitch. "I'm just using that as an example of the things that you could do on the Internet. You could even look into getting a hobby."

"Hobby? What do I need a hobby for? I'm happy with my life as it."

I was spending way too much time talking to my mother. I just wanted her to get out of my way so I could go into my room and start plotting how I could work my way into Cojo's life. "So, what do you know about Cojo?"

"Cojo? Why the hell are you asking about her?" She turned around, walked over to the sofa, and sat down. She turned up her nose like she had suddenly smelled something foul. It was clear from her actions that she seriously disliked my brother's wife.

"She's in the family now, so I just wanted to know something about her."

"She ain't in my family."

If I had any doubt about her feelings about Cojo, they were clear now. "Why don't you like her?" This conversation was about to get interesting to me, so I walked over to the loveseat and sat down directly across from my mother.

"I don't have any opinion about her at all." Now she was lying her ass off. She turned on the television as if she was finished with the conversation.

If I were smarter, I would have used that opportunity to go to my room, but I had to open up my stupid-ass mouth and push the envelope. I had gotten the focus off of me not having a job and on to something else. But by pressing her to talk about something she didn't want to talk about I, brought the focus back to me. "So you're going to just ignore me?"

She turned off the television and gave me her full attention. "You need to stop lusting after your brother's wife and find your sorry ass a job. That is the same shit that landed your ass in prison. You ain't learned shit."

Damn, she busted me out big time. I thought I was being all slick, and she saw right through my mess. I stood up. "I ain't lusting after nobody. I was just asking a damn question." I started to stomp off.

"Who the hell do you think you're talking to? You ain't gonna come up in my house and think that you are going to talk to me any kind of way." She was working on a major neck-snapping attitude, and I wanted to kick my own ass for not following my first instincts.

As much as I didn't want to, I knew that I was going to have to apologize. "I'm sorry, Mother. I didn't mean to be disrespectful."

"Umph."

I continued to walk to my room while she was mulling over her next biting sentence. Lord knows my mother could cut you with her tongue, and I didn't feel like verbally sparring with her. I would not win. "I'm going to take a nap."

She did not answer, but I didn't expect her to. I closed the door and breathed a sigh of relief because she didn't rise up off the sofa and try to continue her argument. I didn't know how much more I was going to be able to take from her. She had the power to make me snap, and I wasn't prepared to do it today.

CHAPTER TWENTY-THREE

MERLIN MILLS

Falling asleep should have been easy. I was back with my wife; we'd just made love. All should have been right with the world, but I still had the little red devil riding my shoulder, talkin' in my ear. The little man had a lot to say, and most of it I didn't want to hear. In fact, if I continued to listen to him, our marriage would be doomed. First he talked about my performance in bed. I didn't last two minutes, but it had been a long time since I'd been inside of my wife. My body was on overload.

Damn, should I start calling you "two"? the devil asked.

Two? I thought.

Yeah, as in two-minute brother. You busted your nut before she could even catch up.

It's been a long time.

Is that your final answer?

She got hers.

But was she faking it? You know women are good at faking it. Stroking our egos, and we're dumb enough to believe it.

Cojo wouldn't fake an organism.

Are you sure about that, buddy?

The seeds of doubt had been planted, and as I sat there waiting for sleep to take me away, I watered the seeds. Dealing with my brother always made me feel this way. The fact that he had actually been intimate with my wife wreaked havoc in my mind. I didn't want to lose yet another woman to him. We'd been down this road too many times before.

The devil said, *Gavin tapped that ass for real. You just played with the pussy.*

"Will you just shut up," I said aloud.

Cojo lifted her head from her pillow and peeked at me. "Huh?" She wiped at her eyes, trying to clear the crust from them.

"Nothin', sweetie, go back to sleep. I had a bad dream."

She snuggled closer to me. The smell of her sex was like an alluring drug. My dick rose to attention. I wanted some more, and this time I was going to last longer than two minutes.

I palmed her grapefruit-sized breast in my hand, kneading her nipple. It became hard as a knot in seconds. That was one of the things that I loved about my wife. Her body responded to my touch. A low purr escaped her lips as she gently pushed her ass against my dick. Even though she was asleep, she responded to my touch, and that made me feel better.

"Can I lick your pussy?" I whispered in her ear. My dick throbbed in anticipation.

She'd never said no in the past, so I didn't expect her to tonight. She complied, flinging her legs open wide, and I slipped down under the sheets to meet her at her V.

This was the first time that I'd ever attempted oral sex on her after we'd had sex, and I knew she would be trippin' because she liked to have her stuff smelling fresh, but there was nothing wrong with what I was smelling. This was the essence of our love, and I was ready to taste the fruits of our love.

"Don't you want me to freshen up?"

"No, I want it just like it is."

As I lowered my head and took the first taste, she moaned.

"Damn, baby, what's come over you?"

She did not want to hear my answer to that question because it would have really hurt her feelings. I wanted to make sure I erased all thoughts of my brother from her pussy.

"I told you, I missed you." I flicked her with my tongue again. That was an understatement. Being stranded for six months with a bunch of dudes was no damn joke. I could have done like some of my boys and taken advantage of the women who were also stationed in the Green Zone in Iraq, but I chose to remain faithful to my wife. That was another reason why it hurt me to find out that Cojo had slept with my brother. I nuzzled my face between her thighs and inhaled deeply. This was my wife and the woman who I chose to spend the rest of my life with. I needed to have her juices all over my face.

You still drinking behind your brother? the devil whispered in my ear.

"Shut the hell up." I shook my head to get the little devil out of my mind.

"What's going on, baby?" Cojo raised up on her elbows to see who the hell I was speaking to.

I felt like a first-class fool. "Your pussy is talking to me and I was telling it to wait. We have nothing but time." Damn, I was proud of myself for coming up with a plausible lie on the spot like that. But I also felt guilty for lying about how I really felt.

The little devil on my shoulder started talking to me again: *You must be doing something different than he did. Why else would she question you? Has she ever questioned you before?*

Shut the fuck up. I never talked shit like this before either, I thought. This little conversation was working on my erection and my desire to have my wife again.

"I'm just trippin'. I have been dreaming about when I would be with you again for so long, my mind is on overload, not to mention my dick."

"Oh, baby, that's so sweet."

Why did it sound like she was placating me for my early ejaculation when I knew she came too? These were the thoughts that I needed to erase from my mind if we were going to continue to have a happy and loving relationship. I couldn't keep those doubts in my head or they would destroy me. "I'm good, baby. I just have something on my mind." It probably would have been a good idea to say exactly what was on my mind since we were trying to rebuild our relationship, but I wasn't feeling so studified. Meaning, I wasn't feeling very comfortable about my manhood right about that time.

There was a pregnant pause in our conversation, and I knew that she could feel the tension building up in me when it should have been the exact opposite. I threw the covers off my side of the bed and swung my legs over the side.

"Where you going, baby?"

"Going to get something to drink. Go back to sleep."

"Can you bring me some too?"

Damn, I was hoping that I could take my time and get myself together before I had to come back in the room with her. "Sure. Can I get you something else while I'm in the kitchen?"

"No, just some water will be fine."

I walked into the kitchen with a heavy heart. Part of me tried to punish my wife with my love-making, but it backfired on me. The shit got so good that I couldn't control myself.

I pulled two glasses out of the cabinet. I really wanted a stiff drink but she would question my drinking so late at night, especially since neither of us really ate that much. I was going to have to suck this up until I could get some time alone.

I carried the glasses back into the bedroom and, to my surprise, Cojo was fast asleep. I could have cried I was so happy. Turning softly on my bare feet, I left the bedroom and went back into the kitchen. I poured out the water and went to the bar and fixed myself a hefty drink. I sat down on the sofa and gazed at the television. I didn't dare turn it on for fear that it would wake my wife.

"Lord, what am I going to do?" I whispered as a tear rolled down my face. I glanced around our apartment. It wasn't bad. Before I left, it had felt like my home, but now I felt as if I didn't belong. I felt like I was a stranger just visiting, even though I knew where everything belonged. I put my feet up on the coffee table as I sipped from my glass. I felt the beginnings of a headache coming on, but I was too tired to go and get some aspirin. Another tear slid down my face.

Just a few days ago I was deep in combat and here I am crying like a little punk 'cause I shot my load off too quickly. My mind was so twisted, it did not occur to me that this was a natural reaction after being deprived of sex so long. It was almost like the first time, especially if you were used to having sex on the regular.

A car pulled into the parking lot; its headlights briefly lit up the living room. I wondered who was coming home so late, so I got up to peek through the curtains. I couldn't see the car because of a huge maple tree.

It was dark outside, but I could see enough to tell that it was a man. He wore dark clothing and kept his head turned so I could not make out his facial features. Something about the man was familiar. He walked toward our breezeway and was blocked from my view. I moved from the window and went to the door. I wanted to see what apartment he was going to enter. The man walked straight to our apartment, much to my amazement. He put his ear to our door and stood there.

I was stunned. Wearing nothing more than my drawers, I yanked open the door. "May I help you, motherfucker?"

The man raised his head. "Hey, bro," he said as he looked me up and down.

"Gavin, what the fuck are you doing here, and why do you have your ear pressed against our door?"

"Uh . . ."

My blood began to boil. He was about to spoonfeed me some bullshit just like he used to do when we were kids.

"Uh, hell," I bellowed. Something just wasn't right about him all of a sudden taking an interest in me and what was going on in my life. He'd been gone so many years, why now?

"I, uh, I was just in the neighborhood, and I was making sure everything was okay with you." He had a sheepish grin on his face.

If I wasn't standing there in my underwear, I would have socked him dead in his face. "Do you know what the fuck time it is?" My fingers balled into a fist, itching to slug him just once.

"Naw, man. What time is it?" He was playing stupid on me and it was making me madder by the second.

I looked past him to see if anyone was watching the spectacle we were causing in the hallway. "Negro, you playing games with me. First you popped up this morning, now you unexpectedly show up after midnight."

"I ain't playin', bro, I just wanted to make sure my brother and his wife were okay, so now that I've done that, I guess I'll be getting on home."

The need to touch him was so strong I had to bite my lower lip just to keep from spitting on him.

Cojo said, "Merlin?"

I quickly turned around; I had forgotten she was asleep in the next room. That was when I realized that she was naked as the day she was born. I swung back around to look at Gavin. His eyes widened as he took in all her naked glory.

"Baby, go back in the room and put some clothes on. I'll be there in a minute."

She jumped back as she realized that we were not alone. "Oh, God!" she screeched as she ran back to our room and shut the door.

That was the second time in the course of two days that she had exposed herself to my brother, and this shit was getting old.

"That's one fine woman you got there. Good to see that y'all knockin' boots again."

If I thought that he was sincere, I would have been touched, but I detected a menace in his tone. "I'm going back to my wife." I started to close the door on my brother's leering eyes.

"Wait, just answer me one question." He put his hands up to stop me from closing the door.

"What is it?" The sight of him was sickening me.

"Why you out here in the living room drinkin' when you could be snuggled up with that dime piece of a wife?"

Damn, he must have seen me peeping through the curtains. That was it. I made up my mind to set this motherfucker straight once and for all. "You got that cell phone on you that I threw in with the clothes?"

He pointed his thumb toward the parking lot. "It's in the car."

"Good. I'll call you in twenty minutes."

Gavin grinned as if I'd made his day. "Oh, yeah? For what? I thought you were going back to your sexy wife."

"I'm tired of drinking alone. Figured we could have a few drinks together."

I stormed into our bedroom and started getting dressed.

"Where are you going?" Cojo said.

"Out. I need to handle something." I put on my Atlanta ball cap.

"Out where?"

"Not right now, Cojo." I grabbed my car keys from the dresser and left.

CHAPTER TWENTY-FOUR

MERLIN MILLS

I jumped in my car and sped out of the parking lot. When I came to the first stoplight, I dialed Gavin.

In the middle of the first ring, he said, "I see you're still Mr. Punctual."

"You know that bar, Central Station, in East Point?"

"Yeah, I remember it. I snuck in there a few times back in the day."

"Meet me there." I started to feel nervous.

"Drinks on you? Bars don't agree with my budget."

Some people never change. Gavin always wanted to freeload off people, getting by without any effort on his part. The motherfucker just took, took, took.

I laughed. "Sure, drinks on me. It's the least I can do."

***

By the time Gavin pulled up, I was tipsy as hell and waiting for him in the parking lot.

He walked up to me. "What's up, fam?" Gavin had a familiar smirk on his face, and it was enough to propel me forward.

I launched my body from the side of the building and slammed into my brother, dragging him to the ground. I punched him in the nose and blood was everywhere.

"Man, what the fuck is your problem?" Gavin struggled to get me off of him, but I was like a dead weight, and I wasn't going anywhere.

"You're my fucking problem. Why the hell you keep popping up at my house and shit? I told you I wasn't fucking with you."

"You tripping, man. I just was in the neighborhood."

"Wrong answer, motherfucker." I punched him in his jaw as hard as I could.

He shook his head. I could tell that I stunned him. We started a back-and-forth tussle in the parking lot.

He said, "Man, you better get the fuck off of me."

Gavin still was trying to catch his breath when I head-butted him. Little did he know that I'd learned a lot in the military, and all my aggression was pouring out on him.

"Stay the fuck away from me and my wife."

"Urg." Gavin finally regrouped and was able to push me off of him. He used someone's car to pull himself to his feet.

I quickly got up and circled my prey, coming in low. I wasn't ready for this fight to end. My brother had caused me a lot of pain throughout my life, and I was ready to inflict some of my own.

He rubbed his hand on his jaw and shrugged his shoulders as if I hadn't hurt him at all. "Nice right. They teach you that in the service?"

I didn't want to talk. I wanted to let my hands speak for me. I rushed him again, but this time Gavin stepped out of the way and I charged past him.

"Stop playing and let's get the drinks you promised." His voice was low.

"Who said I was playing? Now, I am going to tell you one last time, stay the fuck away from my wife." I swung again and managed to hit him in the arm. I could tell that he was finally getting mad, but I didn't give a fuck.

"Ain't nobody stuttin' you." He attempted to punch me in the chest, but I quickly deflected the punch and delivered one of my own.

He said, "Now, I'm going to pretend like you didn't bust my nose, because you're my brother. But make no mistake about it, you're weak. You've always been the weak one, and I will use that to my advantage and beat shit down your leg."

"This is your last warning. You're not welcome at my house." I stepped back.

He opened his trunk, changed his shirt, then got into his car. We were making so much noise in the parking lot, I was surprised someone hadn't called the cops yet.

I said, "You heard what I said."

"Whatever, motherfucker," Gavin said as he rolled down the window and spat at my feet.

I wanted to reach through the window and drag his ass out, but when I reached for him, his car tire ran over my foot. I winced as I grabbed my foot. Gavin pulled off as I danced around on the gravel, trying to make the pain go away.

"Bitch ass," I shouted to his departing car.

Cojo snatched open the front door when I approached it. She covered her mouth and her eyes widened. "Oh my God, Merlin, where did all that blood come from?"

"Leave it alone, Cojo." I limped past her.

"I smell alcohol; have you been drinking?"

"What part of 'leave it alone' is confusing to you?" I slammed the bathroom door shut and locked it.

CHAPTER TWENTY-FIVE

GAVIN MILLS

"Shit, what the hell was I thinking, going o
Merlin's house at this time of night?" I slamm
my hand against the steering wheel. I had
his house looking stupid, but the image of C
naked was burned in my mind; even the fi
with my brother wasn't enough to keep me aw
I had to have her again, there were no ifs, an
or buts about it. I was going to have to devis
way to get Merlin out of the house so I coul
least talk to Cojo and see where her head was

I didn't really want to go home, but I kn
that I had to do something before I broke do
Cojo's door or did something else foolish. I di
quite understand why I was so attracted to h
Maybe it was the forbidden fruit aspect of
Although she was beautiful, there was more t
than that.

Merlin's stupid-ass didn't even know what to do with that little freak. Shit, there ain't no way I would have been out trying to pick a fight instead of in that bedroom tearing that shit up. My dick started to rise as I thought about her round, soft ass and the way that it had filled my hands.

I was sexually frustrated in a way that I hadn't been since I was a teenager, and the thought of going back to my mother's house to beat my meat wasn't the least bit appealing. Knowing her ass, she would knock on the damn door right before I shot my load into my pillowcase. Then I would want to beat her ass for adding to my already blue balls.

I decided to drive down Cleveland Avenue to see if I could see some hoes on the stroll. It had been a while since I'd been in Atlanta. I didn't really know where to go to find some free fun since I had little money in my pocket to pay for a piece of ass. I was hoping to find some hot young thang who wouldn't mind stretching out on the back seat of my car or sucking my dick as I drove around the block.

I rubbed my dick in anticipation. It was late, however, and most young girls were probably in the house, but I was too heated to go home unsatisfied.

***

"Bingo." I slowed my car down as I came up on a woman walking down the street like she had lost her best friend. I rolled down my window. Her shirt was clinging to her skin, and I could see sweat rings under her arms as she walked under the street lamp. She appeared to have been walking for some time because she walked like each step hurt. I drove even slower. I expected her to notice me and solicit her goodies, but she must have been lost in thought because she didn't even look up.

I pulled up next to her at the curb. "Excuse me, miss. I'm a little lost. I'm trying to get back to I-20. Can you help me?"

"Huh?" Her head snapped up and she looked all around as if she was unaware of her surroundings. She was young, very young, just like I liked them.

"I'm sorry. I didn't mean to startle you, but I was wondering if you could help me find the highway."

She stood still for a few seconds before she took a hesitant step toward the car. She didn't come too close, but she came close enough so that I didn't have to speak as loud.

I didn't expect her to be scared, especially since she was on a well-known ho stroll. As she got closer, I was able to get a better look at her face and her perky breasts, which strained against her soaked shirt.

"I'm sorry, I really don't know. I'm not from around here." She backed up a step and looked around as if she were suddenly afraid.

"Oh, okay." I started to pull off because she was giving me a bad vibe.

She looked around again and yelled out to me, "Wait."

I put on the brakes and tried to hide the smile that spread across my face. It was hot as hell outside, so I knew she would prefer being in a car with me to humping down the street in her high-ass heels. My dick throbbed as I watched the indecision play across her pretty face.

"Yes?" I kept my tone even so as not to scare her off. I didn't want her to know how badly I needed her. Truth be told, she could have been bat-shit ugly with one tooth in her head. As long as she looked clean, and had a pussy, I was game. I always kept a condom or two in my wallet, so I wasn't worried about anything else.

"Can I trouble you for a ride?"

"Uh . . ." I didn't want to appear eager so I hesitated.

"Please? I had a fight with my boyfriend, and I want to get out of this neighborhood before he comes back." She took two steps closer to the car and my dick thumped against my zipper.

"I'm sorry, sweetheart, but I don't want no trouble. I'm just trying to find my way home." I sat up straight in my seat as she came closer to the car.

"I won't be no trouble, but I've been walking for a long time and my feet are killing me." She leaned into my open window with her breasts inches from my mouth.

"I hear what you're saying, but what if your man comes running up on me and wants to start something? I can't take that chance, I'm new to Atlanta. I'm stationed at Fort McPherson Army base."

"Please, mister, I promise it will be okay."

I didn't say anything for several seconds. My eyes scanned the streets and my rearview mirror. I even turned around to look out the back window to make it seem like I was worried. In all reality, I wished a motherfucker would run up on me tonight. I was ready for a real fight after that bullshit stunt Merlin pulled.

"Come on." I leaned over and opened the passenger side door.

She ran as fast as her heels would allow to get to the other side of the car. Her face was twisted up in a grimace that wasn't appealing at all. She plopped into the seat and shut the door. "Thank you," she said as she glanced over her shoulder.

"Put your seatbelt on." I pulled back on to the street, happy with this turn of events.

She was fumbling around with the seatbelt so I reached over to help her. She jumped at the contact.

"Relax, ma, I was just trying to help you. I'd hate to get pulled over for driving without a seatbelt."

She visibly relaxed and allowed me to hand her the seatbelt. Once she was settled, I picked up speed.

"The highway can't be far from here. Where do you live?" For a second I thought she didn't hear me, because she didn't answer. "My name is Merlin Mills, what's yours?" I purposely meant to use my brother's name. Old habits were hard to break.

"That's interesting. Never met a black man by the name of Merlin." She took off her shoes and started massaging her feet.

"I smell stinky feet." I was laughing when I said it so she wouldn't take offense.

"My feet don't stink." She attempted to put her shoes back on.

"Hey, I was just kidding. You don't have to ¡
them back on until it's time for you to get out.

She still hadn't volunteered her name, bu
wasn't going to press her until she was ready
talk. Truth be told, I could give two plug nick
about her name. All I wanted from her was so
head and some of that fine, young pussy. I cou
almost smell it, like it was some expensive p
fume she wore.

"So what was the fight about?" I didn't know
she was going to answer the question, but I ¡
it out there. Perhaps if I came across as an ol
brother she would start to trust me.

"How old are you?" She was very good at eva
ing questions.

"Twenty-two." I was really twenty-five, b
that was on a need-to-know basis, and she did
need to know.

"You don't look twenty-two."

"How old do I look?" If she said thirty, I w
going to put her out at the next corner, pussy
not. I waited for a few heartbeats with my fo
hovering over the brake.

"I would have said eighteen." She giggled
she said it, and my ego inflated like a helium b.
loon. She sat back in the seat like she had kno
me all of her life.

I started to feel more confident that I was going to get what I wanted. She was still massaging her foot.

"If you put one of your feet on my lap, I'll massage it for you."

She looked at me with this quizzical expression on her face, and I was afraid that I'd scared her away, but she hesitantly handed me her right foot. It rested on my thigh, and I firmly massaged it while keeping my other hand on the wheel. She folded her left leg on the seat, and I handled her other foot. Her legs were spread like a check mark lying upside down.

"Um, that feels so good," she murmured as her head rested against the window.

I looked over at her and her eyes were closed. I smiled. Things were going a lot better than I thought they would. She had to be young because no experienced woman would allow herself to be in this situation. She didn't know me from Adam, but she was wide open for me.

"Thanks, it's what I used to do before I joined the Army." The lies were just rolling off my tongue.

"What you used to do? What's that supposed to mean?" She raised her head up off the window. She was tall, at least five foot six, and probably weighed about 135 pounds.

"By profession I'm a masseur. The Army is a temporary hustle. I set up in hair salons and fitness clubs to help people relax."

"Oh, that's nice. I never met a masseur before."

We traveled for a few more miles without conversation. I kept firm pressure on her right foot, and she continued to moan softly.

"How's your other foot?"

"It still hurts."

"Put that one up here too, and I'll work on it."

If she were paying attention, she would have realized that we were driving around in a big circle. I knew exactly where I was, and I was in no hurry to get to the highway. In fact, we were now driving down the same street that I'd picked her up on.

She placed both of her feet in my lap. She could have removed the right foot, but she didn't. She must have liked the way my hands felt on her. As I massaged her left foot, her moans got louder.

"You're good. I'd pay money for a full-body massage."

I started trying to calculate how much money I had left in my pocket. I was ready to get a hotel room so I could show her just how good I could make her feel. Inside and out.

"Thanks, it's a job I enjoy."

"Do you do men too?"

"That would be a no. I do this job because I enjoy it, and there is nothing enjoyable about rubbing my hands on another man."

She giggled again, this time louder. "You're funny. I like you, Merlin. You have the hands of a magician." She laughed at her own joke.

"If you only knew." I was growing tired of waiting. As much as I enjoyed touching her feet, I needed more.

She said, "We went to a frat party with some of his friends."

Her voice was so low I could barely hear her. I wanted to tell her to get to the point so we could get to fucking, but I kept my peace, as painful as it was to do.

"He got to drinking and paying more attention to his boys than me, and I was ready to go home. He called me a few ugly names and told me that if I wanted to leave I knew where the door was."

"Wow, how long had you been dating this jerk?"

"For about seven months. I don't know what got into him tonight. He was acting like a stranger."

"I'm sorry that happened to you."

"Angie, my name is Angie Simpson."

"Nice to meet you, Angie." I continued to rub her feet. I was still trying to figure out how I was going to get this little honey in either the back seat or to a cheap hotel room.

"You can stop driving around in circles now and take me home."

Well, I'll be damned.

CHAPTER TWENTY-SIX

GAVIN MILLS

I thought I was going to have to trick my way into Angie's panties but she turned the script on me. As soon as the door closed, she turned into a wild woman. In fact, she kind of scared me for a minute. Now, I don't see nothing wrong with an aggressive woman, but damn, hold the fuck up for a minute. She gripped my dick like she wanted to keep it as a souvenir after I went home.

"Hold up, honey, that shit is still attached."

She looked at me like she was about to punk me and put my ass out, but I didn't want to get this close to pussy and not get any, so I smiled.

"I'm just saying, take your time. I ain't going nowhere." I squeezed her ass.

"Are you out your rabbit-ass mind? This is my parents' house, we've got to hit it and quit it if you want this to happen." She stood before me with her hands on her hips like she was about to change her mind about the whole thing, and I couldn't have that.

I moved in close and pulled her to me. I damn near smothered her with my lips as I tongued her down. I now felt the same sense of urgency that she felt. I began grabbing at her clothes. I wanted her naked in the worst way, and I guess she felt the same way because she also began pawing at my clothes.

Since my clothing was limited, I winced when I heard a button pop off and roll on the floor, but I would make sure to remember to grab before I left so I could sew it back on later. I gently pushed her away from me so I could take off my own clothes. She stood there for a moment, but when she saw that I was removing my own shirt, she started taking off her clothes as well.

We were in the living room and, from the looks of it, this was where we were about to consummate this new relationship.

"I like it rough, daddy." She bent over the sofa and exposed her apple bottom to my eager dick.

I was already excited when I saw her shapely ass, but when she said she liked it rough, I damn near blew my load into the air. What exactly did she mean by *rough*? Did she want me to spank her ass or did she just want me to give it to her hard? I was perfectly willing and able to handle it either way. "Where you want it?" Visions of nasty acts danced in my head. It was rare to find someone as young as Angie who was into the really nasty things. Normally they didn't acquire the really kinky taste until they were at least thirty-five.

"I want you to ram that big dick so far up my ass that it comes out my mouth."

I was outdone. My prayers had been answered. Angie was a nasty girl, and I was about to give it to her. I could not believe that old dude slept on this shit. "Did you let old dude hit it like this?" I normally didn't like to discuss other men while I was about to get my groove on, but this whole night was just like a dream to me. I could not believe that things were turning out just as I had planned.

"Are you just going to talk or are you going to show me what you are working with?" She wagged her naked ass at me.

This chick was bold and brassy. If I wasn't careful, she could very well turn me out. I brought it to her hard, and I stifled the moan that attempted to escape from my lips. She was tight, but access was easy. I was surprised at how receptive she was, and it only excited me more.

"Harder."

Damn, I felt like I had died and gone to heaven. This bitch was allowing me to give it to her like I was grilling her pussy.

"Fuck my asshole harder, goddammit!"

"Oh, you think you can take all of this?" I boasted. I was feeling quite good about myself at this point. Not only was I in those panties, I was dick deep in that ass.

"Stop talking and keep fuckin'." Her voice was guttural and deep.

If I didn't know better, I would have thought that Regan from *The Exorcist* had entered the room. I dug deeper, hoping to give her what she was looking for, and to achieve my own desires as well.

She rammed her ass against my thrusts. "Yeah, just like that, baby. Fuck me like you mean it."

The pressure was on and her nasty talking was about to push me over the edge. I wasn't used to having a woman talk trash to me and it was messing with my mind.

"If you want me to give it to you right, you may want to shut the fuck up." As soon as those words left my mouth, I knew I had fucked up. I felt her shut down and push my dick out of her ass. "Damn, baby, I didn't mean it. I just wanted to let you know that your talking took me out of the moment."

"No problem. Your comment took me out of the moment too, so we're both shit out of luck. Just let me get to my battery-operated dick and I'll be okay." She started to get off the sofa and it pissed me off.

"Bitch, get your ass back on the couch." I was heated.

"Bitch? Who you calling a bitch? I got your bitch." She reached up under the sofa, brought out a baseball bat, and proceeded to hit me with it. Talk about an error in judgment; this bitch was crazy. She cracked me over my arm, and I swore that she broke it.

"Are you crazy?" I started to call her bitch again, but I knew what would result from that. I just wanted to calm her ass down enough so I could bust my nut. As it was, my arms were hurting from the beating she had given me, but I still had an erection. "Damn, baby, I like your attitude. Back that ass up on my dick." I raised up on my knees and scooted to the middle of the sofa. I was about to take this shit to another level. If things went my way, I would have her screaming for her momma.

She backed her shapely ass up in the air, and I plunged into her pussy as if I were trying to

break through to the other side. "That's rig
fuck me," she yelled.

That was it for me. I came and I was throu,
My dick shriveled and escaped her pussy. I ne
felt so dejected in my life. I couldn't hang w
her young ass.

"Don't tell me you're done. I'm not havi
that. You're gonna fuck me longer than tha
am just getting started."

She probably shouldn't have said that beca
I was about to whup her ass. I wasn't about
have some young-ass chick dictate to me wl
she was and wasn't going to have.

"Come again?" I wanted to make sure I hea
her before I choked her 'til she was woozy.

"I didn't stutter. Are you going to give
some dick or not?"

That was it, lights out on the young pussy
snatched her neck and held on until she pass
out and she could not say another word. The
beat the bitch up. Case closed as far as this bi
was concerned.

I continued to squeeze her neck as I jack
off. I rammed my dick inside of her and that v
the biggest nut that I'd ever busted, especia
since she didn't utter a word. I had no idea it v
possible to choke someone with one hand. Fe
about what I'd done did not dawn on me ur

the last little solider had made its way into her pussy.

"I've got to kill this bitch and get rid of the evidence," I said to myself, but I felt like I was in complete control of the situation. It wasn't my fault that she got a little mouthy and wound up dead. I searched around the room for my pants that I had discarded earlier. Most women didn't understand that their wicked mouths brought on most of their problems.

Why did she have to start talking about my performance as if I hadn't been doing a damn thing? If she would have been able to keep control of her pie hole, she would be alive right now and basking in my arms. Once I secured my clothing, I looked around the room to decide the best way to cover the evidence. I didn't touch much in the room, but I couldn't chance a smear of a fingerprint here and there, so I decided to torch the house.

I left Angie's crumpled body on the floor between the sofa and coffee table as I went in search of something that would help me set the place on fire. Time was not on my side since I knew she lived with her parents. If I were caught in the house, I would be facing life for real.

In the carport, I found what I was looking for. A full can of gasoline was sitting next to the push

mower. I was surprised that they would leave
out in the open, especially since the gas pric
were so high, but that was their problem, n
mine. I picked up the can and raced back to t
living room. I wanted the focus of the fire to
downstairs so that all evidence of me being
the home would be destroyed. I even poured
liberal amount of gas upstairs. Once I empti
the entire can, I struck a match, put it into t
can, and tossed it into the living room.

The explosion was minor but the effect w
immediate. I watched tiny plumes of fire et
their way through the house. I jumped into r
car and sped away, hoping that there were
nosey neighbors watching my speedy getaway.

Wow, I had no idea that the house wou
catch fire as quickly as it did. Curiosity got t
better of me, so I drove back and parked my c
on the side of the road to watch. Shit, my di
got hard as I watched those flames leap from t
downstairs windows to the upper floors. Wha
rush! All these crazy-ass motherfuckers out he
just robbing houses and not getting the pus
was crazy. They needed to redo their shit an
get something for their efforts. Once I confirm

the house was engulfed in flames, I was happy. Angie was dead.

I sat and watched as long as I could before I pulled away from the scene. I could hear fire trucks in the distance, and I wanted to make sure that I was long gone before they got there. I wasn't about to be one of those idiots who stayed at the scene and wound up getting arrested because he had no real reason to be there.

I could still smell Angie on my hands because we had gotten very physical. When I get home, I would have to sneak past my mother because I reeked of sex. It was difficult to believe that a random pick up could lead to murder, but I had no regrets. She had no business trying to clown me after I had served it up to her. She wasn't appreciative, so the bitch deserved to die. My mind floated back to when I had sex with my brother's wife. She didn't complain, so why did I have to hear that shit from some random chick? *Fuck that, I don't think so!*

As I parked at my mother's house, I checked the car to make sure the cunt hadn't left any telltale evidence. I looked around, making sure that I wasn't being observed as I got out of the car. It would be just my luck to get away with murder

and get caught by some damn bullshit. Afte
few minutes, I was comfortable that I'd gott
away with murder again. I didn't know about t
next guy, but I was comfortable with escapin
death sentence when I eradicated someone w
was threatening my welfare.

"Bitches beware!" I was ecstatic. I was rea
to go out and do that shit again, especially sir
it was so easy to do. That was one of the pe
of being a good-looking motherfucker. Wom
didn't require much to give up the goodies, an
was Johnny-on-the-spot to provide them.

As I put my key in the door, some of my hi
evaporated. I wasn't up for my mother's sma
ass mouth today. If she knew what I'd done, s
would be careful about how she spoke to
because it wouldn't take much to put her mis
able ass in the ground too. Shit, I'd be doing
a favor.

CHAPTER TWENTY-SEVEN

ANGIE SIMPSON

I woke up and immediately started choking; smoke was everywhere. Fire was eating through the living room. I knew that if I didn't act now, the fire would devour me too. I could hardly move my head; it felt like Merlin still had his powerful hands around my neck. The fire had already crushed my panties and shirt, and now it was working on my pants. Damn.

I shook the pain I was feeling and started to move. The front door was covered by a wall of flames so I stumbled toward the kitchen and froze. There was another wall of flames, but I could see the back door behind it. I tried to hold my breath while I figured out what to do, because I was on the verge of choking to death.

I was trapped. I'd always heard that the three worst ways to die were drowning, suffocation, and fire; but fire was the worst of the worst. With

that thought, I decided that I wasn't going to d
Not now, not like this.

I looked through the flames at the back do
and charged. A guttural scream left my mou
when the fire feasted on my naked flesh. Th
was when I realized that I wouldn't make it
my own.

CHAPTER TWENTY-EIGHT

GINA MEADOWS

I sat on the couch in my favorite spot and ran my mouth on the phone to my best friend. "That boy stayed out all night and didn't have the decency to call."

Tabatha said, "Now, hold off, Gina, ain't no need getting all mad. That *boy*, as you call him, is a grown man."

"Grown or not, it is still common courtesy to call someone you are staying with and let her know that you ain't coming back. He's just like his damn father."

"Gina, you ain't making no sense. First you complain that he comes back to stay with you temporarily, and now you want to fuss 'cause he stayed out all night. Give him a break."

"Whose side are you on anyway, Tabatha?"

"I'm not picking sides. Right is right. You are miserable with your life and you want everyone around you to be miserable. You wouldn't be such a bitch if you had your baby."

I wanted to hang up the phone. I both hated and loved that she always spoke from her heart no matter how much it hurt. "I am not miserable. Maybe a little unhappy, but that's a far cry from miserable."

She had her nerve, like everything in her life was going great and shit.

I said, "Plus, if I like making everyone miserable, why do you continue to hang around me?"

"'Cause I love your miserable ass. Now, what are you doing this weekend? Me and a couple of friends are going to take a bus trip to Biloxi, and I wanted to know if you want to go."

"Girl, I ain't got no money to be throwing away, and neither do you."

"And when did you start knowing what's in my pocket?" She was mad, so I guess I succeeded at making her miserable too.

"I'm sorry, boo. I guess I am being a bitch. When are you leaving?"

"We're leaving at five o'clock on Friday evening. Are you going or not?" Her voice was laced with bitterness.

"Yes, thanks for inviting me. I'm sorry, so please don't be mad at me. Having that boy around me just has me thinking all crazy."

"Yeah, if that's what you want to blame it on this time. I've got to go. I'll pick you up around four-fifteen, late afternoon, on Friday." She hung up before I could even say good-bye.

I was really going to have to work on curbing my tongue with Tabatha, because the last thing that I needed to do was alienate her. I wasn't always the bitch I found myself as today. I used to be a loving woman who always had a smile on my face. That is, until Ronald fucked me over, and I couldn't seem to get past the pain he caused me. I wanted him to pay for it, but he continued to ignore me, and that hurt worse than the betrayal.

CHAPTER TWENTY-NINE

MERLIN MILLS

While Cojo was at work, I reported to the base to pick up my orders for mobilization. My two-week break had gone by so fast it made my head spin. Cojo and I had settled into a comfortable routine at home again. Although we'd managed to mend our fences somewhat, we still weren't where we used to be. It seemed like we were going out of our way to be nicer to each other, and it came off as being fake.

"Communication Specialist Mills, the captain will see you now."

I jumped to attention, startled away from my thoughts. I followed the lieutenant to Captain Jamison's office and waited outside the door to be announced. I was nervous as I entered the captain's office. Rumor was she was a real bitch on wheels, and I didn't need her busting my chops about anything. I marched over to her desk, stood at attention, and gave her a salute.

Captain Jamison was a petite woman who would have turned my head if she hadn't been in uniform with all the medals on her chest warning me to stay in my lane.

"At ease." She hardly looked up at me. She had a stack of files on her desk off to the corner, but she was reading one that I assumed was mine.

I waited for what felt like fifteen minutes, but was probably more like three. That's one thing that I hated about the Army: They stressed about being on time but made you wait for everything. To be such a regimented entity, they were highly disorganized. God forbid the enemy found out just how disorderly we actually were, this country would be doomed.

I had an itch in the back of my throat, but I was so scared to cough for fear of having to hit the floor and knock off fifty pushups. Captains liked to pull their weight like that, especially the women. She closed the file and looked me straight in the eye, which made me even more uncomfortable than when she was ignoring me.

"I said at ease."

I hadn't realized that I was still holding my shoulders straight with my arm cocked at my head. I chuckled a little bit as I lowered my arm.

The smile that slipped across her lips disappeared and was replaced with a frown. "Something funny?"

"No, ma'am." Instinctively, I pulled myself to attention again for what I was sure would be some form of punishment.

She completely threw me off guard with her next statement. "Have you enjoyed your little vacation?"

My eyes widened in surprise because she sounded like she actually cared. I thought about my response before I answered her. "I've been working out on the regular, Captain, so I don't get lazy."

This time she actually chuckled.

"Good answer. I see someone has prepped you well."

I relaxed a little bit, but I didn't allow myself to get too comfortable.

"I have your mobilization package here." She lifted a fat envelope from the file that she was reading.

I could not read the expression on her face. I wasn't sure if she wanted me to reach out and take them; she just waved them at me.

She said, "Do you like Iraq?"

"I will go anywhere the Army sends me." My responses were from the book.

If she was trying to trip me up, she would have to come a little bit better than that. I'd been told that if I were to get too happy about an assignment, they would switch it and send me somewhere completely different. Iraq was okay, but if I had my choice, I would stay my black-ass right there in Atlanta.

"Cut the shit, Specialist. This isn't a trap. I'm just trying to find out where your head is at."

I started to get nervous again. No one had prepared me for this little mind game. I definitely didn't want to leave Cojo alone in Atlanta now that my brother was back in town. He hadn't been by in a minute, but I still wasn't resting comfortably about his late-night visit. I felt like I was being put between a rock and a hard place. Should I trust the captain or was this a trick?

"No offense, Captain, but boot camp taught me that officers don't care about feelings and what we want. We are property of the United States Army."

"See, Specialist, that's where you're wrong. There are some of us who actually care. Off the record, I allowed the Army to ruin my marriage. I, like you, was married when I enlisted. I got my commission based on my college experience so it wasn't that bad, but I still had to travel and leave my husband at home. I thought we had

what it took to make the marriage work. At the
time, like you and Mrs. Mills, we agreed that my
enlisting was the best answer for our situation."
She paused.

I didn't know if she was waiting for me to
say something. I was intrigued by what she was
sharing with me, but I still wasn't sure if she was
setting me up or something.

After a few more seconds, she started speaking again. "At first, things appeared to be okay.
I was told that once I finished officer's training I
could return to our hometown of Fort Jackson,
Florida, but recruiters have a tendency to tell you
what you want to hear and not necessarily what's
the truth. As a result, I stayed away too long and
when I got back, my husband had moved on both
physically and emotionally. He had no problem
spending the monthly stipend I sent home, but
he had no desire to resume what we had because
he had fallen in love with someone else."

I saw what I thought to be tears forming in her
eyes. Instinctively, I wanted to go to her and rock
her in my arms, but I knew that would be the
fastest way to the brig! "Captain, I can't thank
you enough for your candor, and if the opportunity to speak is still on the table, I can honestly
say that I do not wish to leave Atlanta at this time
for personal reasons sensitive to my marriage." I

debated whether to divulge what had happened between my brother and my wife, but the scab hadn't quite healed, so I kept my mouth shut.

She picked up my file and began reading again as if I weren't even in the room. Her face once again became stoic; it made me nervous. While she was relaying her story to me, her face was softer. I could tell she still felt the pain of her husband's betrayal. I wanted to ask her how long ago this had happened to her, but I knew better than to question an officer. If she wanted to tell me, that was one thing, but asking questions was a big no-no.

"I'm not going to be able to keep you here indefinitely, Specialist, but I will personally see to it that you get a job on post for a while. Maybe a month or so, but don't make the same mistake I did. When it's time to ship out, make sure everything that you value is intact."

"Thank you, Captain. I will work on it." All the worry and dread of leaving I carried around on my shoulders had been lifted away with the stroke of a pen, even if only temporarily.

The captain handed me my new job orders. "Your new deployment date comes from upstairs; it'll arrive by mail."

My heart was so full as I exited the captain's office. I didn't know how she knew that this was what

I needed, but she did. Now, maybe I could relax a bit and work on saving my marriage. I would also be around to keep an eye on my brother, at least until he got into trouble again and was run out of town. Although I should have been giving my brother the benefit of the doubt, I knew him well enough to know that his good behavior wouldn't last long.

CHAPTER THIRTY

COJO MILLS

It had been a wonderful week since Merlin had told me he didn't have to go back to Iraq right away. I hoped the war would end before he got his letter. However, my day wasn't starting right at all. First, I woke up late and my stomach was bothering me. All morning long I kept running to the bathroom as if I had to vomit, but nothing was coming out. If I was going to get sick, I wished it would happen already and let me go about my business. By lunchtime I had had it.

I went to my supervisor and asked to be dismissed for the day.

"You ain't pregnant, are you?" she asked as I was leaving her office.

I was too stunned to react to her question. This thought never crossed my mind, but that could be the reason why I had been feeling so yucky lately. Damn, she may have a point, I thought. It was always our desire to have children, so I wasn't shocked at the possibility, but the timing could have been better. After six and a half years, why now? Merlin and I were still tiptoeing around each other, but I was confident that he would accept our child with open arms. I decided to stop at Rite Aid on my way home to get a pregnancy test.

With this resolve I actually started to feel better, but not well enough to stay at work. It was Friday and I wanted to get a jump-start on my weekend. All of a sudden I was excited. Without thinking it through, I called Merlin. "Hey, baby, I'm headed home. I'm not feeling well. My boss said I should go home and take it easy."

"Cool, I'm headed back to the house too. Is there anything that I can pick up for you?"

I wanted to tell him to get me a pregnancy test, but I decided to keep that little secret to myself until I knew for sure. "No, I just want to get some rest."

"How about I fix us some dinner and we watch some movies and call it a night."

I said, "That sounds good to me."

"Is there anything in particular that you want to see?"

"No, surprise me. You're good at picking out movies, so I know I won't be disappointed."

"All right then, I'll see you when you get home."

I hung up the phone with a smile on my face. Although we still weren't where we were before, it was better. I was just glad that Gavin had stayed clear of our house. I still couldn't believe that I didn't realize that the man I was sleeping with was not my husband. Merlin's mother had also stopped her string of confusing phone calls, but that was okay with me too 'cause I didn't like her ass anyway. Girls only get two special moments in life: proms and weddings. Gina fucked my wedding up to where I don't even look at my wedding pictures.

My smile slid from my face at the thought of my mother-in-law. She was such a hateful heifer and I didn't know why. In the beginning and a few times afterward, I did everything I could to make her like me, but she was bound and determined not to. From the first day she met me, she acted as if I wore shit on my face or something. After several attempts to woo her, I gave up.

My thoughts wandered again. I stopped at CVS and purchased a pregnancy test. There were so many to choose from, I just grabbed the cheapest one I could find and rushed back to the counter. I had to go to the bathroom in the worst way and didn't want to risk using a public restroom, especially with that strain of swine flu going around.

The ride home was so fast it was scary. I had just gone to the bathroom right before I left work, but it felt like I hadn't been all day. That's one of the reasons that I thought I might be pregnant. Add to that the fact that my breasts we so sore and sensitive, and the constant feeling of nausea that followed me all day long. I hadn't thrown up yet, but I came close several times.

I turned into our apartment complex doing thirty and didn't put my foot on the brake as I rode over the speed bumps. This didn't help my breasts one bit. I winced in pain.

"Shit." I rubbed my free hand over my breasts. The pain took my mind off the fact that I had to go to the bathroom so badly. I hit the second speed bump at the same pace. I wanted to slow down but my situation was urgent. I could not imagine what my car would smell like if I actually did wet myself. I pulled into the front of our building and had the door open before I had even parked the car. I grabbed my purse and my bag from CVS and dashed up the sidewalk toward my apartment. I ran as fast as my doubled-over body could go.

With keys in hand, I tried to get the key in the lock. "Dear God, please." I could not get the key in the hole to save my life. After several attempts I gave up and rang the bell. A few seconds passed before Merlin answered the door. I had all but resigned to pissing on myself. At least I was at the house and wouldn't ruin the upholstery of my car.

"What, you got to go to the bathroom again?" Merlin was laughing as he stepped out of the way.

"Yeah, move." The end was in sight, and I prayed that Merlin had left the seat down in the bathroom. I was unbuttoning my pants as I raced down the hallway to our bedroom. I could have used the guest bathroom, but in my haste I forgot about it.

"Thank you, Jesus," I said as I sank onto the seat in relief. The hot piss ran into the toilet. I released a heavy sigh of relief. I was so happy that I hadn't peed on myself, I just rested my head on my arms as I allowed myself to finish taking a leak. I completely forgot about the pregnancy test that I had in my purse. Now would have been as good a time as any to take it. However, I was quite sure that I would have to go again within the hour.

"Everything come out okay?" Merlin was outside the door and he had jokes.

"Don't you have something that you need to be doing?" My voice was harsh, and I didn't understand where that mean streak came from. All of a sudden I was mad.

"Dag, I didn't mean to piss you off."

I could tell by his tone that Merlin was hurt. I didn't mean to lash out at him, but the words just slipped out of my mouth. I got up from the toilet after wiping myself and pulled up my pants and zipped them. It wasn't his fault that I had become so moody. I quickly washed my hands because I had to apologize before my behavior ruined the rest of our night together.

"Baby, wait, I'm sorry. I told you I wasn't feeling well, and I'm sorry that I took that out on you." I reached out to touch his shoulder because his back was turned to me.

He immediately melted and turned around and took me in his arms. At that moment things felt just as they used to between us, and I fell in love all over again with my husband.

He said, "Honey, I'm sorry. I was so excited to have you all to myself that I completely forgot that you weren't feeling well." He led me to the sofa and gently pushed me down. Once I was seated, he pulled the reclining lever to elevate my feet. Then, he took off my shoes and began massaging my feet. I was outdone. Merlin was good to me, and he often did sweet things for me, but I could not recall one time that he took off my shoes, let alone massaged my feet.

"I'm fine now that I'm home. I just want to take a nap until dinner is ready. I'm so tired."

He reached over my head, grabbed the throw from across the sofa and gently pulled it over me. Kissing me on the forehead, he left me and headed in the direction of the kitchen. All evidence of his ire had disappeared.

"I wonder what he will say if in fact I do end up pregnant," I mumbled to myself.

CHAPTER THIRTY-ONE

COJO MILLS

I didn't take the test until the following Thursday. "Shit." Positive, both a blessing and a curse. I didn't know whether to shout for joy or yell obscenities at the moon. I so wanted to be pregnant, but I didn't want to be pregnant under these diverse circumstances. If I was pregnant now, there was no way to tell who the father was, and I couldn't imagine how that conversation would go with Merlin.

Thus far, he had been respectful and had been trying to get our relationship back on track, but I had no clue how he would react once he found out that I was pregnant and that there was a very good possibility that the child may be by his own brother. The very thought made me feel like throwing up, so I could only imagine how my husband would feel when I told him.

"Should I tell him?" I uttered the words, even though I didn't believe in the deceit that it would take to carry this out. I had always been a strong proponent for the rights of fathers, but should I risk my family for a mistake? I didn't knowingly have sex with my brother-in-law, so shouldn't I have gotten a pass?

Try as I may, I could not get this image out of my mind. Thank God, Gavin hadn't visited lately, but the visions of him thoroughly fucking me remained in my mind. Merlin was upset because he couldn't understand why I could not tell it wasn't him. What I was trying to make him understand was that he was gone and that I hadn't had none since he left, and a dick is a dick! And I needed one, not to mention that they were identical twins. The difference was in their bedroom skills.

"It is what it is, and I have to face the music." This was a bitter pill to swallow, but I couldn't change what had happened. I left the bathroom and staggered into the living room. I had decided to tell Merlin as soon as he made it home from the base. As much as I loved him, I would not deceive him. He had to know all of the facts. If he chose to leave me, then so be it.

***

I set his dinner in front of him. "Merlin, I need to talk to you and I need you to remain calm. Can you do that?"

"What are you talking about? I'm always calm."

Flashbacks of when he was trying to kick my ass passed through my mind. He paused and I would like to believe that he saw those same images.

He started cutting his steak. "Okay. I understand what you are saying, but I'm cool. Give it to me."

"This is difficult for me to say, but I am pretty certain that I am pregnant." I let the elephant land in the room before I proceeded.

He knew our sexual history and the implication that I left unsaid. I waited for his response with bated breath.

Merlin looked like he had been whipped naked with a leather strap, and my heart went out to him. I felt the same way. *What would I do if I was pregnant by my husband's brother? What would he do? Shit!*

CHAPTER THIRTY-TWO

MERLIN MILLS

"Wow, pregnant. Are you sure?" I didn't know how I felt about it. My stomach was churning and I felt slightly sick. On one hand, I felt ecstatic that I was about to have my first child, but the fear that the child wouldn't be mine overshadowed those emotions. I had to find a way to balance those two emotions before I said something that would drive another wedge between me and my wife. I stuck a forkful of steak in my mouth, even though I'd instantly lost my appetite.

"I took a home test and it was positive, but I haven't been to the doctor yet."

"I see." What did she expect me to say? I felt myself getting angry, but I immediately pumped the brakes because it really wasn't her fault that this happened.

I had to keep reminding myself of that on a daily basis. I looked at her, and I could tell that she was feeling the same emotions that I was experiencing. I rose up from the dinner table and went to her. I opened my arms and she willingly came into them. We would make it through this storm, whichever way it went.

"Baby, it's going to be okay." I wanted her to feel comfortable that I was in it for the long haul with her, even if the baby turned out to belong to my brother. I loved Cojo so much; I could not bear being without her. Whatever feelings this child brought up in me would have to be ignored for the sake of our marriage.

"Are you serious?" She had tears in her eyes.

I could tell that she wanted to say more, but I silenced her with a kiss. I was going to make this work if it killed me. She trembled in my arms and my heart swelled. I knew I was doing the right thing. I pushed her away from me slightly and put my hand on her belly. I looked directly into her eyes.

"I love you and my baby." I left it unsaid that it might not be mine because, as far as I was concerned, if it came out of my wife, it was my baby.

"Merlin, I'm sorry."

"Hush now. Let's not talk about it. In fact, we need a break. Can you get tomorrow off?"

"I think so, what are you planning?"

"Just take off and let me handle the rest of it."

She went to the phone to call her supervisor, who was also a close friend. When she hung up the phone, she told me it was okay for her to be off the next day. Now I had to kick my ass into gear to pull off a fantastic weekend that would show her I loved her more than I loved myself.

In order to keep all my plans secret, I left the house to do some research. I wanted our weekend away to be both romantic and therapeutic. Cojo needed to relax, and I needed to get her back to the funny and sensitive person she used to be before I put my hands on her. I drove a few blocks to the library so that I could get on the Internet to see what was available to us on such short notice.

A friend of mine told me about some cabins that were located up in the North Georgia Mountains. I thought that would be the perfect getaway. Although the cabins were usually built to hold large families, I thought it would be the perfect getaway for a couple who was trying to rediscover the love they had for each other.

I did a Google search, found several cabins, took all the virtual tours, and picked the one that was the most lavish. The cabin had three bedrooms, a pool table, a full kitchen, an outdoor Jacuzzi, and a wraparound porch equipped with rocking chairs. Next, I went to the grocery store so that I could select the food I was going to cook for her while we were there. My plan was that she would not do anything except go to the spa, shop, and whatever else that tickled her fancy.

I booked a spa package for her where she could get her nails and feet done, a facial, and a full-body massage. In fact, I signed up for the massage with her. She had been asking me to do this since we first started dating, but I was hesitant to do it because I didn't like the thought of strangers putting their hands on me, especially if I were in near-naked attire. If it were a man, I might hit him; but if it were a woman, I didn't want to run the risk of getting an erection.

I toyed with the idea of whitewater rafting but decided against it because of the baby, but I did sign up for the wine tasting and grape stomping. This was the only selfish activity I scheduled. I knew she could not do the testing, but she might get a kick out of squishing grapes with her bare feet. I was excited.

As I continued to put groceries in my cart, I froze. I had this amazing urge to share my new-found fatherhood, but I was at a loss for whom to share it with. In a situation like this, the first call should go out to a mother, but that idea instantly soured in my stomach. Knowing my mother, she would say something stupid like, "Why you wanna do that shit for?" Or she might come back with some jacked-up shit like, "Are you sure it's yours?"

I felt lightheaded and sweaty all at the same time. If I were at home, I would have sat the fuck down. *What if it isn't mine?* For some reason, I had blocked out the fact that my wife had mistakenly slept with my brother right around the same time that I came home from Iraq.

Surely, God would not be so cruel as to finally allow us to become pregnant and in the final hour say that it wasn't mine. I was mumbling as I wandered through the aisles. Suddenly, I wanted to cancel the trip and take some sort of paternity test, because there was no way in hell I was going to raise a bastard child of my brother's.

As soon as the thought entered my mind, I felt ashamed of myself. If I was going to allow that to ruin my marriage, I didn't deserve Cojo at all. It wasn't her fault that Gavin had deceived her!

CHAPTER THIRTY-THREE

GAVIN MILLS

I could hear the television as soon as I put my key in the door. If I didn't know better, I would have sworn that my mother was going deaf in her older years. She was watching *Dancing With The Stars* and it was cranked up to what had to be the highest level.

My gut instinct was to yell at her to turn that shit down. This was her house, though, and I wasn't paying any of the bills, so I kept my mouth shut. I didn't understand all that hoopla with the show. Some old, played-out stars grabbing at one last chance of stardom and a glimpse of fame, and the average Joe Blow sitting around the television egging them on and voting for them. I'd be damned if I would spend some of my hard-earned money voting for someone like Jerry Springer to win a fucking dance-off.

I peeked around the corner to see where my mother was. I wanted to be prepared for her attack before it actually happened. I was riding on a high that could likely explode if she came at me wrong. The last thing I wanted to do was kill my mother and end up losing the last place in the world where I could stay for free, at least until she put me out.

Momma wasn't visible when I stuck my head around the corner. That meant one of two things: she was in her bedroom knocked out, or she was passed out on the sofa. I tiptoed up to the sofa, silently praying that she wasn't on it, but in her room instead. I didn't feel like hearing her mouth tonight.

I continued to creep up to the sofa. My heart dipped a little bit when I saw her thrown over the sofa. It appeared that she had flipped over it because her glass was lying on its side and she was spread-eagle on the sofa, naked from the waist down. The phone was not on the base and an annoying message was playing, asking her if she would like to make a call.

I shook my head in disgust. Heaven knows who she was trying to call before she passed out, but more than likely it was my deadbeat dad. For the life of me, I couldn't understand why she was still chasing after his ass when he made it clear that he was done with her.

I tiptoed past her to see if she had anything left to drink in the kitchen. I was still riding the high of my earlier escapade with some chick I met at Club 702, and I needed to come down if I had any intention of getting some sleep tonight.

"Jackpot."

Mom had gone to the store and the entire counter was stocked with liquor. I claimed a bottle of Absolut and retired to my room. Normally, I would not have risked taking a full bottle of her booze, but from the looks of her, she wouldn't even remember going to the store. Hell, I could probably stash all the bottles and play dumb when she asked about them.

I turned my small television, I brought from a yard sale, on low as I cracked open the bottle. I didn't want to risk waking up my mother and her coming in and asking about her bottle before I got my drink on. I searched the channels until I found the news. I wanted to see what, if anything, was being said about the fire on the east side a couple of weeks back. I felt good about covering my tracks since I hadn't heard anything about it so far.

I was halfway through the bottle and still hadn't heard anything about the murder. "Shit, that's good news." I was feeling pretty invincible, even though I was drunk as a skunk. I went out into the hallway to take a piss. I stumbled into the bathroom and peed on everything but the seat.

"I'm gonna have to clean this shit up in the morning." This was not the bathroom that my mother used, so I felt confident that I could hold off on washing the piss off the walls and the sides of the bowl until morning.

I staggered when I peeked back into the living room to check on my mother. The television was still loud as hell and she hadn't moved. However, this time my focus was not on whether she was sleeping, but how good her fat pussy looked.

My mother was not a bad-looking woman. She had gained some weight over the years, but a pussy stays the same size no matter how large a woman gets. Her clit appeared to be winking at me and my dick instantly took notice.

Now I will admit that I was a pretty lowdown dirty dog and would do just about anything for the thrill of doing it, but delivering the package to my mother was a definite no-no. I tried to turn away, but my dick, which was still sticking out of my pants, had other plans. I crept closer. Her scent was tantalizing my nose. "Damn, did her pussy just wink at me?" I didn't even have to touch my dick; it was already throbbing.

***

"Fuck that." The words fell out of my mouth, but those were not my words. My dick was talking through me.

She won't even know we're there. Her ass is out like a light.

In my fucked-up state, I didn't have a choice but to follow my dick, because it was clear that it would not allow me to sleep tonight unless I did.

All right, motherfucker, do what we do.

"Oh, that feels good, Ronald."

I didn't waste time. My dick was already hard and her dumb ass thought I was my daddy. I knew that I had to get in and out before she was conscious of what was really going on. Without wasting another second, I plunged deep inside of her. Her body jerked, but she didn't open her eyes. I felt her pussy wrap around my dick.

"It's been so long, Ronald. Fuck me."

"Damn, your shit is tight, Mommy." I didn't mean to talk but the words automatically came out of my mouth. Shit, she was tighter than the ho I had bagged earlier that week. I worked my dick around in circles, and even though she was unconscious, my mother kept up with me. Even in her sleep, she was following my dick. I took one of her full breasts into my mouth and it was done. I came in my momma. I wish I could have spent more time with her, but I'd taken a big enough risk as it was. I didn't want her drunk ass to realize I wasn't my dad.

I felt remorse for the first time in my life as I pulled my limp dick out of Gina. This was probably the lowest moment in my life, but when I looked up at Gina, she was smiling. That made me feel a little bit better.

CHAPTER THIRTY-FOUR

GINA MEADOWS

I woke up the next day with a serious hangover after drinking myself into a stupor. I remembered that much, but after that everything was but a vague memory or dream. I couldn't tell which. I remember Ronald being in my dreams, though. I sat up, and that was when I realized that I was naked from the waist down.

"Oh, God," I muttered as I remembered getting undressed so I could have phone sex with my so-called husband. He convinced me to get my vibrator from my nightstand and stay on the phone until I could find release.

"Shit don't make no damn sense." I was beating myself up because once again I put myself in the dunce chair, all for the love of a man.

Ronald could talk my panties off on I-285 at twelve noon in the fast lane. That's how powerful his mack game was.

My pussy felt worn, as if I had used all ten inches of the dildo turned on high for an extended amount of time. I leaned over the sofa to see if I could find the purple bandit, my nickname for my high-powered lover.

As I continued to search for the only thing that had shown me love in the last two years, I lost my balance and came crashing to the floor, ass up. "Shit, that hurt." My boobs were smashed into the floor and the dildo lay dangerously close to my mouth. A vision of sucking that dildo flashed through my mind, but in this flashback, I swallowed. "I ain't fucking with that Patron no damn more!" I pushed myself up off the floor and tried to get back on the sofa with as much dignity as my ringing head would allow. My stomach was churning, my brain felt like it was trying to leap out of my head, and my pussy felt freshly fucked. *Damn, that was some good phone sex.*

I needed to go to the bathroom in the worst way, but I felt I'd throw up if I made another sudden movement. The last thing I wanted to do was clean up a mess of vomit. I rocked myself on the sofa, trying to push the pee back up that threatened to leave a brownish stain on my off-white sofa. "Lawd, please." The rocking wasn't helping my head, but it did seem to ease my bladder because instead of the pee being focused in one place, I was spreading it around. My pussy felt swollen, but I attributed that to using the dildo without lubrication. Ronald convinced me that I didn't need it. "Take it like I give it, rough," is what he had said to me, and my stupid ass did it.

My pussy was going to be sore for weeks. I had managed to rock the pee away enough to stand and go to the bathroom. I was ashamed of myself for falling for Ronald's bullshit again.

I stumbled into the bathroom, still a little woozy from the booze and the intense hangover that I was experiencing. It wasn't until my ass found its way to the toilet seat that I remembered Gavin.

With all the booze in my system, I had completely forgotten that he was staying with me until he could get himself on his feet. My mind scrambled, trying to remember if I'd gotten naked before or after he got home. *Oh, shit, I couldn't remember!* I broke out into a cold sweat. Even though I didn't care much for the man my son had become, I still had enough decency not to want him to see me drunk and naked at the same damn time!

I jumped up from the toilet in midstream and raced to his door, trailing piss behind me. "Lawd, please don't let Gavin be in this room." I didn't pray as often as I should, but I was hoping this one time God wouldn't put my call on hold. I swung open the door without bothering to knock. I held my breath. Gavin was lying on his back across his bed. He was butt naked too!

"Damn." This was the first time that I'd gotten to see his dick since he was around six years old. I had to admit that I was impressed. He was hung just like his dad. Even in its relaxed state, his dick was impressive. "Like father, like son." Those words slipped out of my mouth before I could catch them. It wasn't that I was into the incest thing, but truth be told, Gavin was not my biological son. Our only connection was that I'd fucked his father and raised Ronald's child like he was my own.

So was that considered incest? Obviously, the booze was talking for me, because I had to stop myself from rushing the bed and taking his flaccid penis in my mouth. I stood in the doorway with drool practically dripping out of my mouth as I watched my son sleep, with his dick swinging in the wind. A vision of that same dick pounding against my pussy filled my mind. In my head, I knew it was just a vision, but my body felt like it had actually happened. I shuttered inside.

The doorbell rang and there I was stuck like Chuck. I froze. My eyes darted from door to bed and back again. I needed to shut the door before

Gavin could see me standing there practically naked. I had to put some pants on so I could stop the doorbell from ringing again. As my head turned back again toward Gavin, I thought I saw him smile. I quietly shut the door and rushed back to the living room to gather my pants.

CHAPTER THIRTY-FIVE

MERLIN MILLS

Every minute I stood in the vestibule of my mother's apartment was torture. After I finally talked Cojo back inside the church and married her, I vowed never to come back. The news of fatherhood had me acting giddy and I wasn't thinking straight. I had to share the news with someone. I rang the bell again as I placed my ear to the door.

I could hear movement, so I stood back to wait for my mother to answer the door. Each second I waited, I debated whether this was such a good idea. My mother never had a good thing to say about my wife; she barely had a good thing to say about me. I was turning to leave when she finally opened the door.

She was disheveled and her eyes had this wild look to them.

"Are you okay?" I felt genuine concern for h
the likes of which I hadn't felt since I was in h:
school.

"What are you doing here?"

If I thought she'd be happy to see me, tho
thoughts were doused by her sour greeting. I f
like kicking myself for even thinking that sto
ping by her house was a good idea. I should ha
let sleeping dogs lie. "Hello, Mother." I hop
that I could thaw her icy exterior by calling l
Mother, but that only seemed to make her mo
agitated.

"I asked you what you were doing here. H
I haven't seen you in years. What, you want
move in here now too? Did that siddity wife
yours throw you out?"

My good mood disappeared as I realized t
huge error in judgment I'd made. Without sayi
another word, I turned around to leave. I did
need her negative energy hanging around I
neck like an albatross. "Forget it, Mother. I tri
Have a nice life." I stomped down the three ste
that led to her apartment, angry at myself :
making such a stupid mistake. I left a little of I
joy on her stoop, but I was determined to ta
the rest of it back to my house.

"Wait," she hollered a little too loudly for t
enclosed breezeway of her apartment comple:

I hesitated because I didn't know whether she was preparing to strip away the rest of my joy, or if she was actually sorry for treating me the way that she had. I turned around slowly. She was patting her wild hairs back in place. She attempted to straighten out her pants, which appeared to have been put on backward. Suddenly, I didn't want to share my good news with her.

"How are you?" Gina's voice was gentler. She appeared like she almost cared.

"I'm good."

There was a brief moment of silence. She hadn't invited me in, so I felt awkward speaking to her on her doorstep.

"Do you want to come in?"

This would be the first time that I had been inside my mother's house since I got married, and my feet refused to move. A flashing memory of the last time I'd been inside of her house came rushing back to me. I wondered yet again what I was doing here in the first place.

As if she could read my thoughts, she tried to reassure me. "It's okay, I'll be nice."

She smiled again and the sucker in me smiled back. I was so happy about the baby, I lost my friggin' mind. I stepped past her and entered the house. She closed the door behind me. For a second I grew fearful, but I was determined to say to her what I came to say.

"For years, Mother, you've treated Gavin and me like shit." This wasn't the way that I wanted to start the conversation, but the words flew out of my mouth. I heard her inhale sharply, and I saw her pull herself up as if she was ready to fight me, so I quickly finished my thought. "But now that I am about to have a child, I can understand how you've felt all these years caring for my father's children without the benefit of a ring."

The wind was sucked from her sails and tears flooded her eyes and mine. I never thought about how she felt before.

I said, "For years I hated you for the way that you treated us, but I am finally beginning to understand."

"What is it that you are finally understanding?" Her tone was accusing as she mocked me. She sounded like she was about to kick my ass like she did when I was a small child.

"You were acting off of emotions, Mother. I can't imagine how I would feel or react if I had to raise someone's children and not have any of my own." Once again, my words surprised even me. That was not what I had intended to say to her when I came to her door. It was like something or someone planted those words in my mouth. Before I could lose my nerve, I continued. "I didn't understand it when I was a child. In fact, I didn't understand it until today when my wife told me she was having my child. You were reacting to all those years my father treated you like a second-class citizen, and now I understand. I'm not saying I agree with the way you treated us, but I finally understand and I forgive you."

My mother remained speechless. I'm sure she didn't expect this speech from me and was just as surprised as I was that I had made it, but I needed to have her in my life as a positive role model for my child. But she was going to have to change her ways toward my wife if that was going to work, 'cause she would not continue to abuse my wife and the mother of my child.

Gina said, "I don't know what to say."

This was the first time in a long time my mother didn't have a snappy comeback. She opened her mouth to speak but nothing came out. Part of me wanted to hug her, but I couldn't even remember the last time I was physical with my mother.

The tears that had flooded her eyes rolled unchecked down her cheeks. She didn't bother to wipe them away as they slid into her mouth. "I'm sorry, Merlin. All these years I've been wrong and I couldn't see it for the pain Ronald's leaving me caused."

I didn't say anything because I knew that to be true, but I still didn't understand what she had against my wife. She sank down onto the sofa and allowed her sobs to overtake her. Once again I wanted to comfort her, but I wasn't sure how she would react.

I said, "So where do we go from here?"

She looked up at me with what appeared to be hope in her eyes. "Are you willing to give me a second chance?" She was wringing her hands together.

"I will, but you've got to let up on Cojo. I can't have you disrespecting my wife and the mother of my child."

Her eyes narrowed. I thought she was about to do a Sybil on me and flip out. I took a step back just in case I was going to have to defend myself, 'cause she was not about to go upside my head like she used to do in the old days.

"I'll try."

That wasn't good enough for me. I wanted assurances that she wouldn't hurt my baby again. "What is it with you and her? Has she ever done anything to offend you?" I was clearly perplexed about this and I wanted to understand this, too.

My mother took her time with her answer. As far as I was concerned, if she had to think this long, she didn't know the answer her damn self.

"There was never anything wrong with Cojo. I'm sorry about my behavior at your wedding. Cojo's a sweet wife and you are lucky to have her."

This was not the answer I expected. My mother was full of surprises today, but I guess so was I. I never had the nerve to come right out and ask her what the problem was. I just chose to ignore it, hoping that it would go away in time.

I said, "Then what has been the problem? She's tried real hard to be friends with you, but you held her off."

After a painful pause, Gina said, "She had everything that I didn't."

Ah, that made sense. She was jealous of my relationship with my wife.

"When I looked at you two together I saw the woman that your father left me for."

"Mom, you are going to have to get over that or it will destroy your life." I meant those words from the bottom of my heart.

"I know. I tried, but every time I put that man out of my heart and my mind, he calls and says something that makes me fall for him all over again."

"And how long are you going to allow th[...]
go on?"

"So, you're a therapist now?" She laughed
loud.

She might have been joking, but this w[...]
form of therapy. She needed to face the fact [...]
my father just wasn't going to do right, and [...]
would either continue on that emotional r[...]
coaster or get the fuck off.

"He's done with me." She began to sniffle [...]

"How about you saying you're done [...]
him?"

She looked at me strangely as if the tho[...]
never occurred to her. "Hum . . . that does s[...]
better."

"Keep saying it enough and you will belie[...]
Then, the next time he calls talking smack, [...]
can tell him to step off." I smiled to soften [...]
blow. I loved my father simply because he [...]
the man that gave me life, but as far as bein[...]
my life, that didn't happen.

"When did you get so smart?" Gina stare[...]
me.

"I've always been smart, but you were [...]
angry to see that." I didn't say that to hurt [...]
feelings, but the truth was the truth.

"You're right. I couldn't see what was rig[...]
my face. I'm sorry, Merlin."

"I'm sorry too, Mom. We should have had this conversation a long time ago."

"Don't fool yourself. If you'd come to me with this a few years ago, I might have killed your ass." She smiled this time and we both loosened up.

Hesitantly, I stepped forward and gently pulled her from the sofa and hugged her. At first she didn't hug me back. I felt like I'd moved too fast, but then she threw her arms around my waist and hugged me back as if her life depended on it. It was a very special moment for both of us until she roughly pushed me back.

"Did you say you were expecting a baby?"

A wide grin crossed my face.

I guess it finally registered with her that she was about to be a grandma. "Yes, Grandma."

She punched me lightly in the shoulder. "I'm too fine to be a grandma. They are just going to have to call me Gee-Gee." She looked about as happy as I felt. She started patting down her hair and posing for me, even though she looked a hot mess.

I didn't miss the distinct smell of alcohol when I hugged her, either.

"Where is Cojo? I've got to go make friends with her. I don't want her to continue to hate me, because I want to be in my grandchild's life. It's my chance to do what I gave up by not having my own child."

"That's good to know. But that little reunion is going to have to wait until we get back in town. I'm taking Cojo away for the weekend to celebrate."

For a second, my mother's eyes clouded over, but they quickly cleared. "That's nice, baby."

My heart soared 'cause she hadn't called me baby with sincerity since I was six or seven. "You could do me a favor, though."

"What's that?" She looked hopeful again.

"Keep an eye on our mail. I'm expecting my redeployment orders, and I need to know if they come while we are away."

"How am I going to keep an eye on your mail or apartment when I've never ever been there?"

That was a dig, but I knew she knew exactly where it was because she'd visited before and 'cause she gave the address to Gavin. "I'll write down the address and leave an extra key so you can check the mail and leave it in the house. We will be home on Sunday."

"Okay, that's the least I can do for all the damage I've done to our relationship over the years. I'll call you if you get anything that comes from the military."

"Thanks, Mom." My heart felt like it was about to bust. I hadn't felt this good since Cojo told me she was pregnant.

"How far along is Cojo?"

"About four weeks." I handed my mother the extra keys I had on my ring, and she placed them on the fireplace. I got lost in thought thinking about the cute little girl or the handsome son we were going to have.

"Ain't this special." Gavin came out of the guest bedroom clapping his hands.

Rage the likes of which I hadn't felt since I kicked his ass came rushing back at me. I had no idea Gavin was crashing at my mother's house. If I'd known, I would have never come over here. "What are you doing here?" I snarled.

"Oh, no forgiveness for me?" Gavin was mocking me, letting me know that he had heard every word I had said to Gina.

"Leave me alone, Gavin."

"What did I do?" He had this innocent look on his face, as if he'd never done any wrong, but I knew better . . . much better.

"I got to go, Mom. I'll invite you over once we get back." I turned to leave. I needed to get out of here before I said or did something to that asshole brother of mine.

She walked me to the door and we sha
another hug. It felt good to be back in her g
graces, and I had high hopes that she was go
to get her life together.

"Have a safe trip," she said.

"Yo, Merlin," Gavin yelled.

Part of me wanted to keep on walking with
even acknowledging my brother, but I did
want my mother to know the extent of my a
mosity toward him. "What?"

"You sure that kid is yours?" Gavin showed
his devilish grin.

CHAPTER THIRTY-SIX

MERLIN MILLS

How the hell did I forget that bastard was back in town? Shit, I thought he left! I was angry as hell and almost wrecked my car trying to get away from my mother's house. I was very concerned about why Gavin was still here, which only led me to believe that he didn't have any place left to go. However, this was going to ruin any chance of my mother and Cojo getting to know each other.

Hell, Gavin would be in Mom's ear all night trying to get her to hate Cojo again. I felt as if all my efforts today had been wasted. "I'm gonna fuck that bastard up! He has screwed up my life for the last time." I banged a fist against the steering wheel as hot tears burned my eyes. Gavin brought back the doubt I felt about my child—that, more than anything else hurt me. Gone was the anger that I felt against my wife, but I had to know for certain that she was carrying my child and not Gavin's.

I drove around for at least an hour before I got my emotions under control. I was going to take my wife away for the weekend and leave these troubles behind. Regardless of who fathered the child, it would still be mine. Turning the car around, I headed home to my wife. With any luck, I could get a quickie in before we got on the road. I pulled out my cell phone and called Cojo.

"Where are you?" she said.

"I'm almost there, sweetheart. Are you all packed?"

"Yeah, I've been done for hours. I was beginning to think something happened to you."

"I'll explain everything when I get there. Do me a favor and pack the small cooler with ice and water, and grab a few snacks so we won't have to stop but for gas and to go to the bathroom."

"Where are we going?"

"You are going to have to wait and see, but make sure you packed some sweaters."

"Sweaters? It's eighty degrees outside."

"Humor me." I didn't know if she would need them, but it would be better to be safe than sorry. Despite how I was feeling an hour ago, I still wanted to make this a memorable weekend for my wife.

The drive was approximately two hours. It had begun to rain, and I had to slow down my speed considerably. We also had to make frequent stops because Cojo just couldn't hold her water, but I didn't mind. I was enjoying the quality time we were spending. She spent her time reading and wasn't really paying attention to where we were going. When I pulled up to the cabin rental office, I could see the look of disdain on her face. I could tell she was not happy, and to be honest, I wasn't either. This shack didn't look anything like the cabins I had seen on the Internet.

"Be right back."

She didn't say a word. Hopefully, the cabin wouldn't look as bad on the inside as it did on the outside. When I got back into the car, there was a chill in the air and it had nothing to do with the mountain air. I put the address to the cabin into our GPS system and turned the car around. Cojo had even cut off the radio and her book was closed on her lap. All of a sudden she was focused on our destination. I said a silent prayer.

The cabin was about twenty-five miles from the rental location and farther up the mountains.

I had never driven in the mountains before and was a little nervous, especially since it was still raining and starting to get dark.

Finally, we found the road that led to the cabins. I had to drive slower because I didn't want to run into any wild animals. I glanced over at Cojo. She was sitting up straight in her seat, peering into the approaching night. We traveled straight up; it was very scary. At one point, as we were going down again, the road narrowed to a single lane. I don't know what I would have done if I had to back out to let another car pass.

As the GPS announced that we'd arrived at our destination, I let out a heavy sigh. I was tired and the pressure to please had worn me out.

"Merlin! Are you serious?" Cojo looked at the cabin in awe.

"Yes, baby."

"We're really going to stay here?"

"Did you think I was going to make you sleep in a shack?" I handed her the key so she could check out the house while I unpacked the car. I had groceries and our suitcases in the back. I wanted to get everything inside before it got totally dark. She leapt out of the car and raced to the house.

What the fuck was I thinking about? I am no mountain man. I am a city boy, I mused. As I looked up and saw the way Cojo was acting, all my fears went right out of my head. Her reaction was enough to make anything I had to go through worth it.

"Sweetie, this place is to die for!" Cojo twirled around the living room, flapping her arms.

"I'm glad you like it, honey." I had just brought in all of our provisions, and I was tired as hell. I hadn't even had a chance to look around at our surroundings. I flopped down on the first available chair and tried to catch my breath. I didn't know what Cojo had put in her suitcase, but that bitch was heavy as hell.

Cojo plopped down in my lap. "It's got a pool table downstairs, a Jacuzzi; I've died and gone to heaven."

She didn't have to tell me all the amenities, but I let her go on and tell me. I was happy she was happy. Before I started dinner, I decided to light the fireplace. Although it was comfortable in the cabin, I thought the fire would be more romantic.

***

I had been fucking with the fire for a full fifteen minutes, and I was starting to lose my patience. This was just another reminder that I wasn't a mountain man. I was also getting spooked because there were no curtains on the first floor of the cabin and all I could see outside was darkness. My imagination was running wild as I envisioned bears rushing the windows and glass doors.

"Honey, take a break. Let me do this," Cojo said as she patted me on the shoulder.

I wasn't annoyed at all that she volunteered to help me out. I was sick of that fucking fire and couldn't care less whether we had one. "Go for it. I think the wood is wet. We should have brought one of those starter logs." I got up off the floor and went into the kitchen to start dinner. I'd planned a surf-and-turf meal for my baby. Now that we were in the cabin and most of my duties were done, it was time to relax. I fixed myself a drink. "Babe, do you want a soda or something?" I knew not to offer her booze because of the baby. If she weren't pregnant, I would have probably served her champagne. I looked into the living room to check on her since she didn't answer, but she was laid out in front of the fireplace that was giving off this hearty blaze!

"Well, I'll be damned." I could not help but laugh 'cause she had that fire lit in three minutes flat.

CHAPTER THIRTY-SEVEN

GINA MEADOWS

"What the hell was that all about?" I turned to Gavin when Merlin walked out the door. I knew that there was bad blood between the brothers and a lot of it was caused by me. I was not happy with the role that I played, but I never noticed it 'til tonight.

"What?"

"Don't play dumb, boy." I knew it would piss Gavin off that I called him a boy, but I didn't care. Merlin came to me after all those years of neglect and told me he forgave me, and I'd be damned if I allowed my other so-called son to fuck that up.

"I'm not playing dumb. I just asked Merlin if he was sure it was his kid. After all, he's been away doing the patriotic thing, so it ain't no telling who his wife was keeping company with. You told me she was a little slut."

"I was wrong about that. I didn't even know her."

"So you lied on her? I'm ashamed of you for maligning Cojo's character." His tone was totally condescending.

"What would you know about maligning someone's character? Hell, I didn't even know you knew that word, since you barely went to school."

He had me heated as no one else could do. As a child he was always a selfish bastard who had to have everything his way. Between him and Merlin, he had been the most difficult to raise.

"I didn't need school. I was also smarter than the average child."

"You were street smart. I'll give you that, just like your daddy. Always talking somebody out of shit. But you still don't have the skills to survive on your own, 'cause if you did, you wouldn't be here shacked up with me."

"I'm just down on my luck. But if you had shown me half the love that you are willing to give my brother and his skank-ass, I'm sure I could come up."

His words hurt me more than his fists ever could. I was guilty of not showing them love, but was I that bad? I don't think so. They had a roof over their heads and food in their mouths. Second of all, they were not my kids. I allowed them to call me mama, but I was not the biological mother of either of these kids.

"Why are you directing all your anger at me? I'm not your mother!" I was mad now.

"You were the only mother I knew." Gavin was foaming at the mouth. All of his pent-up aggressions were coming forth, and I started to get scared thinking that he might do something to me.

"You should talk to your father about that," I said.

"I would if I ever saw his ass." He was pacing back and forth like a wild animal.

"He will be here next week to close the deal on our new house." I turned and went into my bedroom. Part of me wanted to warn Ronald that he was going to have to deal with Gavin when he got there, but the other part felt like Ronald had made his bed and now he had to lie in it.

"Fine. Next week, what day and time?"

"You know your father, he gets here when he gets here."

"Knowing my father, that's a laugh." He didn't smile when he said it. "I don't know that motherfucker any more than the man on the moon."

"You're going to have to have that conversation with him, not me."

He turned and walked away. I thought he was about to go into his room when he turned back around. "New house?"

Shit, I hadn't meant to say anything about that to Gavin, at least not until I knew for sure it was going to happen. "Yeah, your father says he's finally coming home."

"He's moving back to Atlanta after sixteen years?"

"Yes." I figured if I kept my responses to one-word answers he would let up, but I was wrong.

"So what, y'all going be this one big, happy family?" The sarcasm dripped from his mouth.

"I hope so." I tried to sound confident, but I'd been down this road before.

"Am I part of that family?"

I could sense the vulnerability in his voice, but I didn't have an answer to his question since he was a grown-ass man, and Ronald felt like grown-ass men should live like grown-ass men. "You can discuss that with your father when he gets here." I was ready to go get cleaned up and try to make myself presentable if Ronald actually showed up.

"Why can't I have that discussion with you? You're the one who raised me, not him."

"That's true, but when your father gets here, he will be the man in the house, not me."

"You just accepted Merlin back in your life. Why can't you accept me?"

There was no denying the pain he was feeling this time, but he didn't melt my heart completely. I remembered all too well what he had been like growing up. He was a mean-spirited child, and it appeared he hadn't changed much.

"Why does it always come back to the same thing?" I was sick of all this rivalry between them. I accepted my part, but damn.

"'Cause I can't stand his pansy ass." This time he did go into his room and slammed the door.

I started to go after him and tell him that only I was allowed to slam doors in this house, but I decided not to press the issue. I grabbed my things from the sofa and went to take a shower. "I hope he stays his ass in his room until I get out of here."

CHAPTER THIRTY-EIGHT

MERLIN MILLS

After dinner, Cojo and I went downstairs to check out the hot tub. I hadn't had a chance to check out the rest of the house since I was busy preparing dinner while she took a nap. The basement was just as impressive as the main floor. Unlike the main floor, which had shiny hardwood floors, this area was carpeted. "This is nice."

"I know, you should see the upstairs, too. These people thought of everything."

"I saw the pictures on the Internet, but it looks even better in person."

She turned to me and gave me a big kiss.

"What was that for?"

"For being you."

"Think you can work your magic on that fireplace while I crank up the hot tub?"

"Sure. The instructions for the tub says it's already on. All you have to do is take the top off."

"The instructions? Where did you see the instructions?"

"There's a book on the coffee table in the living room. They also have this picture book that inventories everything in the house, down to how many knives they have in the kitchen. It says if anything is missing or moved, we will be billed for it."

"Damn, that's a good idea."

"I told you they thought of everything." She knelt down to start the fire, and I went outside to the tub.

"It's creepy out here," I yelled to Cojo.

"Stop being a wuss."

I could tell she was joking so I didn't let it get to me, but it really was creepy. The area where the tub was had a light, but other than that, I couldn't see a thing. The temperature had dropped, but it really wasn't that bad. I laid our towels on the heated towel rack and took the cover off the tub. I tested the water with my arm, and it was definitely on. "Hey, babe, we're good to go."

"Here I come."

I stripped down to my boxers and got into the tub. The warm water felt good. I looked up as my wife came out of the cabin naked as the day she was born. "You getting in naked?" Not that I minded. But, still, what if someone came by?

"Of course, silly. Can't nobody see me but you." She had a point, but I wasn't about to take off my boxers.

If a bear came charging out of the woods, I would feel better having something covering my package. I just couldn't see myself trying to defend us with my shit dangling in the wind.

She climbed into the tub and settled between my legs. It felt like the water instantly heated up when she stepped into the tub, and my dick got hard as she leaned on me.

"Stop poking me in my back."

"I can't help it, babe. You have that effect on me." I could tell she was smiling, and I couldn't even see her face. The night was picture perfect.

"The next time we come we will have the baby with us," she said.

"You like it that much to come back?"

"Who wouldn't? It has everything."

"Babe, remember when you asked where I was earlier?"

"Yeah."

"Well, I wasn't exactly truthful with you. I stopped by my mother's house."

Immediately Cojo tensed up in my arms. I pulled her closer to my chest. I expected her to say something, but she didn't.

I said, "Having this baby means the world to me. I had to share our news. I want so much more for our child than I had. I want our child to have a family." I let my words settle in.

Cojo was still tense and felt cold to the touch, even in the warm waters of the hot tub.

"Relax, babe, it went better than I thought it would go."

"What did she say?" She was trembling.

"First I told her I forgave her for being such a shitty mother."

"You said that?" She tried to turn and face me, but I didn't want her to, so I held her tighter.

"Yeah, I told her that now that I'm about to be a father, I could understand how she took out her anger at my father on us, and I wanted to break the cycle and have her be a part of our lives."

"Umph. Well, I wish you good luck with that."

I could tell she didn't mean it, but I let it go. "I also told her that if she was going to be a part of our lives, I would not tolerate any more disrespect to you. I said you were the love of my life and the mother of my child." I felt her inhale sharply.

"And?"

"She said you were a good woman and she didn't dislike you, but she was jealous because you had all the things that she wanted." I thought about telling her about Gavin, but I refused to bring him into our lives. I was willing to forgive my mother, but Gavin was a whole other story.

"Are you serious?"

"Yeah. It was a touching moment. I think we have a chance, if you allow it."

When she tried to turn around this time, I let her.

"Merlin, that's all I've ever wanted." She gazed into my eyes.

We shared a passionate kiss, and the next thing I knew, I was naked. If I didn't know any better, I could have sworn the water started to boil.

CHAPTER THIRTY-NINE

GAVIN MILLS

"That bitch." I was pissed. Not only was my bitch-ass father coming home, but Gina all but told me that I would not be welcome in their new house. This was going to put a serious monkey wrench in my plans. I was trying to stick around long enough for Merlin to go back to playing war games so I could get next to his hot wife. I still couldn't get the image of her round ass out my mind as I banged her from behind.

I started pacing back and forth, trying to come up with a way to buy more time.

I needed to find a job quick, fast, and in a hurry. I hoped my dad would be more compassionate if he saw that I was at least trying to do something with my life. As much as I hated to do it, I was going to have to put in work. Living off of people was much easier. Problem was, I wasn't trained to do anything. I was twenty-five years old and had never held down a job.

***

After my shower I went to the kitchen and fixed myself a bowl of cereal. My stomach yearned for a hot meal, but I didn't feel like fixing it myself. Since Gina had already left the house, I had to settle on what I could get. I started to leave the bowl in the sink just to piss her off, but I thought better of it since I was trying to buy myself some time.

As I was preparing to leave, I saw the keys that Merlin had given my mother. Without even stopping to think about it, I grabbed them and put them in my pocket. I drove to AutoZone, which wasn't far from her apartment. I needed to get some keys made.

A slow smile spread across my face when the clerk handed me the keys. I paid my tab and doubled back to put the keys back where I found them. No one would be the wiser.

"Bingo." I was feeling pretty good as I walked out of Tiffany's on Northside Drive. I had managed to snag a job as a bartender/bouncer. I would work from ten to two as a bartender and from two to four as a bouncer. It was the perfect job. I don't know why I didn't think of it before. Tiffany's was a strip club that catered to both gay and straight patrons. I wasn't too thrilled about the gay guys, but I'd take their money the same as I would take a chick's.

I was feeling pretty good. All in all it was a productive morning, and I would start work later on tonight. As I drove home, I was mentally searching my closet for something to wear that would have those faggots and bitches lining my pockets. Unfortunately, I couldn't think of a thing that would really set me apart from the other bartenders. Then I remembered the keys that I had made earlier. Since Merlin and his wife were still out of town, I decided to stop by his place and go shopping.

I walked with confidence into my brother's home. I wasn't afraid of anyone trying to stop me since we looked exactly alike. Merlin's neighbor tried to stop me, but I told him that I was in a hurry and I'd talk to him later. After I closed the door, I flipped the double bolt.

Memories of the last time that I was in their home flooded my brain. "Damn, this is me!" I could get comfortable in a place like this. It actually felt like a home, and I was eager to have one. Not just any home, but this one with the perfect wife beside me. I grabbed a beer from the refrigerator and went into the master bedroom. It was immaculate, as was the rest of the house. Gone was the chaos from the fight that had ensued the last time I was here. In fact, everything that was broken had been replaced as if it had never happened.

Their apartment was huge, unlike the one that I shared with my mother. In the master bedroom, they had his-and-her closets. I went into hers first. Her scent lingered in the air as if she had just left the room. I breathed deeply as a small smile tugged at the corners of my mouth. My hand slipped down to my dick, and I gently tugged at it.

Her closet was filled with bright colors and business suits hanging neatly on plastic hangers. "No wire hangers for her." My baby had class. On the far left wall hung her dresses and pants, on the right, blouses and jeans. Her jeans had that dry-cleaners look with deep creases. I fingered the blouses and my dick got harder.

The hamper was in the center of the closet. I flipped open the lid in search of a dirty pair of her underwear. It was almost empty, but I found a blue thong. I sniffed the tiny patch that covered her pussy, while lost in a fantasy world.

"Ah." A guttural sound coming from deep inside my throat escaped my lips. I unzipped my pants and grabbed my dick. I needed to get some relief. I went to the chest of drawers, found one of her sexy teddies, and wrapped it around my dick as I stroked myself. I sucked the lining of the tiny underwear, and it was as if she were sitting on my face all over again. I exploded in her teddy as I fell back on their bed.

"Shit." It wasn't as good as the real thing, but it was a close second. I lay there for a few minutes until the blood started going back to my head instead of my dick. I licked the lining one more time before I shoved both items into my back pocket.

"I'm keeping these." With a satisfied smile on my face, I stuck my dick back in my pants and went through my brother's closet. His clothes were just as organized as hers. Envy threatened to rip a hole in my heart. *All this shit should be mine,* I thought. I grabbed three pairs of jeans off the bottom rack and a couple of shirts. I kept them on the hangers so it wouldn't be noticeable that they were gone. I would have preferred a muscle shirt, but I didn't see any of those. I was about to grab his Tims but decided against it.

Nah, he might miss those. I spread his remaining jeans apart so that he wouldn't readily realize that some were gone. Satisfied that I had enough to get me started, I turned to leave. I stopped in the kitchen to get a large garbage bag to throw my loot into. I drained my beer and tossed the empty bottle into the trash. It clanked against what I assumed was another bottle.

I opened the door and was startled by the postman, who appeared to have been just about ready to ring the bell. I jumped back, and my heart began to pound harder. "C—can I help you?" I stuttered.

"Certified letter for Merlin Mills," the postman chimed.

"Sure, that's me." I took the envelope from him and signed my brother's name. I waited for the postman to get in his truck and leave the parking lot before I locked the door and went to my car.

That was close. Next time I come over here, I will check the peephole before I open that bitch. It probably wasn't such a good idea to sign for that letter, but I couldn't very well decline since I was standing right in front of the man.

"Oh, well." I dismissed the thought and went home to take a nap.

Gina still wasn't there and that was just as well, because I didn't want her to ask me about the bag.

CHAPTER FORTY

GINA MEADOWS

"Tabatha, I'm so glad you answered the phone."

"Hey, girl, what's up?"

"I just need an ear. Are you going into work today?"

"Actually, I was planning on working from home."

"Can I come by?" I was already in the car, headed to her house. I had so much on my mind, I just needed to talk to someone.

"Sure, see you in a few."

I knocked on her door ten minutes later.

"Damn, that was quick," Tabatha said, opening the door.

"Yeah, I was already in the car when I called. I was hoping you would be at home instead of the office, but the way that I'm feeling I would have even driven down there."

"Wow, things must be deep 'cause you hate my office."

"I don't hate your office, I just hate those fake-ass folks you work with." I walked right into the living room and sat down on her sofa. I didn't begin to speak right away because I was trying to figure out how much I was going to tell my longtime friend. She didn't rush me, and I appreciated it.

"Merlin came by today."

"Say what?" She paused. "Are you serious?"

"Yeah, I know. I still can't believe it myself."

"So what brought that on?"

"He came by to tell me what a lousy mother I was."

"Oh, shit. I think I need a drink, do you want one?"

"Naw, I tied one on last night and my stomach still don't feel too good." My pussy didn't either, but I wasn't going to tell her that. I waited until she came back into the room before I continued talking.

"Okay, go ahead." She seemed too eager to hear the story, and I almost regretted even coming over here.

"Actually, I'm glad he said it because he forced me to really look at myself. He also said he forgave me."

"I'm speechless. First of all, you didn't slap him upside the head, and second, he forgave you."

"I was horrible, wasn't I?" A tear slipped down my face.

"Yeah, girl, you were, but now you can start over. Everyone doesn't get a second chance, so be grateful."

"Trust me, I am."

"What about his wife? How are you going to handle that?"

"I'm fine with that, too. She never was a bad girl, I just couldn't see it. Hell, she's about to have my son's baby."

"That's wonderful, congratulations. It's about time you let all that anger go. What about Gavin?" She sipped her drink as she eyed me.

"I'm not ready to let go with him yet. The jury is still out on him. I don't trust him. Gavin's so jealous of Merlin it scares me. He has so much anger pent up inside him."

"Hmm . . . sounds a lot like you."

If she had said that to me yesterday, I would've probably stormed out of her house and wrote her out of my life, but today I allowed the comment to slide.

"No snappy retort?" She sat back in the chair, observing me.

"Nope, you speak the truth, so I feel like I'm healing."

She rushed off the sofa and threw her arms around me. We rocked back and forth as tears flowed from our eyes.

Tabatha looked at me. "So when are we going shopping for your new grandchild?"

"As soon as I find out what it is. I'm going to love this one like it's my own." I had one more thing to get off my chest, but I decided to keep that information to myself. "Thanks for listening, girl. I'm going to get out of your hair so you can get some work done."

"Any time, you know you and me are down like two flat tires."

I chuckled as I grabbed my purse and went out the door.

I knew I was less than honest with Tabatha when I didn't disclose that Ronald was coming home, but she would have given me a lecture about letting him into my life again. I think she assumed that I'd let him go when I said I was healing, but that was furthest from the truth. I still loved that man, regardless of all the pain that he had caused in all of our lives.

"I'm just going to have to wait and see."

CHAPTER FORTY-ONE

GAVIN MILLS

I had only been working six days, and I was making mad money at the club. The sissies loved me, and the women kept begging me for dick. It was the perfect world; things were finally looking up for me. I used some of the money that I made and bought me a few muscle shirts and the shit was on and popping.

Nobody in the club, including the dancers, could touch me. I was easily the most handsome man in the club, and I had bank in my pocket to prove it. Management was pleased because bar sales were up, because most of the sissies sat at the bar and stared me down rather than throwing dollars at the dancers. This kept more money in the club. The dancers weren't feeling me, but that was their problem.

I hadn't seen Gina in a week because my work schedule was so completely different from hers, so I had no idea what was going on in her life. I had no idea if my father had even made it home, but that was her problem now. I had enough bank to get a small, furnished apartment. Fuck Gina. I didn't need her anymore.

I packed my meager possessions and carried them to the car. As I took one final look around the room, I noticed the letter that I'd taken from Merlin's house. I ripped it open, surprised that I had forgotten all about it. "Well, now, looky here." The letter said that Merlin was supposed to be redeployed to Iraq two days ago. This was the break that I had been waiting for. "Oh, well, fuck him." I could not worry about his shit right now. He'd have to deal with that shit by his damn self. I tossed the letter into the trash. I had bigger fish to fry. I needed to get settled into my place and take a nap before my shift started tonight.

My new job was so time consuming I hadn't had time to think about my brother and his wife. Right now it was about stacking paper, fuck the bullshit. I hadn't forgotten the scent of Cojo's pussy, but I had to come up first before I could step to her.

If things keep going like they were, I'd be ready for her in a few months. Hell, one bitch offered me $500 just to suck my dick. I almost took her up on the offer, but I figured if I made her sweat, she'd offer me more, and I planned on making her wait. Last week, I'd let a bitch suck my dick for free, so things were already looking better for a brother.

The club was packed when I strolled in. I felt all eyes on me as I stuck out my chest, as if I needed to do anything extra to draw attention to myself. My bald head gleamed like a magnet, turning all male and female eyes on me.

"Damn, when I think of all the years I wasted avoiding a job, I could kick myself," I muttered under my breath. I waved my hand at a few of the regulars as I made my way to the back of the club to clock in. I was early, but management didn't mind 'cause I was a moneymaker. I came early so I could sit on the other side of the bar and talk to the customers. It was a win-win situation for me and the house. At home I had a small box with numbers for pussy all over Atlanta. So far I hadn't had time to call any of those numbers. Now that I was living by myself, I was sure that was going to change.

I was wearing a black muscle shirt, black jeans, and a pair of black Tims that I had bought with some of the money that I'd been making. From the looks that I was getting, I knew I was looking good enough to eat. I took a seat at the end of the bar and studied the crowd. It was still early, but there was an equal mix of men and women.

I noticed that the women came out early and were mostly gone by the time I started my shift. My guess was that they had to go home to their husbands. After midnight the club was dominated by men, but there were a few exceptions to that rule.

"Can I buy you a drink?" a seductive-sounding female whispered in my ear.

I smiled before I turned around to see who was macking on me. The face that greeted me was pretty enough, but she had an Adam's apple bigger than mine. But hell, a free drink was a free drink.

"Sure, I'll take a shot of Remy Black." I turned away as if I wasn't interested in conversation. I didn't really like dealing with the shims. All they wanted was to be fucked and there was no way I was putting my dick in someone's ass unless they were one-hundred-percent female.

"Are you new around here?" she asked as she pushed my glass toward me.

"Kind of, I've been working here for about a week."

"You work here?" She raised her eyebrows, which were nicely arched, at me.

"Yeah, I'm one of the bartenders."

"Well, hell, you should be buying me a drink then." She batted her false eyelashes at me.

"Look, I'm flattered and all, but I've got a wife at home, and she doesn't have to tape her dick to her ass."

"You son of a bitch," she hissed at me as she grabbed her drink and vacated the chair.

I threw my head back in laughter. I normally didn't come off as rude because I was still about stackin' paper, but I knew I wasn't going to get any from that shim. So I used her for what she was worth and kept it moving.

I turned my drink up and emptied my glass. I wanted it to be empty before someone else sat down next to me. I had no intention of drinking a lot because I still had to function when I went on duty in an hour, but I wanted to get my buzz on as well so I could deal with all the flaming fags that would be hitting on me for the next several hours.

I didn't have long to wait for someone to be bold enough to sit next to me. This time the voice was all female.

"Hi, handsome, are you one of the dancers?"

I turned slightly in my seat to see who was speaking to me. She was a good-looking woman, although she was a little short for my taste. I'd fuck her if I didn't have anything else to do. She was about five foot two with deep chestnut-brown-colored skin, deep brown eyes, and a short and sassy haircut.

"You flatter me but, no, I'm not a dancer," I said with a smug grin on my face. If I had a dollar for every time someone asked me if I was one of the dancers, I would have been rich.

"You should be."

"Thanks, but I prefer to shake my ass in private."

"Is that an offer?" She had a hopeful look in her eyes.

I glanced at her ring finger and saw that she was indeed married. "Sorry, I don't do married ladies." I was lying my ass off, but she didn't have to know that.

She tried to hide her hand from me, but it was too late; I'd already seen it. "Shame, I could make it worth your while."

She had my attention now. I looked her over again. I noticed the bling around her neck and wrist. She had to be stupid to come into a club such as this with all that glitter, but it had the desired effect. I was all ears.

"So what did you have in mind?"

"Everything that you can imagine. And trust and believe it will be worth your time." She never said how much, but I was pretty sure she could afford me. Any other time I would give it to her for free, but once again, I was about stackin' paper.

She pulled her business card out of her clutch and handed it to me. "This is my private cell number. Call me during the day when you have some time."

I took her card and slid it into the back pocket of my tight-fighting jeans. I made sure I turned around so she could see me slide it into my pocket.

"Damn," she murmured under her breath. She waved her hand across her face as if she were getting hot or something.

"I'll call you." I slipped off the seat so that she could watch me walk away. I went into the back so I could put on my apron. As I got to the back door of the employees' lounge, I was approached by someone else. A familiar face—the same person who had offered me money for some of my time.

"Hey, there," I said without breaking my stride. I wanted her to run behind my ass like a lovesick puppy.

"Can I talk to you for a second?"

I slowed my roll. I was ready to take the money that she had to offer, especially since I had moved into my new place. Plus, I needed my dick sucked. I stopped and turned around. She wasn't a bad-looking girl. I would just close my eyes and pretend she was Cojo.

"Sure, what is it?" I glanced down at my watch because I didn't want to be late checking in for my shift.

"Can I taste that big, black dick of yours?"

"What's in a taste? Do you want to give it just a lick like a lollipop or do you want to taste the center of a Tootsie Roll Pop?"

"I want the Tootsie Roll Pop."

"You know that shit ain't free."

"I understand that, Gavin; I'm willing to double my offer." She didn't have to say no more 'cause I grabbed her arm and led her back to the employee lounge.

"Show me the money," I demanded as I started to unbuckle my pants. I watched as she counted out ten $100 bills and handed them to me. I folded the bills and put them in my pocket. I sat down in a chair and the thirsty bitch dropped down on her knees and went to work. I had to admit, homegirl knew her shit. I allowed my mind to think about Cojo as she worked my dick.

Either this sister had mad skills or it was the thrill of the easy money that was being made. Either way, it didn't take long to get me off. I exploded in her mouth, and she swallowed every single bit of my precious cum.

"Umm, I knew it would taste good," she said, licking her lips.

"Thanks, baby. Nice doing business with you." I stood up and zipped up my pants.

She was still on the floor, staring at me as if she wanted more, but I was done for the moment. If she wanted seconds, she was going to have to reach deeper into her purse. I reached out my hand to pull her to her feet. She looked like a little kid who had her toy stolen.

"I'd like to see you again."

"Get your money right and we'll see, but no promises." I was ready to get her out of the lounge so I could get to work stackin' more paper.

"I wasn't talking about inside this club. We could go out to dinner or something."

"Look, I enjoyed what just happened, but that's about as far as I'm willing to go. I'm strickly about the money."

"I understand." She ignored my outstretched hand and got to her feet on her own.

That was fine with me, 'cause I would hate to have to bust this bitch in her face if she started to get out of hand. She walked out the door without even looking back. I went over to the sink and washed off my dick. If my luck held up, I might be able to get someone else to come off the money and wet my dick.

CHAPTER FORTY-TWO

ANGIE SIMPSON

I opened my eyes and realized I was in Grady Memorial Hospital. I recognized this place because I had to research its trauma center for a term paper last semester. Then it dawned on me: *Trauma center? What the fuck?* I tried to sit up, but the agonizing pain that shot through every inch of my body caused me to sit my ass still. I didn't even want to breathe too deep after that shit.

One by one I started noticing things. A morphine drip hung over my head to the left; an intravenous drip to the right. Then I remembered the fire and my skin crawled. I really didn't want to do it, but I had to know. I peeked under my sheet and started to cry. Most of my body was covered with bandages.

A nurse came into the room, carrying a bedpan. "You're back with us." She started checking my vitals, then noticed my tears and handed me a tissue.

"I'm hurting."

"I would imagine so with seventy-five percent of your body burned. God was with you because He saved this pretty face of yours." She tinkered with my morphine drip and the pain instantly went away.

I remembered asking for God's help as I ran through the fire. I didn't remember anything after that. "How long have I been here?"

"Twenty-one days and counting. You're healing well. With some physical therapy, you'll get along just fine."

"My parents," I said. "I need to see my parents."

The nurse checked her watch. "It's two o'clock now. They've been here like clockwork every day at five o'clock since your accident."

Two men walked into my room. They both wore cheap suits and worn-down walking shoes.

"Oh, no, you don't," the nurse said. "She just came out of a coma. She hasn't even seen the doctor yet."

The white man with a coffee stain on his Tasmanian Devil-printed tie stepped up. "Nurse Graham, we'll only be a minute."

I saw the bulge of guns under their suit jackets, and gold badges clipped to their waists.

Nurse Graham said, "Every time you come here you ask for a minute and take twenty, as if you have no concern for the patient. I'm going to get the doctor. When I get back, you two have to leave."

"Fair enough," the other guy said.

Nurse Graham left the room.

The guy with the Tasmanian Devil tie said, "I'm Detective Adams, and this is my partner, Detective Lyle."

Detective Lyle waved. "Glad to see you pulled through."

"Thanks," I said, feeling like I was in trouble about something.

Detective Adams looked at my morphine drip. "You must be feeling pretty good, Ms. Simpson. They got you on the good stuff."

If he was attempting to be funny, I missed the damn joke.

"Let me tell you what we know," Detective Lyle said, sitting in the chair beside my bed. "There was an accelerant used to burn your house to the ground. My guess is gasoline, but we won't know that for sure until our lab results come back."

Detective Adams stroked his mustache. "I really don't think it was a suicide attempt on your part because you were found by Atlanta PD in your backyard, unless it was suicide motivated but you chickened out at the last minute."

Detective Lyle leaned forward. "But what's been keeping me awake at night is that you were naked. Why? My cop instincts tell me someone left you for dead."

"The doctors can't definitively say because of the severity of your burns, but they're pretty sure you were beaten," Detective Adams said.

Detective Lyle sighed. "How about you tell us what you know so we can stop guessing."

I looked between the two as a dose of morphine hit me. If I wanted to lie to make myself look better in this ugly mess, the drugs wouldn't allow it. "I got in the car with this stranger on Cleveland Avenue. We went back to my place and had sex. We got a little aggressive with each other, and the last thing I remember was him choking me. I woke up and the house was on fire."

"So you got burned trying to get out?" Detective Adams started taking notes.

I nodded.

"What can you tell me about this stranger, Ms. Simpson?" Detective Lyle said. He too was writing on a notepad.

"His name is Merlin Mills. He's twenty-two, and he's stationed at Fort McPherson Army base. He's six-two, approximately 190 pounds. He drives a 2002 Malibu, brown, with a dent on the back door, passenger side. License plate number is JE619."

The detectives looked at each other as if they were amazed.

"Well, I'll be damned," Detective Lyles said. "I've been in law enforcement going on twenty-two years, and I've never had anyone give me such a thorough description."

I said, "Maybe because you've never asked for a suspect description from a criminal justice major. Would one of you mind getting Nurse Graham for me?" I didn't like these condesending cops and I wanted them to Leone.

CHAPTER FORTY-THREE

GINA MEADOWS

"Babe, I'm at the airport, can you pick me up?"

"Airport? I thought you were going to drive."

"Something came up and I couldn't. Are you coming?"

"Yeah, I'm on my way." Something didn't feel right about this. Why would Ronald leave his car in Ohio if he intended to move here? What could have come up at the last moment? I tried to push all those warning signs to the back of my mind as I rushed to the car to go pick him up. Once I got in the car, I had to call him back because he hadn't told me what airline he was at.

"Why won't he pick up the fucking phone?" I had called him three times, and it kept going straight to voice mail, which either meant he was on the phone or he was ignoring me. Neither scenario left a good taste in my mouth.

Lord, don't let this motherfucker try to play me again. I knew I was wrong for saying "motherfucker" in the same sentence with the Lord's name, but I was tired of being taken for a ride like a broken-down pony at the fair. Then my phone rang. I answered.

"What's up, where you at?" Ronald asked, sounding upset.

"I was calling to find out what gate you are at. You didn't tell me what airline, so I need to know where to find you." I wanted to ask him so badly why he didn't answer the first three times, but I also didn't want to start this visit off with an argument.

"I flew in on Delta. I'll be at the end of the Delta platform."

"Okay, I should be there in about fifteen minutes."

"All right then." He hung up.

It would have been nice if he said something nice like "I can't wait to see you" or even better, "I love you, babe." For a second, I wanted to cry, but I sucked it up. I was going to ride this bike until the wheels fell off. If he tried to play me again, I would know for certain it was over. I was getting too old for this shit.

***

"So what happened?" I moved over and allowed Ronald to drive my car.

"I wasn't able to tie up all my loose ends in Ohio so I decided to fly in, handle the business, and drive back when I was done."

As explanations go, his sucked. No kiss, no hello, and no "baby, I missed you." I could have kicked myself for expecting it.

We drove to the house in Alpharetta to do the final walk-through. The house was beautiful, and I couldn't wait to move in. The Realtor gave Ronald the keys, and Ronald left them with the gatekeepers so they could let the furniture people in.

Ronald said, "We should be ready to move in two weeks from now."

I didn't know about Ronald, but I was ready to move in that day. "Where to now?" I asked when we got back in the car. I was all fired up and ready to discuss our plans for the future. Now that he had the keys, I wanted to tell him I could start moving right away and have the house all set up by the time that he got here.

"We need to pick out some furniture."

I hadn't thought about that because I assumed we would take the furniture that I already had, but I liked his idea better. My stuff was old. We now had this fantastic house, so it was only fitting that we get new furniture.

***

We walked into the furniture store and Ronald said, "Pick out whatever you want, babe."

It felt like when we first got together, and I was so happy. We got all the rooms furnished, and the furniture would be delivered the following day.

We spent the longest time in the furniture store. The rest of our business didn't take long to finish. Ronald arranged for cable, electricity, water, and phone service. And the next thing I knew, we were back at the airport. He didn't even bother to stop by the house for a quickie, which I was really ready for after that vivid dream last week that wore my pussy out.

"Why do you have to leave so soon?" I tried to keep the whining out of my voice, but it wasn't working. We'd spent so many hours playing out life, but never talked about anything concrete as it related to us.

"I told you, baby, I am on a tight schedule. I'll be back in two weeks, and we can get everything straight then." He pulled up to the drop-off point and grabbed his carry-on from the back seat.

I didn't know why he even bothered to bring a bag, because he didn't open it one time. I got out of the car and went around to the driver's side.

Ronald kissed me on the forehead and headed inside the terminal.

"What just happened here?" I had a really weird feeling in the pit of my stomach. Something just didn't feel right. Ronald and I hadn't seen each other in months, and all I got from him was a peck on the forehead? What the fuck?

I drove home in a semi-daze with thousands of questions running through my mind. I tried not to think too hard as I finished packing up my house. I'd been packing for three solid days. I wasn't going to take any of my furniture, but I certainly needed all of my clothes. I also wanted all of my pots and pans. It didn't make sense to buy that stuff again when the pans that I had worked perfectly fine.

As I was packing a sense of joy filled my spirit, and I forgot about all the misgivings I felt when I was with Ronald earlier. For the moment, I felt like everything was going to be okay. Since it was close to the first of the month, I notified my landlord that I would be moving. My lease had already expired, and he was on notice that my plans were to move, so it was no big deal. I just needed to make sure my place was clean before I left.

I hadn't seen Gavin in at least a week, but from the looks of it, he was gone. I went into his room to inspect it for any damage and confirmed the fact that he had moved. All of his clothes were gone. "Good, now I don't have to have that conversation with him." I started to strip the linen from his bed. I had no intention of taking them to my new house. Underneath his pillow I found a blue thong and a red teddy. I didn't want to pick them up, so I just smashed them together with the soiled linen and dumped it all into a large trash bag.

Ugh, ain't no telling who the tramp was who wore these. I couldn't believe that bastard had the nerve to bring one of his whores into my house. I finished clearing out his room and cleaning the bathroom. I was tired, but I still couldn't rest. I was full of nervous energy. I called the Realtor I'd been working with so closely for months.

"Hey, Dan, it's Gina Mills." I loved how the last name Mills sounded coming out of my mouth.

"Hi, Gina. Congratulations."

"Thanks, listen. I know we said we would move in two weeks from now, but I've packed up a lot of things from my old house and I can't see with the boxes. Is there any way that I can start moving things tomorrow?"

"I'm out of it now. Whatever you decide is fine. That house is sold. Congratulations again."

I hung up the phone feeling satisfied that I could accomplish something while I was off from work. I would have felt better if I had keys to our new house, but since my credit was less than perfect, I was not listed on the mortgage papers. I would just have to get a copy of the keys from Ronald. I finished packing the rest of my kitchen items and fell asleep, totally exhausted.

CHAPTER FORTY-FOUR

COJO MILLS

I was skipping work today and going to the doctor's for the first time without Merlin. It was imperative that I find out if the baby was actually my husband's. So far, Merlin had not mentioned his fears about raising a child who might belong to his brother, but I was sure he had done the math in his head.

"Lord, please let this baby belong to my husband." I got up off my knees and started to get dressed. I hated to deceive Merlin in this fashion, but the guilt and shame were killing me. I'd lost weight instead of gaining it, and I knew it was because of the stress.

Even though I knew Merlin knew it was a possibility that the child was not his, he never ever expressed that to me, and that made me love him more than ever, especially since it had not been my intention to cheat on him in the first place. I had gotten tricked.

***

"Cojo Mills?" the nurse called out.

I stood up and followed her to the back, even though my nerves were wreaking havoc with me. I knew I was making the right decision by having a CVS, but I hated that I didn't have the nerve to tell Merlin about it before I did it. The correct medical terminology was Chorionic Villus Sampling. Typically, this test was done to confirm the health of the baby, but it was also used to detect growth abnormalities on the fetus.

"Undress, and put on this robe. The doctor will be in any moment." The nurse handed me the robe and left.

"Thank you." I waited until the door was closed and started taking off my clothes. Once again I started praying. *Sweet Jesus, please be with me through this process and make it all right. Please don't let me be carrying the son or daughter of my husband's brother. Amen.* I got up on the table and waited for the doctor.

"How are you doing, Mrs. Mills?" An Indian doctor came in the room. He was a small man.

"I'd be better if I weren't spread-eagle on this table in front of you."

He chuckled. "I can't tell you how many times I've heard that before." He may have thought he was being funny, but I saw no humor in the situation.

His nurse entered the room to assist him with the procedure.

With his strong accent, he said, "This isn't going to hurt, but it will be a little uncomfortable. I am going to place a catheter through the cervix and take a small tissue sample of the chorion villa cells for biopsy. CVS was used to find genetic disorders but it could also be used to determine the sex of the child. It should only take a minute, so please lie still."

"How long should it take to learn the results?"

"The results are usually available within seven to ten days. I will have preliminary results within forty-eight hours, but they will not be one hundred percent accurate. Would you like those preliminary results e-mailed to you?"

"Yes, I would."

"Okay, I will make a note to the file. It is common for women to experience mild uterine cramping. This may be slightly uncomfortable, but it is usually not painful. If you experience pain, contact me immediately."

"Okay." I was feeling a lot better knowing that my mind would be at rest soon. Even if it wasn't my husband's child, I just had to know. The unknown was killing my joy.

"You will be fine," the doctor said.

***

"Are there any restrictions on my part?" I asked this question as an afterthought. Since I felt no pain, I assumed there would be no worries.

"It is recommended that you refrain from strenuous physical activity, heavy lifting, sitting in water—such as bath or pool—and sexual intercourse for approximately twenty-four to forty-eight hours. In addition, you should avoid the insertion of anything vaginally, including suppositories, for twenty-four to forty-eight hours."

"Aye aye, sir."

He spit out his orders to me as if he were a naval captain and I was on one of his boats, but I got it. I didn't plan on doing shit. Hell, I didn't have to. Merlin took care of everything at the house. I walked out of the doctor's office feeling better than when I went in, because I knew that I would have an answer soon.

"So, whose baby is it? Mine or his?" Gavin stood beside my car with an evil grin on his face.

Immediately, my heart started beating faster. He was the last person on God's green earth that I wanted to see, and I certainly didn't want to see him today.

"You need to get the hell away from me."

"Where is this animosity coming from, sis? I just want to know whose child you are carrying."

I didn't hate many people, but I could honestly say that I hated Gavin. "None of your fucking business."

"Oh, I beg to differ, 'cause if it is my child—and I have the right to know—I will not allow anyone else to raise it other than me. Let's be clear about that shit."

"Are you serious?"

"As a heart attack."

My mind was spinning. The fact that he knew about my doctor's appointment, when my own husband didn't, spoke volumes. It was apparent that Gavin had been following me or had other insider information. That didn't bode well for Merlin and me. I also knew that I couldn't allow him to see me sweat.

"I tell you what. If I find out that the child I am carrying does not belong to my husband, you can follow me right back here while I abort the bastard." I got into the car and slammed the door.

Outside the car, Gavin was acting an ass. I ignored him and pulled out of the parking lot. It unnerved me to know that he was following me. Initially, I had no intention of telling Merlin about the test, but I now knew I could not afford to keep it from him. He needed to know. And now that Gavin had showed his ugly face, the sooner I told him, the better.

I pulled over to the side of the road and sent Merlin a text message: When you get a chance, I really need to speak with you.

My phone rang back almost immediately, and I used my Bluetooth to speak with my husband.

He said, "What's wrong, baby?"

This was not the way that I wanted to have this conversation, but I felt it was better if it came from me rather than Gavin. "Honey, I went to the doctor's today to have a paternity test. I felt I owed it to you to make sure that I wasn't carrying your brother's child. I'm sorry I didn't tell you about it, but I wanted to be certain that this child is ours. I wasn't trying to deceive you, but I didn't want to worry you, either." I started driving.

"Baby, I fully understand what you did. I have had my doubts, but I'd already made up my mind to accept this child as my own, regardless of who the father is."

"You did?"

"Yes. You're my wife. You didn't cheat on me, you got cheated."

"Oh my God! I've been so worried that you wouldn't love me anymore if you found out that I wasn't carrying your child." I had to pull over to the side of the road again because the tears from my eyes blinded me.

"Sweetheart, hush. It's all a moot point."

"Wait, baby, you have to hear this. Gavin showed up at the doctor's office. I don't know how he knew that I was pregnant, but he asked if it was his. I think he has been following me."

Merlin didn't answer right away, and I could tell he was battling with his own emotions when he finally spoke. "I'll deal with Gavin. Go home and get some rest." His words had a bite to them that I was unfamiliar with.

I could tell he was mad. "Are you okay, baby?"

"Yeah, just go home. If he comes to the house, call me back."

CHAPTER FORTY-FIVE

MERLIN MILLS

"Son of a bitch." The coffee cup that I had been holding in my hands shattered all over the floor. It wasn't like me to lose control at work, but I felt like I had been pushed over the very edge of the earth. "How dare the fucker follow my wife."

"Specialist Mills, are you all right?" my job supervisor asked.

"No, I'm not all right. I need to take a personal day starting right now."

"Report to the captain. I'm sure it can be arranged."

I had no doubt my request would be granted after the last Army soldier went ballistic and shot up half his camp, but I didn't want to go out on a bad note. I went to find the captain. I had found her to be completely human the last time I had to speak with her.

"Captain, I have a family emergency and I have to leave."

"At ease. Shut the door."

I turned and closed the door behind me. I didn't want to take the time to explain the situation, but I also didn't want to fuck myself in my haste to get off the base.

Captain Jamison looked at me with genuine concern. "What's going on, Specialist?"

I did some soul searching before I was ready to admit to the circumstances of this new emergency. "Captain, you've been more than just an officer with me. You have shown me true compassion since I've been on base and I appreciate it. However, my brother is trying to make a move on my wife, and I can't let that happen. I thought he had moved on, but I found out a few minutes ago that he hasn't. I need to handle this situation." I could not bring myself to tell her that there was a good chance that the child my wife carried might not be mine.

"Go handle your business. If you can't make it tomorrow, call me." She reached across her desk and gave me her personal card with her cell and house phone numbers on it.

"Thank you, Captain. You don't know how much this means to me."

"Yes, I do."

Our eyes locked for a second. She had told me her story, and I believed that she understood what I was going through.

I rushed off the base, intent upon setting Gavin in his place once and for all. He must have really lost his mind if he thought for one minute that I was going to allow him to come into our life and ruin our marriage.

I didn't give a flying fuck if it was his child. He was going to leave my wife alone. I was so angry I almost ran my car into a truck in front of me that stopped suddenly. I stomped on the brake, causing myself to push up against the steering wheel.

I drove over to my mother's house so that I could talk to my brother. I really didn't want to see him, but he wouldn't answer the cell phone I had given him. When I pulled up to my mother's apartment complex, I didn't see his car or my mother's. I was so far removed from her life, I had no idea what shift she was working.

I sat in the car for several more minutes, hoping that one of them would show up, but it was to no avail. As a last-ditch effort, I wrote a note to my mother.

Mother, I am trying to get in touch with Gavin. When he comes back, can you please have him give me a call on my cell? Better yet, if he shows up, could you please call me and I'll come back over. What I have to say to him, I need to say it to his face and not on the phone.

Thanks for your help.

Merlin.

I wasn't happy about this unexpected delay, but it was what it was. I would just have to wait and deal with my wayward brother later. Of course, this could have been a blessing in disguise because I really didn't know how I would have reacted if I saw Gavin at this exact moment.

With no other options, I drove home to comfort my wife.

CHAPTER FORTY-SIX

GINA MEADOWS

I packed as many boxes and bags that I could fit into my car. It was so loaded, I could barely see out the windows. For the first time, I wished that Gavin were here so that he could help me and I wouldn't have to make so many trips.

"Shit, I should have rented a U-Haul truck." As soon as the words left my mouth, I realized just how stupid it would have been because I had no idea how to drive a truck. *All right, Lord, I'm just going to do this the best way I know how.* I looked around for my purse. Once I found it, I locked the house up and took the long drive to Alpharetta. I started getting excited the farther I got away from the city. I was looking forward to the peace and quiet of the new neighborhood.

When I arrived at the gated community, the guard waved me in. He had gotten used to seeing me during the construction phase of our home.

He leaned out of the booth to speak with me. "Good afternoon, the door is open because some delivery men have already arrived with the furniture."

"Thanks, I'm just going to drop off some of my things and be out."

"No problem."

I was absolutely giddy when I pulled up in front of our new home. Leaving my purse in the car, I carried two boxes to the stoop before I tried the door. I walked into the foyer and marveled at how nicely the furniture that I picked out went with our living room.

I bent over and pushed my boxes over to the corner. As I was standing up, a lady walked out of the kitchen. She appeared to be in her late twenties/early thirties. She smiled at me in a greeting manner, and I returned the smile.

"I'm just dropping off a few boxes," I said as I headed to the door.

She didn't say anything, and it didn't dawn on me to ask who she was. I went back to the car and grabbed a few more boxes. I was getting tired and sure would have liked to have had some help with all this lifting and shit. I practically dumped my next box of household items all over the white carpeting.

"What company are you with?" she asked, still standing in the doorway of the kitchen.

I started to tell her that it was none of her business, but I decided to be nice. "I'm not with any company. I live here," I proudly announced.

"Excuse me?" Her eyebrows rose significantly as she placed her hands on her hips.

If I weren't so tired, I might have noticed her defensive posture. "My husband and I are moving in over the next few weeks." I knew I didn't have to explain myself, but my exhaustion got my tongue to wagging. Plus, I was proud of our new accomplishment.

"What's your husband's name?" Her tone was even and held no hint of attitude.

"Ronald." I turned around to go get some more boxes.

"That's interesting."

I didn't know who this nosey bitch was, but she was starting to get on my nerves. "How so?"

"Because this is my house and my husband just so happens to be named Ronald too."

It felt like the floor just rushed up and smacked me in the face. Before I knew it, I was face down on the carpet. I looked around to see who had pushed me, but there was no one else there but the lady, and she hadn't moved. "There has to be a misunderstanding," I stuttered. Surely Ronald did not play me like this. He wouldn't be that heartless.

"Oh, yeah, there is some misunderstanding. I think you made it."

I pushed myself off the rug trying to figure out what was really going on. I wasn't upset because I knew there had to be a mistake. "How long have you been married?" I asked in a whisper.

The woman practically glowed at the mention of her marriage. "Three months."

I staggered back. I needed to get out of that house before I did something that landed my ass in jail. I stumbled toward the door.

"What are you going to do about these boxes?" She was pretty calm given that I had just barged into her house claiming ownership.

"Keep them." There was no way I was going back into that house after learning that Ronald had duped me again. It was inconceivable that he would treat me this way. As I drove away, I was numb and was operating the car on autopilot. I was so void of feeling I couldn't even cry.

"This is crazy. I mean, really crazy." But I could not deny any longer what was placed right in my face. Ronald gave me his ass to kiss with a big-ass bow on it. I tried to remember every conversation that we'd had over the last few months, and he never gave me any indication that I wouldn't be moving into the house with him. In fact, he kept saying we would be a happy family.

How the hell were we going to be a happy family when he had some other heifer living with him? Hell, he even married her and that was something that he never did for me. I was having a hard time processing this information. It was all so bizarre.

Why would he let me pick out the furnishing to a house I wouldn't even be invited to? I was ready to call him and cuss his ass out, but I needed to pull myself together first. Over the years Ronald had done his dirt, but he'd never just thrown it in my face like he did today. I dealt with the cheating, the long-distance relationship, and the money he hoarded, but when it was all said and done, I felt confident that he loved me on some level. It hurt me more than anything to know that he married this woman after stringing me along for damn near twenty years.

Hell, as far as I was concerned, I was his wife. I thought he felt the same way. I was trying to get up the energy to go into the house, but I just didn't have the strength. I looked at all the boxes lining my car and felt like screaming.

"This is some *Jerry Springer* bullshit." I looked toward my door and saw a note attached to it. It had to be from Ronald. He's was going to tell me it was a sick joke and that we were all right. Suddenly energized, I quickly undid my seatbelt and rushed to the front door to get the note. My blood was rushing through my veins. I thought my heart was going to leap right out of my chest. I snatched the note from the door and read the opening line, hoping for the best.

It read: *Mother, I am trying to get in touch with Gavin–*

I crumbled the note without reading anything further. I used my key to open the door before I started crying on my front stoop. My hand was trembling so badly, I could barely get the key in the lock. I leaned against the door to keep from falling. When the lock finally unlatched, I fell into the house and landed on the floor. I kicked the door shut.

"I'm going to lay here until I feel better." The tears came, and I was happy that I had been able to hold them back until I was alone.

CHAPTER FORTY-SEVEN

GAVIN MILLS

Damn, things hadn't gone anything like the way I'd planned. I was back in my car, speeding to my apartment to regroup. I could not believe I had underestimated the effect I would have on Cojo when I showed up at her doctor's appointment.

Shit, I thought she would've been happy to see me, especially since her own husband hadn't taken the time to come himself. Women are such a fickle group. Half the time you're damned if you do and damned if you don't. I should have been getting some rest for my shift tonight. Instead, I took my precious time to let Cojo know I was there for her and our baby, but she acted like I had stepped in shit and tracked it all over her carpet.

I slipped into my room as quickly as I could. I didn't want to get too close to my neighbors.

The less they saw of me, the better. It was not my plan to live in this dingy one-bedroom apartment for long. As soon as I could get Cojo to see I was the better man, I planned to move in with her. She needed a real man, and I was more than enough for the job.

Hell, I was even wearing the lucky Polo shirt that I'd taken from Merlin's closet, and she didn't even notice. I said it was my lucky shirt because every time I wore it, the women and shims just threw panties at me. I could not understand why Cojo resisted her inner instincts.

"She's gonna mess around and lose me if she doesn't change her attitude." I was talking shit and I knew it, but it made me feel better to say it out loud. I knew it was going to take some convincing to get Cojo over to my side of the bed, but I really was willing to put in the work because I recognized her for the jewel she was. I just had to convince her I was the better man, which wouldn't be hard to do since Merlin has always stood in my shadows.

My room was a mess. I hadn't fully unpacked, and I hadn't bothered to do any cleaning since the day I moved in. I had dirty dishes in the sink and clothes strewn all over the floors. Even as a child, housework was never my thing. But if I ever hoped to bring someone back to my place, I knew that I needed to clean up.

I scooped up all the dirty clothes from the floor and hid them in the tub. I didn't have a washer so after I had worn my last piece of clean clothing, I would go over to my mother's house while she was at work and wash. There was no way that I was going to pay seventy-five cents a load to wash and dry my clothes when I could use her utilities for free.

I took off the clothes I was wearing, threw them into the tub, and took a shower. I had just enough time to catch a couple hours of sleep before I had to go to work.

CHAPTER FORTY-EIGHT

ANGIE SIMPSON

Detective Adams said, "You're looking a lot better."

I was sitting up in bed, sipping ice water. "I feel much better. I can go to the bathroom on my own."

"You're making progress then. You'll be out of here in no time."

"I'm having a difficult time shaking the morphine, but they're weaning me off it with Demoral."

"The lesser of the two evils." He pulled up a chair and straddled it. "I need you to ID this guy, Ms. Simpson. Here's a pen." He gave me an expensive pen; it probably cost more than his suit. "I'm going to show you a photo card with six pictures on it. If you see the guy who did this to you, I need you to sign your name right beneath his picture."

"Okay," I said.

He gave me the photo card. I recognized Merlin as Detective Adams was passing me the photo card. There was absolutely no reason to consider the other five potentials.

"This is Merlin Mills." I put a fingertip on picture number four. It was a mug shot from when he was younger, probably around seventeen or eighteen, but it was him. "This is him." I signed my name under the picture of the unsatisfying piece of dick who'd tried to kill me.

Nurse Graham came into the room. Clearly something was bothering her. Since she'd been caring for me, I'd learned that she wore her emotions on her face.

Now I was concerned. "What's wrong, Ms. Graham?"

She nodded at Detective Adams. "Do you mind giving us a few minutes?"

"It's okay," I said. "It can't be that bad. He can stay."

Ms. Graham shook her head as if she pitied me. "You're pregnant."

I lost my breath. I prayed that I did not have a monster growing in my womb.

CHAPTER FORTY-NINE

MERLIN MILLS

My heart was heavy when I put my key in the door. For all my bravado, I accomplished nothing as it related to getting Gavin to leave my wife alone. I had been by my mother's several times. Even though her car was back in the parking lot, she didn't appear to be home. I wanted Gavin's ass so bad, I could taste it.

"Any luck?" Cojo asked after I closed and bolted the door.

"Not yet. I could not get in touch with my mother, and Gavin is not answering the cell phone I gave him. He could be hiding because he knows that I would be coming for him, but for some reason I doubt that. Gavin has always had a problem with boundaries." As soon as I said it, I realized that wasn't the best thing to say to my pregnant wife, who was being led around by wild hormones.

"What's that supposed to mean?" She was clearly agitated.

"No, sweetheart, you misunderstood me. What I meant to say was that Gavin's sense of right and wrong are different from the normal person's."

"Oh, that's supposed to make me feel better?" She burst into tears.

I rushed to her to take her in my arms.

I knew that I was not explaining myself well, but I was never good at discussing the enigma that Gavin was. "Let me run you a bath. Have you eaten yet?" I was trying to remain calm for her; but, inside, my emotions were raging just like hers.

"No, I can't take a bath for forty-eight hours." She sniffed.

I led her to our bedroom. I turned on the shower and went to whip up a light snack for her. While she was in the bathroom, I continued trying to reach my mother. The bad thing for me was that I knew nothing of her life, so I didn't know any other number but her home.

I had just heated up some soup and made a sandwich for Cojo when the doorbell rang. I wasn't expecting anyone and the disruption really irritated me. Whoever it was on the other side of the bell was practically lying on it.

Don't tell me that bastard Gavin has the nerve to come over here after he's followed my wife, I thought. Putting my tray to the side, I strode to the door, ready to knock this fool's head off his shoulders. I snatched open the door ready to do battle.

"Merlin Mills?"

Facing me were two military police officers.

"Uh, yeah, what's this about?" For the life of me, I couldn't understand why two police officers would be standing outside my door.

The tallest of the two said, "You are under arrest."

They stepped forward, turned me around, and cuffed me.

"What in the hell are you talking about? What did I do?"

In the meantime, Cojo had emerged from the bathroom in her robe. Her eyes were wide as saucers as she witnessed me being arrested.

"In other words, Specialist Mills, you have been listed as AWOL, absent without leave, and in violation of a direct order," the shortest officer said.

My eyes swung wildly between the two officers and my wife. "I'm sorry, there must be some mistake. I'm not AWOL. I was at work today. Call my captain, she can vouch for me."

"Merlin, what's going on?" Cojo's eyes were bucked.

I said, "I don't know, sweetheart, but don't worry."

They were trying to drag me through the door, but I wanted Cojo to assure that I didn't do anything wrong and I would be back by her side in no time.

"Call Captain Jamison, let her know what happened and ask her to please help me." At this point I was practically screaming this to Cojo as the other officer grabbed the door and shut it in my wife's face.

This day had turned into a nightmare, and I didn't know how to stop it from getting any worse. It was killing me to leave my wife at this emotionally vulnerable time especially when my stupid-ass brother was running amuck and following her.

"Where are you taking me?" I assumed that they would be taking me back to the base so I could clear up any problems that they had, but we were traveling in the opposite direction.

"I suggest you put a lid on it, Specialist. We don't owe you any explanations," short stuff said.

"No disrespect, sirs, but I still think this is a big misunderstanding. I've been to work every day since I was assigned a temporary job on base while awaiting my redeployment orders."

"Well, your orders called for you to head back to Iraq on June thirteenth. Obviously, one of us is wrong, and I guarantee it's not us."

"Stop talking to the prisoner. You don't owe him shit." The tall one frowned.

"Wait, hold up for a second. If I was going to go AWOL, why would I be at my house instead of going somewhere else?" It was like I was talking to a wall. "Think about it, if I was going AWOL, why would I report to work every day as if things were normal? If I were truly AWOL, I would have left the state or even the country, but I didn't do that. Come on, people, think."

"Maybe you're one of those crazy niggers!"

Since both of my arresting officers where white, I saw nothing funny about his remarks.

"Please, before you put me on a plane and waste taxpayer money, please just look into this. If I'm wrong, then I should be punished, but I promise you that I did nothing wrong."

"Shut your pie hole, Specialist."

CHAPTER FIFTY

GINA MEADOWS

I was not believing this shit. And the worst part about it was that I couldn't even call Tabatha and tell her about the shit that had just gone down, 'cause she warned me, and my hardheaded ass wouldn't listen.

Everywhere I looked I saw boxes. It seemed like it had taken forever to pack the boxes, and now I would need to spend the next week unpacking them. That was, if I could get my landlord to allow me to stay. If not, I would be out there pounding the pavement, trying to find an apartment that I could afford.

This whole situation was a nightmare that I could not believe I was living. Part of me wanted to start unpacking immediately just in case someone dropped by and I had to explain to them why all my shit was in boxes, but I just didn't have the energy.

I went into the kitchen and fixed a drink. If I ever deserved a drink it was now. I had never been so humiliated in my life. Ronald had been giving me the shaft for years, but no one outside of us knew what was going on.

I embarrassed myself in front of a total stranger. I wanted to get mad at the woman and go back out there and kick her ass. The reality was that it wasn't her fault. She probably didn't know jack shit about me.

Ronald was the motherfucker at the root of all this shit. If she knew anything about me, things might have gone differently.

Hell, she could have shot me for walking up in her spot like I owned it. I had no idea what was in the boxes that I left at their house. I figured it was just a matter of time before Ronald showed up and dropped them off. Seeing that he was a coward, I wouldn't have been surprised if he'd just dropped them off one day when I was at work.

That bastard really didn't want to see me. Just thinking about Ronald started my blood to boil. I was angry, no doubt about that, but I was also curious as to why he would treat me in this fashion. Hell, I was a good woman to him. Mentally, I went through all the conversations that I had had with Ronald over the last several months when he announced that he was moving home. At no point did he indicate that I would not be living with him.

If that was the case, he didn't even have to tell me he was coming. He could have just shown up, and I wouldn't have been the wiser. It ain't like I traveled to Alpharetta on the regular. He could have lived his life to the ripe old age of one hundred, and I would have never known the difference. Shit just wasn't adding up. I lay down on the sofa, too tired to think anymore.

I was going to have to find a way to get past this hurt and move on with my life. I wanted to call Tabatha so badly, but I could not hear "I told you so." Not tonight. I was whupping up on myself already. I didn't need any more help in that regard.

CHAPTER FIFTY-ONE

MERLIN MILLS

I wasn't able to speak to Captain Jamison when I saw her come through the door, but I immediately began to relax knowing that I had someone on my side coming to the rescue. I could tell by her stride that she was pissed. She went into the commander general's office and slammed the door.

"Yeah!" I screamed.

She didn't take too well to people fucking with her folks, but she didn't appear as confident when she came out of the office. My heart sank. I still couldn't figure out what the fuck I could have done to get myself in trouble. She came into the room they were holding me in, with a confused look on her face.

"Specialist, I'm trying to fight this, but I have to know why you signed these orders."

"Orders? I haven't received any orders."

She slid some papers across the table to me. I could tell from her demeanor that she was pissed.

"Captain, I've never seen these papers before. Why would I sign something without speaking with you? This makes no sense." I picked up the papers to look at them more closely. They had been sent by Certified Mail and someone signed for them the same day that I had taken Cojo to the mountains. "Captain Jamison, remember I told you I was taking my wife to the mountains because I had just found out she was pregnant?"

"Yeah."

"These papers were signed for after I left. There is no way I could have signed them!" Things were finally making sense, but I still didn't know who signed for them.

"Someone signed for those papers, and that is why we are both here."

"But I didn't do it. Can't they compare the signatures?" The only other person who knew I had orders coming was my mother, and I didn't want to believe that she had thrown away our newfound understanding. I just couldn't believe that, so I wouldn't throw her under the bus yet.

"That might be enough to get you out of here tonight, but we have got to get some answers.

Specialist Mills, I have gone out of my way to make concessions for you. Don't let this bite me in my ass!"

"I have one more question, how did you know about the orders?"

"That's a good question.

It took another few hours before I was finally released. Captain Jamison agreed to take me home because I didn't have my car with me. She started speaking after we got into the car. "They were gunning for you for some reason. Is there anything else that I should be aware of?"

"I promise you, Captain, I'm as squeaky clean as they come. I don't have any surprises in my closet that will come back to bite you in the butt."

"I hope you're telling the truth, 'cause I take objection to folks chewing on my ass."

I wanted to laugh because it was a funny comment, but the severity of the situation made it impossible for me to laugh. "Do you really believe that I would have traumatized my wife over some bullshit? Oops, I'm sorry, Captain, but this has really pissed me off. My sick-ass brother is running around trying to hit on my wife, and now this."

"That's crazy your brother would do something like that."

"Yeah, we look just alike. He tricked my wife into thinking he was me and had sex with her. Lord, I can't believe that I'm telling you all this."

"Go ahead, I think I need to hear this."

"It was while I was on my way home from my last tour. I never told her about him, because he did some foul shit that he blamed me for. But the truth came out and he went to prison for a long time. Hell, I forgot all about him. Anyway, he got out of prison and showed up at my house. My wife thought he was me and one thing led to another. I made it home right after they finished. Now my brother wants to claim the baby as his."

"Oh, damn."

Hearing Captain Jamison cuss somehow made her seem more human to me. "I know, it's jacked up. I left today because my wife went to the doctor's today to take a paternity test because she was afraid that it might be my brother's. She didn't tell me because she didn't want to stir up some shit, but my brother showed up at the doctor's. My guess is that he has been following her."

"Wow, some *Jerry Springer*–type shit."

"Yeah, tell me about it. I had just gotten home when they arrived to arrest me. Talk about bad timing."

"Have you spoken with your wife yet?"

"No, I didn't get a chance to grab my phone before I was forced to leave the house."

She fished around in her purse and handed me her phone. I was grateful for the chance to put Cojo's mind at ease, but I didn't feel all that comfortable speaking to my wife in front of her.

Despite my misgivings, I called her. "Hey, babe."

"Merlin? Whose phone are you calling from, and what in the hell is going on?"

"Hold on, baby, calm down. I'm with my captain, and she is bringing me home. I told her what we've been dealing with, and she let me use her phone to call you to put your fears to rest." I heard her exhale, and I could tell that she'd been worried out of her mind.

"Thank God."

"Is everything okay at the house?"

"Yeah, just been waiting to hear from you."

"I'll be there soon. Love you."

"I love you too."

I closed the phone and handed it back to Captain Jamison. "Thanks, I really needed to do that."

"Don't mention it. I shared a lot of my story with you, so I understand what you're going through. I only wish that someone would have taken an interest in me when I was going through similar situations after I enlisted. The biggest problem that I see is when people get these positions in the military they forget that they were people first, and with that comes life's problems. My CO didn't care about anything unless it was connected with the Army."

"I'm glad I didn't enlist back then, 'cause I probably would have gone AWOL."

"I understand what you're saying, but don't even joke about that. My ass is on the line for this. They really wanted to ship you out tonight. I had to call my direct supervisor to get it stopped. I don't want to have to shine a spotlight on my stuff like this again."

"You won't have to. As I said, I'm squeaky clean. Once I get my sick-ass brother under control, you'll probably never hear about me again."

"I'm gonna hold you to that!"

CHAPTER FIFTY-TWO

COJO MILLS

Merlin was on the way home, and I wanted to look extra nice for him. I took a hot shower and swept my hair into an updo. I went into the bedroom and oiled my body down. I didn't know if his captain would come in, so I wanted to put on something under my clothes that I could strip down to.

I had a red teddy that would be perfect for the occasion. I was very meticulous about my clothing and knew where every item was placed, but I could not find it to save my soul. I pulled out every drawer and sorted through each item in them, but I couldn't find it.

"That's so strange." After wasting a good fifteen minutes, I decided on a white teddy. I liked the way my chocolate skin contrasted against the white. I pulled on a pair of jeans over the teddy and put on a shirt to cover it. I decided against a bra. My boobs were feeling extra heavy and wearing a bra for eight hours was enough for me.

I was in the living room when Merlin came through the door. I launched my body toward him and damn near knocked him down.

"Damn, baby, I haven't been gone that long."

"I know, but when you left it scared me so bad, I just couldn't help myself."

"Shit scared me too." He gently pulled me from his chest and turned toward the door. "Babe, let me introduce you to the person who is responsible for getting me out."

I didn't even wait until he finished his introduction before I was rushing forward to greet and thank his captain for her help. "Thank you so much for helping my husband. I don't know what I would do without him."

Captain Jamison said, "You are very welcome. He's a good guy, and I can tell he loves you."

My heart swelled with her comment. It was one thing for him to tell me that, but it was something entirely different when a stranger said it. Without warning, I burst out in tears. My hormones had been raging, and I wasn't in control of anything. Not my bladder, not my emotions, or my crazy-ass brother-in-law.

"Sweetheart, why are you crying?" Merlin had a terrified look on his face, but I couldn't make him feel better when I was raging out of control.

"I don't know," I wailed. I walked toward my husband and wrapped my arms around his neck. I needed him to hold me and reassure me that everything was going to be all right.

"It's going to be okay, baby. Just calm down." He stroked my back, and I began to feel better.

In fact, I began to feel ashamed for acting out in front of his captain. I pulled away from his arms to face her. "I'm so sorry. I didn't mean to carry on this way in front of you."

"Girl, shut up, I was pregnant too. I know what you are dealing with." She came to me with open arms, and I cried on her shoulder too.

There was a heavy knock at the door.

"I'll get it." Merlin went to the door and opened it while still looking over his shoulder at us.

Two white men wearing the cheapest suits I'd ever seen were standing there with their guns trained on Merlin. I gasped and my eyes bucked.

"What?" Merlin asked when he saw of my expression. He turned toward the door.

"Merlin Mills," the white man with the Looney Tunes–printed tie said, "get on the ground and place your hands behind your back."

That's when I noticed the badges clipped to their waist.

Merlin laughed. "We just got that little situation taken care of."

The guy with the tie charged Merlin and knocked him to the ground. The other guy kept his gun pointed.

"I said get on the ground." He put his knee in Merlin's back and pulled out a set of handcuffs.

"My captain is standing right there," Merlin said. "Ask her."

"Merlin Mills," the man said while cuffing him, "you're under arrest for attempted murder and arson."

My eyes damn near jumped out of my head. Just when I thought things could get no worse, they did.

CHAPTER FIFTY-THREE

GAVIN MILLS

"You ready to go?"

"Damn, don't be rushing me." I was aggravated. I never should have promised to meet up with the trick. Now I was mad at him and myself.

"I ain't rushing you, boo."

My stomach turned a little. I started to check him right there at the club, but I didn't want to draw any attention to us. "What's your name?" I was stalling, trying to figure out exactly what I was going to do.

"It's Wayne." He didn't ask for my name, and if he had, I would have most definitely told him a lie.

"All right, Wayne, let's bounce." I followed him out of the club.

"My car is right across the street." He walked off, and I got in my car to follow him. His arrogance reminded me of Merlin and it made my blood boil.

I followed him to his house, which wasn't too far from the club.

"Do you want a drink?" Wayne asked as he left the living room and went into the kitchen.

"I could use a beer." I looked around his modest apartment. From the looks of things, Wayne did okay for himself. His apartment didn't have that run-down look that mine had and that only made me madder. "I like your crib."

"Thanks," Wayne said as he handed me a beer. He took the top off of his bottle and took a generous gulp. He appeared to be nervous as he walked over to the television and turned it on. I took a seat on the sofa. "So what do you do?"

"I'm a pharmacist."

I didn't expect that. I thought he was going to tell me that he was into interior decorating or some other gay shit like that. "Oh, yeah, that's good."

He sat next to me on the sofa. I got nervous.

"You are really cute. Do you dance?" Wayne said as he scooted over closer to me.

"No, my talents are limited to pouring liquor."

"I wouldn't say that," Wayne said suggestively. He ran his hand up my thigh, and I had to suppress the urge to punch him in his fucking face.

"Hey, I've got to use your bathroom." I jumped up from the sofa.

"It's down the hall on the right, sweetie."

I took my time in the bathroom, looking through his medicine cabinet and underneath the sink. I was surprised to find a bottle of Rohypnol.

Rohypnol was the date rape drug. I flipped open the top and poured out two tablets into my hand. I was formulating a plan in my mind. I casually walked back into the living room. I needed to find a way to get the pills into his beer. "Can I get a glass of water?" I asked.

"Why, you trying to kill your high with water?"

"Nigga, I ain't killing shit, I just need some water."

Wayne went into the kitchen and got my water, and I was able to slip the pills into his open bottle of beer.

I sipped at the water and drowned the beer waiting for the pills to take effect on Wayne.

"Can I go and get comfortable?" Wayne asked.

"Sure, do your thing. I'm going to go into the kitchen and make me a drink."

"That's cool, I'll be out in a minute." He was shaking his hips as if he were enticing me. Little did he know, I had no interest in what he had to offer. I just wanted to teach his ass a lesson that he wouldn't soon forget.

I had settled onto the couch and was watching the news when Wayne came out of the bedroom. He was naked and appeared to be very proud of his tiny dick. I almost laughed when I saw him appear in the doorway. He struck a pose.

"Where are you clothes, bro?"

"We both know what you're here for. Just tell me how much it's going to cost me."

"I don't get down like that. Put a towel around your ass. I get with men who I connect with mentally."

"Wow, I'm sorry." He turned around and went back into the bathroom to get a towel.

I stifled a laugh. Little did he know, I wouldn't get with him no matter how big his mind was.

Wayne walked back into the room, and I could tell that he was embarrassed.

"Don't worry about it man, I get this all the time. I like to know who I'm sleeping with so I take my time."

He picked up his beer and drank the rest of it. He did exactly what I wanted him to do. All I had to do was wait. He sat on the sofa with me and we watched the news. However, I could not sit still when I heard the top story. My brother Merlin had been arrested for attempted arson. Under normal circumstances, I would have been happy that he was out of the way, but he being charged for a crime that I had committed.

The news was unexpected but it came right on time. I needed to get to Cojo. This was my chance to get close to her.

Wayne passed out, and I took out all my aggression on him. I pulled off the towel and exposed his flaccid penis. I pushed him back on the sofa so he was completely laid out. The razor that I had removed from his medicine cabinet was in my hand. I used this razor to sever the pulsating vein running down his dick. He wouldn't be able to use that piece of flesh ever again. I cleaned up and headed over to my true love, Cojo.

CHAPTER FIFTY-FOUR

GINA MEADOWS

One week had passed since I had made that trip to Alpharetta and Merlin had been arrested, and I still could not get my shit together. I called my job and took off another week. I still was having a hard time understanding what had happened.

I did manage to unpack my shit, only 'cause I didn't want Gavin coming in and seeing the boxes and asking me a bunch of questions. But, strangely enough, I hadn't seen him. This only confirmed my suspicious that he had moved. I was fine with that since I didn't want him living with me in the first place, but still . . . I started to cry again. My heart felt like it had a hole in it that would never heal, and I didn't know how I would be able to go on with my life.

The doorbell rang. This wasn't the first time that I ignored it, but it was the first time that I was standing near it when it rang.

"Gina, answer the motherfucking door," Ronald screamed. He nigga-knocked on it to let me know that he meant business.

I wasn't ready to see his sorry ass, so I went back into my bedroom, hoping his ass would go away.

"I'm not going away, so you might as well open the fucking door."

I wondered what happened to the fucking key that I made sure he always had, but I guess he had amnesia or some shit like that. "You've got a key, you fucker, use it." I was not about to make anything easy for him after all the shit he had just put me through.

There was silence on the other side of the door for a few minutes before I heard him fumbling with the lock. Obviously, he had confused me with one of his other chicks, who hadn't given him the key to their life.

When he finally got it opened, he pushed against the door like a superhero. In his arms he had the boxes I had left at his house. "What the fuck is your problem? I've been trying to get in touch with you for days."

"What the fuck is my problem? Nigga, please. My problem is the wife you have posted up in a house that I thought I was going to occupy."

"I never said that I was going to live in the house with you."

As if that shit made it better. I wanted to beat his head in with an iron skillet. "You never said I wouldn't. In fact, you told me that we were going to be a big, happy family." I started making my way to the kitchen. He had really pissed me off, and I didn't want to look at him.

"I never said I was going to marry you."

I adjusted my voice so he could hear me from the kitchen. "I see, I had it all wrong."

"Yeah, it was a big misunderstanding." He had the nerve to chuckle like it was a big-ass joke.

That was when I snapped. I grabbed the biggest knife that I had left in the kitchen. "So let me make sure I understand what you are telling me. You married a woman nearly half your age and moved her into a home that I picked out the furniture for and did all the planning for. Is that what you came over here to talk to me about?"

"Well, I guess so."

I heard enough. I raced toward my "husband" with the knife. I wanted him to hurt as bad as I did. I stabbed him as hard as I could. I was aiming for his heart but only managed to cut him on the shoulder. I tried to whack it off.

"Bitch, are you crazy? You damn near took off my arm!" Ronald was pissed, but I didn't give a rat's ass.

He had hurt me for so long, it was time I gave him a dose of his own medicine.

"Yes, I'm crazy. You made me this way. How dare you treat me like a jump off and move some other bitch into your house instead of me? Why would you marry her when I did the work?" I tried to get close to him so I could cut him again. I realized that I was going to go to jail along with Merlin, but I didn't fucking care. Ronald had trampled on my feelings for so long, I felt like this was the only option.

"You can't help who you love."

No, he didn't just say that shit to me. I hit rewind in my mind, but I heard the same words. I let the knife hit the floor 'cause it wouldn't matter how many times I stuck him, he would always come back with the same response. I could only pray that he wouldn't want to press charges against me.

I crumpled to the floor. My wails were so loud, I didn't even recognize them as coming from me. I felt as if my heart had been broken in pieces. It wasn't the first time that Ronald had hurt me, but this was the ultimate. I now knew that all my years of work had been in vain. And I didn't know if I could go on with that knowledge.

I got up from the floor and went into the bathroom. He was still in the kitchen trying to stop

the blood flowing from his arm. I went straight
to the medicine cabinet. I was done with this life
that refused to treat me fairly.

I wasn't a bad person. In fact, I had spent so
many years in service to others, if this was the
thanks that I got. I was done. I didn't have anything else to live for. His children were grown,
and I was going to wind up an old maid thanks
to his trifling ass.

Ronald was still in the kitchen cussing, but
he wasn't running up behind me to get even. I
guessed that was a blessing. I wanted to leave
this world, but I wanted to do it on my terms. I
went through the cabinet looking for the most
lethal medicine I could find.

"Ain't this a bitch." There was nothing in there
stronger than an aspirin. I didn't know what I
thought I would find since I wasn't into popping
pills or any hard drugs now that I'd managed
to get clean. That was another thing that I did
for Ronald's stinking ass. When he was slinging
coke, I was high all the time. I raced back into the
kitchen to see if he had anything in his pockets
that would help me out, but he had already left
the house. I followed the trail of his dripping
blood all the way out to the parking lot. He was
gone. I went back inside.

Fear set in at this point. I was going to jail for sure. After all the dirt and shit I'd done, I was going to finally see the other side of a jail cell. "Lord, I'm sorry but he made me do it," I wailed as I once again fell to my knees on the kitchen floor. Above all, I didn't want to go to jail. I didn't want to have to fight off some lesbo bitches trying to make an example of me.

"I talk a lot of shit, Lord, but I'm a coward." Once I realized that I didn't have anything in the house that would allow me to leave this world painlessly, other ideas started floating in my head. Ronald left for the hospital and with that the police would be en route to my house. I called my best friend.

"Tabatha, I need to come over. Are you busy?"

"No, I'm just chilling. Do you want to order some pizza and veg out?"

"That sounds good to me, I'm on my way." I wasn't the least bit hungry, but I needed to get away from this house just in case the cops were lining up to get me. Eventually, I knew I would have to face the music, but I wasn't ready to do so right now.

Tabatha said, "Stop and get some beer, too."

I almost told her what was really going on, but I didn't want to admit to it over the phone. I had hit Ronald pretty hard. "I've got to get the fuck out of here." I rushed into my room and grabbed several outfits that would hold me for a couple of days. I wouldn't be able to stay there long because if Ronald lived, he knew exactly where Tabatha lived. If I was going to jail, I was going to go on my terms with my own lawyer and bond practically set before I got there.

I don't know what made me make the call, but I decided to call my daughter-in-law as I was leaving the house. "Hello, can I speak to Cojo, please?"

"Who is this?" Cojo asked.

"Gina."

"I'm sorry, Ms. Meadows, I didn't recognize your voice."

"It's okay, sweetie, we don't talk often."

I held the phone away from my face shocked that she was being nice but I realixed Merlin must have told her about our talk. "I know, I've been a real bitch to you, and I would like a second chance. Do you think we could try that?" I knew my time was running out, but I wanted to at least put that shit behind me.

"Are you serious? I would like nothing more. I could use a mother figure in my life."

"Mother figure? I didn't say all that, but I would like to try." I laughed. I never thought this would be possible between us.

"I'd like to try too."

***

"Girl, what the hell is the matter? You look like shit."

I pushed past Tabatha into her apartment. I didn't need her to remind me about how bad I looked. I was on the run and looking good was the least of my concerns.

"Shut the door, you're letting out all this air conditioning." I was trying to decide how much of the drama I was going to mention. I took a seat on the sofa as she shut and locked the door.

"You still haven't answered me. What the hell is going on?"

"Uh . . ." I was still shaking and nervous as hell.

"Uh, hell. Spill it, girl. You know you can't keep shit to yourself for long."

She was wrong there. I'd kept a lot of stuff from her over the years, and if I told her any of it, I would have to tell it all.

"It's all good. I just had to leave the house before I went stir crazy."

"Stop bullshitting me and tell me what is really going on."

I started to cry again, and she came over and wrapped her arms around me. She didn't press me to talk. I just rocked in her arms until I got my emotions under control.

"It's kind of a long story," I said.

"Can I get the abbreviated version?"

I pushed away and moved over to the other side of the sofa. She was watching *Jerry Springer* on television. And, for a second, I got caught up in all the drama on the set.

"Ronald finally agreed to move home. I've been meeting with builders to design a house for us, and we did the final walk-through last week. He said we were going to move in next week."

"I know I should be happy for you, but you know how I feel about him."

"I know. And as much as I hate to admit it, you were right."

"Say what?" She raised a brow.

"Yeah, he was lying to me all along."

"What did he do?" Her voice was pinched, like she was about to go off on his ass.

"I jumped the gun. I was so excited about the new house and the new furniture that he let me pick out that I went home right after the walk-through and started packing. I didn't realize that I'd accumulated so much shit. I had so many boxes, I couldn't even walk through my apartment. So I had the bright idea of taking some of the boxes to the house and dropping them off."

"Okay, that sounds reasonable."

"It sounded good to me too. I went to the house and the guard let me in because I hadn't had the chance to get a key yet."

"Let me guess, the house is in his name only."

"Yeah, but he said it was because my credit was less than perfect. Anyway, I get to the house and the door is unlocked because the furniture people were still delivering furniture. I go in and start dropping boxes and this heifer I'd never seen before comes out of the kitchen. I thought she was someone that Ronald hired to decorate."

"Oh, shit."

"You can say that again. I asked who she was and she said Ronald's wife."

"Damn, now that's some foul shit."

"I've never been so embarrassed in my life. I hightailed it out of there. I didn't even have the strength to get back my boxes. I told her to keep the shit."

"Damn."

"You said that."

"Shit, I don't know what to say. I knew the motherfucker was lowdown, but even I didn't think he was that low."

"Well, go on and say it," I said.

"Say what?"

"I told you so."

"Sweetie, I was kidding when I said that. There is no way I would taunt you like that after something this traumatic happened to you."

She surprised me. I just knew those would be the first words out of her mouth, that was why I hesitated to even tell her about it. She moved closer to me.

I said, "Needless to say, I've been a raging bitch for the last two days."

"Have you spoken with the bastard?"

"He had the nerve to show up today with my boxes and it wasn't pretty."

"I'll bet. I would have chopped off his dick," she said, laughing.

"I didn't get his dick, but I damn sure got his arm."

"What did you say?" She leaned in closer so that our faces were practically touching.

I could see tears welling up in her eyes. "You heard me. I asked him why, and he started telling me some lame-ass shit, and I grabbed the biggest knife I could find and I swung at him."

"Oh, God!" She fell back against the sofa as if I'd hit her too.

"I got his ass good, too, but now I'm afraid that I will go to jail."

"Oh, no, boo. This can't be happening. Why did you even let his sorry ass in?"

"Because I had to know why he did that to me. If he didn't want me to live with him, why would he keep filling my head up with that nonsense? Why take me shopping to furnish a house that I would never live in?"

"That rat bastard. He can't just play with your heart like that." She shook her head.

"He doesn't care. You've told me that for years, but I was too much in love to listen to you. I always thought that I would be the one he married and I just snapped."

"Sweetie, you have to go home. If Ronald went to the cops and you've left the scene, it will only make you look more guilty. If you go home and the police come, plead temporary insanity. Once you tell them all the shit he has put you through, I'm sure no jury will convict you."

"I can't go to jail! I am not about to fight off some butch-ass bitch and wind up spending the rest of my life behind bars."

"Relax, honey, they will just arrest you and then you get arraigned. Since you have no priors, they will give you bail. I will be waiting to post bail, then we get you the best lawyer we can afford to go to court with you."

"We?"

"Girl, you are like a sister to me. Do you think I would let you go through this by yourself?"

"Thanks, Tabatha. I know I don't deserve it, but I'm glad you are my friend."

"Go home and call me when you get your first phone call." Tabatha made a lot of sense.

As much as I didn't want to, I drove home.

CHAPTER FIFTY-FIVE

COJO MILLS

I hadn't heard from Merlin since his arrest the week before, and it was taking its toll on me. I needed information, but the cops refused to speak with me about his case. I hired an attorney, but thus far, he hadn't furnished any information.

I called his attorney once again to get an update.

"Mosby Law Group."

"Yes, I would like to speak with Attorney Ricardo Mosby."

"Ma'am, he is not in the office at the moment but I do expect him. Would you like to leave a message?"

"Yes, would you please tell him that Cojo Mills called, and I would like an update on my husband's case."

"I will give him the message."

I hung up the phone, frustrated. I felt a pain deep down in my soul, and I knew that the only way to fix it was to have my husband home with me.

What happened to the phone call he was entitled to make? The phone had been ringing off the hook since the news started broadcasting his arrest, but none of the calls were from my husband.

I knew this stress wasn't good for our baby, but I didn't know what else to do but worry and cry. This wasn't like the first time that he was led out of the house in handcuffs; this was serious. They were charging him with attempted murder and arson.

For the life of me, I couldn't understand why they would accuse my mild-mannered husband of such a heinous crime. Over the last few days, Merlin's mother had called, but I couldn't speak to her because I didn't know what the circumstances were of his alleged crimes. Even with my wild imagination, I could not imagine Merlin setting a person on fire.

I was pacing the living room floor crying when the doorbell rang. I rushed to it and yanked open the door. I was so distraught I didn't even bother to check who was on the other side of the door. I gasped when I saw who was standing there. "Merlin?"

"Try again, sweetheart." Gavin wore a sickening grin on his face.

He was the last person I wanted to see, especially since I was in such a vulnerable state of mind.

"What are you doing here? Didn't Merlin tell you to stay the fuck away from us?" I was mad, but I could not deny the sexual attraction that I felt just looking at his wonderful body.

"I know, and under normal circumstances, I would have stayed away, but I was concerned about how you were holding up."

I stepped back from the door. I didn't expect Gavin to even care about his brother after all the things that Merlin had told me.

Gavin stepped into the apartment and closed the door behind him. I looked at him suspiciously. Today, he was different. He didn't have the arrogant swagger. He actually acted as if he cared about me and Merlin. Ever since he had come into our lives, it had been nothing but turmoil. I needed my life to get back on an even keel.

"I saw it on the news and I just had to come."

"Oh, God." Fresh tears rolled down my face. I didn't like the fact that our dirty laundry was being viewed on television.

Gavin rushed toward me and took me in his arms. Instinctively, I tensed up, but I couldn't hold on to that because it felt good in his arms. As much as I wanted to deny it, I was sexually attracted to Gavin. He continued to hold me in his arms and, for a minute, I relaxed and allowed him to comfort me. His hot breath against my neck excited me. It took me several minutes to remember that he wasn't my husband and his arms should not be around me.

I pulled away. "Gavin, you need to leave. When Merlin comes home, he won't be happy to see you here."

"Cojo, he may not be coming home."

A low moan escaped my lips. "Merlin is innocent." I tried saying it with conviction, but my delivery was weak.

"Are you sure? The police wouldn't have arrested him if they didn't feel like they had a good case against him."

I pushed away from him and started pacing the floor. Gavin was taking me to a place that I didn't want to go. What would I do if they actually kept my husband in jail?

"Why are you here?" I demanded.

"I came for you. Regardless of whether or not you are ready to accept this, we connected. I don't want my brother to spoil another relationship for me."

I looked at him as if he had lost his happy mind. "What are you talking about?"

"This is not the first relationship that I've had that my brother ruined. He killed my first girlfriend and fingered me in the scheme and I wound up doing time."

"Huh?" I was so confused.

"My first girlfriend. He killed her and fingered me. I did seven years in prison behind that shit, but I still have mad love for my brother."

"Wait, I don't understand. He said that you blamed him and he got arrested." I was feeling dizzy so I sat down on the sofa.

"Of course he would tell you that. It wasn't me, it was really him. He has a violent temper. Remember when he tried to choke you?"

"He had every right to be mad, I slept with his brother."

"So why did he take it out on you and not me?" He sat back on the sofa with a smug smirk on his face.

I was so confused I didn't know what to think. Suddenly, I wasn't so sure of my convictions that Merlin was innocent. I remembered the night when he left the house in the middle of the night and came home with blood on his clothes and refused to speak about it. That was the same night of the house fire.

Gavin came over to the couch and sat next to me. "Things aren't always the way they seem. You need to hear both sides of the story." He planted a seed, and I had enough water at my feet to make it grow.

"Cojo, I think we belong together and this is God's way of making sure it happens."

I jumped up off the sofa again. Gavin was talking some bullshit. How in the world was I going to abandon my relationship with Merlin and take up with his brother?

"Merlin has lied to you, Cojo. I know my brother. He probably tried to blame me for all the shit he's done over the years, but it isn't true."

"I need to lie down." I left the living room and went into the master bedroom. My mind was on overload, and I didn't know what to believe. I didn't even consider the fact that I shouldn't have allowed Gavin to stay. I just needed to be by myself so I could think.

"I don't think that you should be alone. Can I stay here until we know more about Merlin's case?"

"I don't care." I wasn't thinking straight. Gavin had me thinking that I didn't know my husband at all.

"I'm going to go and get some clothes. I will be back." He followed me into the bedroom and kissed me on the forehead. There was nothing sexual in the kiss.

"Let me hold your key so I won't have to disturb you when I come back." I reached into my bag and pulled out my key. I wasn't thinking straight. My mind was on overload. I passed the key to Gavin and climbed into the bed with my clothes still on.

"Okay." My mind had shut down. I needed to think about my relationship with my husband. Who was this man I married? At this point, I was having second thoughts about having a child at all.

I'm not sure when Gavin came back. I'd been sleeping off and on since he left, but I felt him when he climbed into the bed with me. At first, I thought he was Merlin, but I recognized Gavin's distinctive smell. My body tensed as Gavin eased up to me.

"Gavin, stop," I didn't have the energy to fight him and I couldn't deny the attraction I felt for him.

"I just want to comfort you."

"This is wrong. The first time was a mistake but if we do it again, it's intentional," I said.

"Well, I'm going to keep it one hundred with you. Getting with you again is definitely intentional with me. I know we are destined to be together so I'm not even going to lie." His words shocked me and I turned around in his embrace.

"What do you mean?" I asked.

"Have you heard Jaheim's new song, 'Ain't Leaving Without You'?" He summed it up in a nutshell: I ain't leaving without you. Part of me was flattered, but the rest of me was scared as hell. His lips dipped dangerously close to mine, and for a second or two, I allowed myself to dwell in the fantasy.

I was tired and didn't try to fight him. Truth be told, I wanted to get another opportunity to be with Gavin, but I didn't know how to admit it. Merlin's arrest offered the perfect opportunity.

I allowed Gavin to peel off my clothes. I tried to pretend like I was asleep, but I was aware of everything that was going on around me. I stifled a gasp when he took my extended nipple into his mouth.

"I want you so bad," Gavin whispered as he positioned himself to enter me. I kept my eyes closed, as if this would protect me from committing adultery a second time with my husband's brother. I knew that I was dead wrong, but I couldn't stop myself. Gavin was right: we did connect in a way that Merlin and I never did.

He spread my legs and positioned himself between mine. Without any fanfare, he inserted his dick into my vagina and I could not believe the intensity of the feeling that I felt when he gently rocked his dick into me. The feeling was intense. There was no need for foreplay; I was already into the moment the second he had taken off my clothes. I never felt so close to a man in my entire life. We rocked this way for twenty minutes before he busted a nut inside of me. The entire time, I kept my eyes closed.

"Damn, that was amazing." The words spilled out of my mouth without my permission, but Gavin heard them.

CHAPTER FIFTY-SIX

COJO MILLS

My phone rang. "Cojo, I really need to speak with you. Are you alone?" Braxton, my husband's closest friend, said from the other end of the line.

"Hey, Braxton." I was trying to wake up. Gavin and I had had sex so many times, I was still feeling woozy.

"I drove by your house a while ago. What is Gavin doing over there?" Immediately, I began to feel nervous. This was not how I had expected our conversation to go.

"Ah . . . he came over to see if he could do anything while Merlin was locked up." I knew this was a piss poor example.

"Cojo, be careful, there is a lot about Gavin that you probably don't even know."

"Well, according to Gavin, there is a lot of things that I don't know about Merlin."

"Don't get caught up in his hype, he is a born con man. He is good at deceiving folks." I was tired of the lies and since I could not speak to Merlin directly, I needed to have some answers.

"Braxton, if you know so much, could you please tell me what is going on?" I tiptoed out of the bedroom to see where Gavin was, but it appeared as if he'd left.

"Cojo, normally I would mind my fucking business but this shit is scaring me. A couple of months ago, I saw Merlin's car and followed it. He went to the same woman's house who got killed. When I spoke to Merlin, he informed me that Gavin was driving the car during that time. Gavin is dangerous."

I was nervous as hell. I would have gone straight to the cops if I knew for sure where Gavin was. I had a doctor's appointment and he always appeared at them. I can't believe I let him trick me twice. The waiting room was crowded. If I didn't want to know the results as badly as I did, I might have left, but I took a seat and pulled a novel from my purse and started to read. I was really trying not to think about what Braxton told me. I wasn't here for a checkup, so I hoped they would call me soon to give me the results. As I waited, I got lost in my newest read, *The Cartel*, by Ashley & JaQuavis. This was the first novel that I'd read by them. So far it was holding my attention, which said a lot with everything going on.

My intent was to finish the book, but my body had other ideas. I quickly drifted off to sleep. The vitamins I had been given weren't doing anything to give me more energy.

"Cojo Mills?"

I woke up and realized that they were talking to me. "I'm sorry, here I am." I looked around the waiting room and it was deserted except for me. I glanced at my watch and realized that I had been there for over an hour.

"Come this way," a nurse instructed.

"Can I go to the bathroom first?" I had to go the second I stood up.

"Of course." She smiled at me as she directed me to the bathroom. "The doctor will see you in his office."

My nerves started to get the best of me again. Part of me wanted to walk right out of the office and let the chips fall where they may. Regardless of the outcome, I wasn't going to abort the baby, so what difference did it make?

"'Cause you owe it to Merlin," I said softly.

He deserved to know and so did our unborn child. As much as I hated to think about Gavin as the father, I would tell him if the results indicated that he was. I would even allow him to have a small portion of my child's life, but I would fight him like a banshee if he attempted to get any form of custody.

I finished up in the bathroom and went into the doctor's office to wait again. "I wish doctors cared enough about our time as we have to care about their time." I started to read my book again and before I knew it, I was sleep again.

"Mrs. Mills?" This time it was a male voice that was interrupting my nap.

I wiped the drool that had seeped out of my mouth and sat up in my seat. "I'm sorry," I offered the apology, but what I really wanted to say was that I wouldn't have fallen asleep if he had scheduled his time better to not have me wait so long.

"There's no need to apologize. I'm sorry for the delay, but we've had a couple of emergencies today."

He must have been reading my mind because I had half a mind to tell him he couldn't just let a pregnant woman sit.

"Can I go to the bathroom?"

"Sure, there is one right through that door. I'll be here waiting for you."

I was feeling a little self-conscious because he knew the results of my test and I didn't.

Does he think I'm a whore because I had to get a test to find out who my baby's daddy was? I dismissed the thought as I flushed the toilet. I didn't owe him any explanations. He was going to get paid regardless of who the father of my child was. But I still held on to the hope that Merlin was the father.

"Your husband won't be joining you today?" I could not tell if he was being condescending, and it made me nervous all over again. Had he seen Merlin on the news?

"No, he was busy at work. Can we do this before I have to go to the bathroom again?"

He opened the file that he had on his desk and studied it for a moment. "Your husband . . . is the father." He paused for dramatic effect.

At first I didn't understand what he said because I was so afraid that Gavin was the child's father, but slowly his words sank in. In the back of my mind, I knew there was still a possibility that Gavin could have fathered the child, but for the moment I was ejecting this from my memory banks.

"Are you sure?"

"As sure as we can be with identical twins."

I jumped up and ran to the door. I couldn't wait to go to the jail and tell Merlin the good news. "Are you done with me?"

"Yes, I will see you next month. Take care of yourself and don't overdo it."

"I won't, Doctor, and thanks." I snatched open the door and practically danced all the way to the parking lot. I rummaged through my purse to find my keys and my phone, but I kept pulling out everything else.

I couldn't wait to tell Merlin the good news. Braxton went to the cops and they were checking out his story. Hopefully, Detective Adams would be able to get Merlin out of jail so that we could celebrate in a major way. I was practically bouncing, and all the weight that I'd been carrying on my shoulders felt like it had been lifted.

"Shit." A hand was placed rudely over my mouth, and I was dragged away from my car kicking and struggling to scream.

CHAPTER FIFTY-SEVEN

MERLIN MILLS

"Braxton I think something is wrong. I had been calling Cojo for the last few hours and it kept going straight to voice mail. I've got to go home to be with my wife." As we were running to Braxton's car, I dialed my mother. I needed to know if she knew where Gavin was.

"Hey, Mom, I can't get in touch with Cojo. Have you talked to her by any chance?" I hadn't told her that Gavin had slept with my wife.

Gina said, "Are you okay in there?"

"It was a big misunderstanding. Thanks to Braxton, I just got released. I'll explain that later, though. So have you talked to my wife?"

"Yeah, we had a nice conversation, and I'm looking forward to spending time with her. I have something to tell you, do you think you could drop by my house?"

I was torn. I wanted to find out what was up with Cojo. I was also curious as to why my mother wanted to see me. Since we were just rebuilding our relationship, I thought it was important that I go over there.

"Okay, I can come over there, but I can't stay long. I want to see Cojo."

"It won't take long." She sounded strange, but I quickly dismissed the thought because we hadn't been close in years and she could have changed.

"I'm on my way."

"If you get there before me, wait for me. If the police are there, call me."

"Police, what are you talking about?" I paused. "It's Gavin, isn't it? He's done it again."

"I'll explain when I get there." She hung up the phone without giving me any more details.

I believed yet couldn't believe that Braxton had seen my car at the home of someone who was almost killed in a fire. That motherfucker Gavin. I just hoped the cops caught up with him before he went around my wife again.

"Oh, shit." I tried to call Cojo again to let her know I needed to stop by my mother's house before I came home, but her phone went straight to voice mail. "Damn, where is she?"

CHAPTER FIFTY-EIGHT

GINA MEADOWS

I managed to make it to the house before Merlin and at least comb my hair and wash my face. I didn't want anyone else commenting on how bad I looked, especially my son, who I had just formed a new relationship with.

"Hey," he said when I opened the door.

"Hi, come on in." I was trying to think of the best way to tell him all that had happened in the last twenty-four hours. I was stuck. I wasn't used to confiding in anyone. Since I had been excluded from Merlin's life for so long, I didn't know how he felt about his father and how he would react.

"I actually came over here a couple of weeks ago to see Gavin, but neither of you were home."

"Why didn't you call?"

"I didn't have your number in my cell."

I could understand that I could not blame him for anything because I wasn't the best stepmother that I could have been. In the beginning, I was gold, but Ronald changed me and it affected the way I dealt with his kids. "I understand. So why are you suddenly interested in your brother? And how did you get out of jail?" I knew I should have been talking about my situation, but I was grateful to have the focus off me for a minute.

"Trust and believe, I couldn't care less about Gavin, but several things have happened that I'm sure you're not aware of. Gavin is the reason I was in jail. He tried to set me up again."

Gina's eyes widened. "Please tell me he isn't responsible for that girl getting hurt in the fire? I knew you couldn't have anything to do with that."

He said, "I think so, is he still staying here with you?"

"He was but he moved out and I haven't seen him in a few weeks." Gina paused. "He didn't come here the night of that fire. I'm sure of that."

There was an urgent knock on the door. It was a nigga-knock, and it scared the shit out of me and Merlin. Merlin started toward the door.

"Merlin, wait before you answer the door, there is something else that I have to tell you."

Whoever was there knocked again, this time more violently.

"What is it?" Merlin asked.

"I stabbed your father and that's probably the police to arrest me."

He staggered, and I lunged to catch him.

"You did what?"

I didn't bother to answer him. I just went to the door. If this was my time, I was ready to get it over with. I peeked through the peephole, and sure enough, it was the cops. My heart started beating really fast and sweat popped out on my brow. I didn't expect them this soon.

"Is it the cops?" Merlin whispered.

"Yes," I said as I unlocked the door. Part of me was relieved that I could get this behind me, but the other half was scared as shit that I was going to spend the rest of my life behind bars.

CHAPTER FIFTY-NINE

MERLIN MILLS

My mind was melting down. I had just received too much information in too short an amount of time. First I learned that Gavin set me up again, and that my mother stabbed my dad. "What the fuck?"

I watched my mother open the door and two armed officers entered her apartment. It wasn't until they had come into the room that I noticed all the boxes packed from floor to ceiling.

"Can I help you?" my mother asked.

Even if she had become a bitch over the last ten years, she still was the only one who showed me love as I was growing up, and the thought of her going to jail made my heart hurt. My real mother had left me on her doorstep, and I hadn't seen her since I was three.

"Good afternoon. We are here looking for information about Gavin Mills."

She exhaled deeply; it was clear to me that she thought they were there for her.

I could not wait to hear why she stabbed my father and if he was still alive.

"What type of information?" I probably would not have come off that way with the cops, but Gina was under a lot of pressure. In light of what I had just gone through with cops, my patience was wearing thin.

"Does he live here with you?" a black cop asked.

"He did, but I think he may have moved because I haven't seen him in at least two weeks." My mother said.

The white cop asked, "He didn't tell you he was moving out?"

"His moving in was a temporary situation that neither of us were happy about."

"I see. Do you have any way to contact him?"

The black officer was busy looking around my mother's apartment, and didn't appear to be following the conversation. He kept staring at me. Finally, he pulled out a picture. "You look very much like the person we are looking for."

Shit, the last thing I needed was to be dragged into Gavin's bullshit again. I reached into my back pocket to pull out my wallet and the officer immediately pulled out his gun. "Wait, hold up. I wasn't thinking. Gavin is my twin brother and

I was reaching for my wallet. Call Detectives Adams and Lyle. I know why you're here. I was arrested for it the week before last. I was released when they found out they were looking for Gavin and not me.

He didn't lower his gun until he had read my name off my license. He gave it back to me slowly. "Do you know where your brother is?"

"I actually came over here to ask my mother where he was." That wasn't the only reason that I was here, but it worked so I was sticking to it.

My mother said, "Could somebody tell me what's really going on with Gavin?"

The black officer said, "We're not at liberty to talk about it, but we need to speak to him as soon as possible."

"Mom, I can explain everything."

All eyes turned to me.

"Oh, really?" the white cop said.

"Yeah." I retold the story that Braxton told to me and the detectives, and I didn't feel bad.

The black cop turned to my mother. "Mind if I use your phone to call the station?"

When he hung up, he said, "You were right. We did get an eyewitness account from your friend. Detectives Adams and Lyle are investigating, and since this isn't the first time that Gavin has been charged with violent crimes again women, the department has given the case high priority."

I said, "I need to add something to the case. And while it is not a crime, I'm concerned about it. In the first case that you are talking about, my brother claimed he was me and I got arrested then too. Recently, he fooled my wife into thinking he was me and had sex with her. Since then, he's been hanging around my house stalking us."

"Merlin, no! Please tell me that isn't true," my mother cried.

"Sorry, Momma. This was one of the reasons that I came to talk to you today. I wanted to let you know in case he should up over here."

"He's been asking me questions about your wife."

The officers looked confused as if we had given them more information than they came to collect.

"Where is your wife now? Will she corroborate what you told us here today?"

"I hope Gavin hasn't done anything to her."

"What type of car does he drive?" the white cop asked. "I just want to verify that make and model again."

"He's driving my old car. It's a 2002 Malibu. Brown, with a dent on the back door. The plate number is JE619."

"I'll call in the APB," the white cop said.

"Wait, there may be a better way to find him. OnStar. It comes standard on some models, but my car was the type that people loved to steal so I added it to my car. All we need to do is call them and they will tell us where the car is. As long as he is near the car, we will find him."

"Officer, I'm so afraid that he may have my wife. She always answers her phone and—"

"Calm down, Mr. Mills. If he has her, we'll find him."

Gina said, "I just don't understand that boy. He's been a handful since the first day he was brought to my house. I'm so sorry I didn't do better, Merlin, to protect you from him, but I honestly didn't know he was capable of this."

"It's not your fault, Mother. Perhaps if our dad had been around more, things would have been different."

It appeared as if my mother went into a trance or something because her eyes got this blank stare. She swayed before me, and I moved closer to support her.

"We found the car," the black officer said after getting off the phone with OnStar.

"Can we come with you? My wife is expecting a baby."

He nodded. "That is totally against regulations, but if you just happened to follow us, well, there's no law against that." He smiled.

I quickly grabbed my mother's hand and followed the officers out the door.

As we were buckling up our seatbelts, I said a prayer. "Lord, if he has her, please make sure she is all right."

"Amen," my mother replied, and looked at me. "Why am I feeling like I did when I was pregnant?"

"What do you mean?"

"I'm feeling"—she rolled her window down—"morning sickness. I feel like I'm about to throw up."

I shrugged. "Probably because you've been doing the nasty. Imagine you being pregnant at your age."

"Yeah, imagine that. I'm fucking forty years old and now this!" She held her stomach. "And I have not been doing the nasty with anyone in a long time."

"Then, you're not having morning sickness. It's probably just stress."

She threw up in my lap.

CHAPTER SIXTY

GAVIN MILLS

Cojo came out of the doctor's office practically dancing. That could only mean one thing: I wasn't the father. I watched her in disbelief because I was so sure that I had planted a seed in her. Something in me snapped, and she was acting weird earlier. I leaped from my car and snuck up behind her.

I looked around to see if there were any witnesses. I didn't know what I was going to do, but I knew that I needed to speak with her and plead my case. I slipped my hand around her mouth and dragged her away from her car and into mine. Roughly, I pushed her into the back seat and climbed in after her.

"What the hell do you think you are doing?" she yelled. "You'd better let me the fuck go."

I locked the doors. "Not until I've had a chance to talk to you."

She came at me like a caged animal scratching and kicking. I wasn't prepared for her attack. She was punching me like a man. Before I knew it, I punched her back and knocked her out. Luckily there was no one around or I would have been in jail.

"Damn, baby, I didn't mean to hit you," I whispered to her unconscious body. I quickly got into the front seat and drove to the Alamo, a seedy motel. I planned to use the room to plead my case. I checked in, and carried her into the room. While she was asleep, I got some duct tape from my trunk and taped her wrists to the headboard. For good measure, I placed a piece across her mouth to keep her quiet.

Her eye was swelling up, which reminded me of the last time that I saw her that way, but this time I caused it. The last time it was her jaw, but seeing her face all swollen affected me just the same. I went into the bathroom and looked at my reflection. I had railroad track–type scratches down both sides of my face. It immediately made me mad. Part of me wanted to go into the bedroom and strip her clothes off and fuck her into submission, but my intent wasn't to make her madder. I just wanted to have the opportunity to speak to her and tell her how much I loved her.

I wanted to tell her how well I was doing at the strip club and explain what I would do for her if she would agree to be my wife. I wanted her to know that the last three days were the best of my life. We bonded in a way that I didn't know existed and the sex was incredible. My eyes wandered again to my face, and I snapped again.

"How dare she do this to me?" I ran back into the bedroom and began to hit her repeatedly. I felt like a child again receiving a whupping. For the first time, I was able to defend myself.

She woke up and started to fight back as best she could with her hands bound. I was out of control, but could do nothing to rein myself back in.

"Settle down, bitch," I snarled. I was still mad at her, but I needed to find out if the baby was mine.

She was crying profusely and so was I. Her eyes widened as if she had just realized who I was. She started bucking against the bed even more. "Are you trying to hurt our baby?" I demanded.

A calm came over me. I was ready to convince her that I was a better husband than my brother. She stopped bucking immediately.

I reached over and rubbed the slight bulge that she was developing. "Pregnant women are so sexy in the early months." I was trying to let her know that I would be supportive of her gaining weight. I unbuttoned the first two buttons of her blouse. She started to cry even more and this made me upset.

With an open hand, I smacked her across the face. "What the hell you crying for?" This was so unlike earlier when I held her. Even though I hadn't penetrated her again, we had developed a closeness, and that was rare. She didn't pull away when I touched her. She continued to cry. I did not understand why she was acting so strangely.

"Hell, I should be crying too. Look what you did to my face. How am I going to explain this shit?"

Her tears stopped. She followed my every move with dilated eyes.

"Did I scare you?"

She didn't answer right away, but after a few seconds she nodded and something in me cracked. My heart moved and my anger disappeared.

"I didn't mean to scare you and I'm sorry I put my hands on you, but you confused me when you attacked me. I just needed to speak with you alone. I could tell that something changed between us when I came to your house today, right when everything was perfect. Do you know how badly I want to touch you, taste you, feel you?"

Her eyes got wider.

"Yes, I was staking out your apartment but my intentions were good. I saw Braxton leave today. You see, I've not been able to get you out of my mind since the first time I slept with you, and after the last few days of closeness, I can't wait to sleep with you again. Am I wrong for wanting to feel that from you again? Can you deny the energy between us?" I removed the tape from her mouth.

"Did you forget I'm already married."

This was not what I wanted to hear from her, and I had to stop myself from punching her in the fucking face again. I was still going to have to go slow with her, but with Merlin locked up, I had time. "I want to let you go, but you've got to promise me that you are going to behave."

She just looked at me as if I were speaking a different language.

"Did you hear what I just said?" I raised my voice because I was getting tired of this whole episode. I wasn't used to having to woo women. Normally, women flocked to me. This was the first time that I actually cared enough to put my best foot forward. Cojo shook her head, and I took that to mean she would cooperate. I let one hand loose.

"Ouch," she yelled.

"I done told you, you need to be quiet."

She nodded again. I was about to release her other hand, but she hadn't proven to me that she was going to fully cooperate with me yet.

"What do you want?"

"That's easy. I want you, and if you are honest with yourself, you would realize that you want me too. I want to kiss you, taste you, and lick you. After the time we spent together, I know you love me." I was prepared for her initial denial, but it didn't come.

"What about your brother? Are we gonna just let him rot away in jail, pretend like he doesn't exist?"

"My brother? Fuck my brother. This isn't about him and me, it's about us. We connected and you know we did."

She really pissed me off when she brought my brother in the room. I was sick and tired of people bringing my brother into my life. I'd spent the last seven years without a care in the world for him, and now, all of a sudden, he was in practically every conversation that I had and I was sick of it. I had half a mind to beat her ass to death just for mentioning him.

"But he's still my husband."

Damn, she had a point. For me, it was so easy to dismiss him; I forgot he had first dibs on the woman I wanted to claim as my own.

"So what did the doctor say?" I needed to change the subject so I could figure out a way to convince her that I was the man of her dreams and not my brother.

"How do you intend to support me and a baby?"

I started to get mad all over again. Everyone, including my mother, was focused on me working a nine-to-five. Why couldn't they understand that a nine-to-five job was not for me?

"There are other ways to support a family beside a nine-to-five."

"Oh, really? Name one."

"I could go into business for myself." I just pulled that answer out of my ass. She was not ready for the strip club.

"Doing what?" She had me there.

When I mentioned going into business, I was talking about going back to my old ways of robbing and stealing. "That ain't none of your business. I just want to know if you want to be with me or my brother."

"I know the truth now. I want to be with my husband."

I jumped up from the bed as my blood pressure rose. This was just another slap in the face. As much as I loved her, I couldn't allow my brother to walk into the sunshine with the love of his life. That just wasn't going to happen.

As I approached the bed to put Ms. Smarty Pants out of her misery, the door to my hotel room burst open. The noise startled both of us. Cojo started screaming as I backed up against the wall trying to find out what I was dealing with.

"Police, get down on the floor."

Son of a bitch, how did they find me? I slowly lowered myself onto the floor as my mind started thinking of a defense for being in a hotel room with my brother's wife bound to the bed. I would probably get at least ten years for kidnapping, but if I got a good lawyer it could possibly be reduced. I was going to enter a plea of temporary insanity.

The third person through the door was my brother. At that point, I knew that I was screwed because he would go above and beyond to make sure that I was locked away behind bars with no options of a release. For the first time in a long time, I prayed.

My hands were cuffed behind me. The first officer in the room began to read me my rights.

"Gavin Mills, you are being arrested for attempted murder, arson, and kidnapping."

"Shit!" *I wish that bitch would have burned to death.*

"You have the right to remain silent—"

"Fuck you."

The officer snatched at my cuffs hard enough to leave a gash. "I'd watch my mouth if I were you."

I turned my head and looked my brother in the face. He had a satisfied smirk on his face. I didn't realize that my mother was with him until I gritted on him. I wanted to tell him so badly how much I wanted to fuck his wife again, but seeing my mother shut my mouth. Admitting my intentions in front of the police wouldn't have been such a smart idea.

My mother said, "I'm ashamed of you. I can't believe that you could be this lowdown."

"Shut up, woman, you don't know anything about me." I didn't have to worry about holding my tongue now because she would not be supporting me. I was now custody of the state of Georgia, and I was quite sure they would not allow me bail.

"You're right, I don't know you. And if you want to take it a step further, I don't want to know you. You're an animal, and completely out of your mind. I would like to blame this on your father. But truth be told, it probably came from your hoodrat mother. I'm done with you. Do not, I repeat, do not call me again—ever!" My mother yelled.

"Oh, you're that type of bitch who would kick a brother when he was down? No wonder my father left you. Your pussy ain't that good, either." My mother lunged at me, and if it weren't for the armed cops in the room, I was sure she would have tried to kill me.

She said, "You lucky I can't get to you like I want to. But that's okay, you're about to get yours. I've done everything that I could and should do for you. You're a grown man now, and it's time to face the music for the things that you've done. And you don't have a clue what my pussy is like."

"Whatever, bitch." If she had any objection to being called a bitch it was lost on me, because I was roughly hauled to my feet and shuttled into the waiting police car. I saw Merlin rush to his wife from the corner of my eye and my heart ached. He won again.

CHAPTER SIXTY-ONE

MERLIN MILLS

"Sweetheart, are you okay?" I held Cojo in my arms.

"How did you find us?"

"Later. I just want to know if you and the baby are okay."

"We are fine. He hit me in the face to get me into the car, and slapped me around a few times. Other than that, he hasn't touched me."

I breathed a sigh of relief. I didn't know if I would have been able to handle it if my brother had sexed my wife twice. It was bad enough the first time, and I was still trying to get those images out of my mind. "Thank God!"

"I've got good news." She was smiling like there was no tomorrow, and it caused me to smile as well.

"What's that?" I started to work on untying her.

My mother was right by my side.

"It's your baby. The test results are ninety-nine percent accurate. I think that is what set your brother off 'cause he followed me to the doctor's office again."

"Sweetheart, I love you." I was happy about the news, but I still worried about what had happened from the time that he'd snatched her until now. Although I vowed to love the child, regardless of who the father was, I knew I would eventually have a problem with it that could jeopardize our relationship. I leaped in the air and screamed, pretending all was right with the world. "I'm gonna be a daddy!" With all the excitement, I forgot to finish untying my wife.

"Do you think you could untie me? I prayed that you would come and rescue me, but damn, my arms have become numb."

"I'm so sorry, sweetie. I just lost my head. You don't know how bad this whole thing has been stressing me."

"Let's not talk about stress, just unhook me. I've got to pee." When she was finally free, she hugged me and my mother then ran to the bathroom!

CHAPTER SIXTY-TWO

MERLIN MILLS

Cojo snuggled with me in our bed. Our interaction had been different since we started going to counseling. I was thankful and I was looking forward to the birth of our child. "I can understand now how you wanted to forget your brother. He's one piece of work."

"You don't know the half of it. He made all of our lives miserable, and I'm glad that he's finally off the streets."

"Well, I forgive you for not telling me about him. I might not have married you if I knew he was floating around in your gene pool."

"Are you serious?"

"Yeah, 'cause crazy doesn't fall far from the tree."

"That's not fair. We're brothers because we share the same parents, but I don't really know shit about them."

"Well, he is about to find out 'cause I just got off the phone with your momma and she don't want to have anything to do with him." She paused then said, "I love you."

"I love you too, boo, and our daughter." I rubbed her round belly. I felt like I was given a second chance at happiness. Everything was working out in my favor and I was thankful to God.

DISCUSSION QUESTIONS

1. Should Merlin have forgiven Gina?

2. Why didn't Merlin and Gavin confront Ronald?

3. Why did Gina continue to love Ronald?

4. Was Cojo a fool for trusting Gavin?

5. Why did Gavin continue to torment Merlin?

6. Why didn't Merlin take his anger out on Gavin instead of Cojo?

7. Should Cojo have left Merlin?

8. Do you believe Cojo and Merlin will live happily ever after?

9. Why did Braxton wait so long to speak to Cojo?

ABOUT THE AUTHOR

A native of Baltimore, Maryland currently residing in Covington Georgia, Tina wears many hats, as she balances her time among being wife, mother, talk show hostess/interviewer, and the creative force behind the drama trilogy: *All That Drama* in 2004, *Lawd, Mo' Drama* in 2007, and, *Fool, Stop Trippin'* in 2008. All are published under the imprint of Strebor Books, a division of Simon & Schuster's Atria Books.

Deep Deceptions was the first book published with her new publisher, Urban Books, LLC, under the Urban Renaissance imprint and it released in November 2009. Tina is currently working on the sequel to *Deep Deceptions II*.

As an avid reader, taking in everything she could get her hands on, Tina decided to share her love of books with the world by hosting an Internet radio show called *Real Talk With Tina Brooks McKinney*. Tina's show focuses on both traditional and self-published authors whose voices are seldom heard. To learn more about this show, log onto: www.blogtalkradio.com/tinabrooksmckinney. The show airs on Tuesday nights at 7:00 EST, but previous shows are available in the archives.

Tina uses fictional characters to address real issues occurring in the world. Known for her "tell it like it is" banter, Tina hopes to enlighten and entertain her reading audience. Thus far, she has been successful.

Tina loves to interact with her readers and is always interested in meeting more of them. You can contact Tina at tybrooks2@yahoo.com. She is also available for book club meetings, chats, and conferences. Check her tour page to see if she is coming to a City near you!

www.tinamckinney.com

Notes

Notes

ORDER FORM
URBAN BOOKS, LLC
78 E. Industry Ct
Deer Park, NY 11729

Name: (please print):_____

Address:_____

City/State:_____

Zip:_____

QTY	TITLES	PRICE
	16 On The Block	$14.95
	A Girl From Flint	$14.95
	A Pimp's Life	$14.95
	Baltimore Chronicles	$14.95
	Baltimore Chronicles 2	$14.95
	Betrayal	$14.95
	Black Diamond	$14.95

Shipping and handling add $3.50 for 1st book, then $1.75 for each additional book. Please send a check payable to:

Urban Books, LLC

Please allow 4-6 weeks for delivery

ORDER FORM
URBAN BOOKS, LLC
78 E. Industry Ct
Deer Park, NY 11729

Name: (please print):_____

Address:_____

City/State:_____

Zip:_____

QTY	TITLES	PRICE
	Black Diamond 2	$14.95
	Black Friday	$14.95
	Both Sides Of The Fence	$14.95
	Both Sides Of The Fence 2	$14.95
	California Connection	$14.95
	California Connection 2	$14.95

Shipping and handling add $3.50 for 1st book, then $1.75 for each additional book. Please send a check payable to:

Urban Books, LLC

Please allow 4-6 weeks for delivery

ORDER FORM
URBAN BOOKS, LLC
78 E. Industry Ct
Deer Park, NY 11729

Name: (please print):_____

Address:_____

City/State:_____

Zip:_____

QTY	TITLES	PRICE
	Cheesecake And Teardrops	$14.95
	Congratulations	$14.95
	Crazy In Love	$14.95
	Cyber Case	$14.95
	Denim Diaries	$14.95
	Diary Of A Mad First Lady	$14.95
	Diary Of A Stalker	$14.95

Shipping and handling add $3.50 for 1st book, then $1.75 for each additional book. Please send a check payable to:

Urban Books, LLC

Please allow 4-6 weeks for delivery

ORDER FORM
URBAN BOOKS, LLC
78 E. Industry Ct
Deer Park, NY 11729

Name: (please print):_____

Address:_____

City/State:_____

Zip:_____

QTY	TITLES	PRICE
	Diary Of A Street Diva	$14.95
	Diary Of A Young Girl	$14.95
	Dirty Money	$14.95
	Dirty To The Grave	$14.95
	Gunz And Roses	$14.95
	Happily Ever Now	$14.95
	Hell Has No Fury	$14.95

Shipping and handling-add $3.50 for 1st book, then $1.75 for each additional book.
Please send a check payable to:

Urban Books, LLC

Please allow 4-6 weeks for delivery

ORDER FORM
URBAN BOOKS, LLC
78 E. Industry Ct
Deer Park, NY 11729

Name: (please print):_____

Address:_____

City/State:_____

Zip:_____

QTY	TITLES	PRICE
	Hush	$14.95
	If It Isn't love	$14.95
	Kiss Kiss Bang Bang	$14.95
	Last Breath	$14.95
	Little Black Girl Lost	$14.95
	Little Black Girl Lost 2	$14.95

Shipping and handlingadd $3.50 for 1st book, then $1.75 for each additional book.
Please send a check payable to:
    Urban Books, LLC
Please allow 4-6 weeks for delivery

ORDER FORM
URBAN BOOKS, LLC
78 E. Industry Ct
Deer Park, NY 11729

Name: (please print):_____

Address:_____

City/State:_____

Zip:_____

QTY	TITLES	PRICE
	Little Black Girl Lost 3	$14.95
	Little Black Girl Lost 4	$14.95
	Little Black Girl Lost 5	$14.95
	Loving Dasia	$14.95
	Material Girl	$14.95
	Moth To A Flame	$14.95

Shipping and handling-add $3.50 for 1ˢᵗ book, then $1.75 for each additional book

Please send a check payable to:

Urban Books, LLC

Please allow 4-6 weeks for delivery